FLY ME TO MOONGATE MANOR

Also by Kate Forster

Fly Me to Moongate Manor
Christmas Eve at Cranberry Cross
Christmas Wishes at Pudding Hall
Finding Love at Mermaid Terrace
Starting Over at Acorn Cottage
The Sisters

FLY ME TO MOONGATE MANOR

Kate Forster

An *Aria* Book

First published in the UK in 2023 by Head of Zeus,
part of Bloomsbury Publishing Plc

9 7 5 3 1 2 4 6 8

A catalogue record for this book is available from the British Library.

ISBN (PB): 9781803281445
ISBN (E): 9781803281421

Cover design: Cherie Chapman

Typeset by Siliconchips Services Ltd UK

Printed and bound in Great Britain by
CPI Group (UK) Ltd, Croydon CR0 4YY

Head of Zeus
First Floor East
5–8 Hardwick Street
London EC1R 4RG

WWW.HEADOFZEUS.COM

For my beautiful Fiona.
A fellow gardener, wise woman and the best friend anyone could ever wish for.

1

Amanda

Amanda Cox closed the door to the apartment she shared with her mother, ignoring the mess that was slowly creeping towards the front door.

'Tomorrow,' she promised the apartment and headed downstairs and onto the New York street and to the coffee stand where a flat white and a bagel were waiting for her.

'Thanks, Arnold,' she said to the man who ran the coffee stand. Arnold had left her bagels by her mailbox when her mother, Wendy, was sick.

'You good, Manda?' he asked, busy making coffee for the waiting patrons.

'Great,' she said as she left the exact money on the counter and picked up her standing order.

'You lie like a rug, lady,' he said, and she gave him a half-smile then headed to the subway.

Arnold had been at the coffee stand ever since she could remember. He was a constant in her life, always on the corner, making bagels and coffee and chatting with the locals in Astoria, Queens.

The neighbourhood had changed over the years, but Arnold hadn't and neither had the other mainstays of Wendy and Amanda's life. They had the same rent-controlled apartment, the same bodega, passed the same faces until some of the old stores went, replaced with Starbucks and Whole Foods. A dog grooming shop replaced the bookstore and, to Amanda's horror, a yoga studio replaced the art supply and studio store where she had worked through college, while still living at home.

For twenty-six years Amanda had been in Astoria, watching the world shift and turn while her little pocket of the planet stayed largely the same with her mom, and Arnold and the coffee and the bagels.

Until the pocket was emptied and Wendy fell over in the street one day, writhing in pain. The next day, the scans showed a brain tumour.

Incurable but they could treat it to prolong her life, they said.

Wendy had said no treatment and Amanda was so furious at her mother's selfishness that she hadn't spoken to her for three days until her best friend Lainie reminded her that she might as well consider her mom dead already if she was going to treat her like that when she was dying.

Only Lainie could put it in a way that was an emotional slap to wake her up from her pain.

And it was pain. Every moment of her mother's death was painful, but it was also so beautiful being able to express the love without any conditions attached. The privilege of being with someone as they died was not lost on her. When Lainie asked her if there was anything about death that she wasn't prepared for, after all was said and done, Amanda had pondered. Lainie always asked thoughtful questions.

It was all so unusual, she had replied after she had

sugared her coffee and they sat in the park watching the well-groomed dogs play with coloured balls and chew-proof rubber bones.

'The laughter,' she had answered finally.

Lainie had looked at her, confused. 'What about death is funny?'

'I don't know. I can't really explain it. It's not funny so much as it's life without any edits. It's all raw footage. The body makes peculiar noises when it's shutting down, which we would scream laughing at, or you say stuff that you think you shouldn't but it's perfect at the moment. You're honest about stuff, like Mom and I talking about our mutual hatred of folk music and Gerard Butler movies. I can't explain it, but there was laughter, and love, so much love.'

Now, sitting on the train to work, Amanda would have handed over her coffee and bagel to anyone who could have made her laugh again at that moment, or anyone who would call her boss and tell him she wouldn't be in today, but she knew she couldn't take another day off from work. She was already in the red for sick days, and there had recently been another hire at the talent agency to book the models and the photographers for shoots.

If she could, she would resign tomorrow, but that wasn't possible. In her perfect world, she would spend the day drawing and working on the illustrations for the children's book her mom had written but never published. That was her only regret on her death bed, she had told Amanda.

'I should have done more of what made me happy, like writing. I didn't trust my voice until I was older. I should have known I knew what I was doing sooner, or at least tried.'

Amanda had tried to tell her it was fine; she had raised Amanda as a single mom, who had moved to New York from England when she was twenty to become an important writer. Then she became pregnant with Amanda and gave up on her dream; instead, she worked as a court stenographer for twenty-five years, giving them stability and food on the table but at the cost of quashing her dreams so Amanda could have hers.

But was the dream of being an artist a reality? she thought as she left the subway and walked the three blocks to work. She hated her job, but it wasn't like her door was being knocked down with offers for her drawings. She had seen so many agents to try and get one of them to take her on. All she needed was one important commission and then she could leverage off that. But the response was always the same.

Your style is too old-fashioned.

We already have a Beatrix Potter style of illustrator.

No one cares about flowers anymore.

She didn't think her work looked like Beatrix Potter's; it was inspired by her style but not the same. Just characters living in New York, doing New York things but as animals.

There were the ferrets who ran the local bodega. And the warthog traffic cop. The elegant frogs who dined at Gramercy Tavern wearing pearls and gloves and heels, and the tiny little puppies all in school uniforms, tumbling through the fancy iron gates for their posh school.

Amanda pushed her non-existent art career out of her mind as she threw the coffee cup in the rubbish bin outside the building where she worked. She took the elevator to the fourteenth floor and nodded at the receptionist who scared her most days. She was an ex-model who never quite got enough bookings, who was now working her way into a role in the office that involved duties other than looking predatorily beautiful and bored. She was a hyena who Amanda tried to avoid whenever she could.

'Amanda, Greg wants to see you,' the hyena hissed and Amanda swore she was smirking at Amanda's outfit of a denim pinafore and a red checked shirt. In hindsight, she realised she looked like Raggedy Ann with her red curls and black boots. The dress was the only thing that was clean though, and the red shirt had been her mom's. The collar still smelled of Diorissimo and there was a tiny hole where her mom used to put one of her many ebullient brooches over her beautiful, warm heart.

Amanda wanted to go to her desk and do her work and count down the hours until she could go home and lie in bed and cry, but if Greg – her very exacting boss – wanted to see her she had no choice.

Greg was sitting at the small round table in his office instead of at his desk. In front of him were some papers turned upside down. Her stomach started to churn at the sight of them and Greg's very serious face when she sat down in the chair he gestured to. Greg was a bull, and he didn't ever spin any bullshit.

'How are you, Amanda?' he asked, and she wondered if it was a trick question.

'Fine,' she lied.

'Listen, I'll get right to it. This is a hard time in the industry, and I know you have had a hard time personally.'

She nodded because she wanted him to know she understood, even though she didn't.

'Which is why we need people who are entirely focused and passionate about bookings.'

Amanda heard the train coming down the track. She was tied down; she couldn't move.

'Okay,' she encouraged. *Just run me over already*, she wanted to say. *Get it over and done with*.

'So, I'm letting you go. You seem to have your priorities elsewhere and while we have been patient and accommodating, you have hardly been in to work.'

'That's not true,' she argued.

'You were in two days last week – no word on the other days. I mean, we can only do so much. I have a business to run.'

Amanda tried to think back to the previous week. She thought she had been in every day, but Greg had just told her it was only two days.

Her mind flicked over the week before. Admittedly, the days blurred into each other and she couldn't say if it was true or not. All she knew was that every day since her mother's death even waking up felt like a punishment.

Greg was speaking and she tried to bring her attention back to her own firing.

He was pushing the papers across the table towards her.

'We have been very generous we believe, with a pay-out of two months' salary and of course we will be your reference to whatever job you decide to apply for when you get better.'

What could she say? It was generous. She wasn't doing her job properly; she hadn't been since her mom had become ill. There was only so much of her drama and anguish the company could take on.

'I'm sorry,' she said, and her voice cracked with pain and embarrassment.

'Don't be sorry. You're having a hard time, kid. Be good to yourself and do what you need to do to remember your mom in a way that doesn't feel like you're betraying her by living.'

It was the most profound and right thing anyone had said to her in the eight weeks since Wendy's death.

Every decision she made that moved her forward felt like treachery to her mom's memory.

Amanda picked up the pen that was on the table, scrawled her signature on the papers and pushed them back to Greg.

'Thank you for being so kind and I'm sorry I let you and the business down.'

Greg shook his head. 'You didn't let anyone down. Now go and find some peace, okay?'

When Amanda left the building, the receptionist didn't even look up at her, and she didn't bother to collect anything from her desk. She had nothing of herself at work, not even friends. It was always supposed to be a layover job until she found something that she liked more. Two years later it was a longer stay than she would have liked but leaving after so much change hadn't been an option until Greg decided for her.

She needed to go home and gather her scattered thoughts and tackle the mess. Perhaps today would be the day she could put some order into her world.

The train ride back was quiet and when she passed Arnold at the coffee stand on the way home, he laughed and asked her if she had forgotten something.

She just half waved and pretended to laugh as she climbed the stairs to her apartment.

And there on the door was a notice taped roughly with sticky tape at each corner.

Intention to sell. Eviction notice. Thirty days.

2

Simon

Simon adjusted his helmet and looked in the side mirror on his motorbike, waiting for a car to pass, and then took off with a roar. The roads heading north were not as busy coming into early summer but he knew it would be crowded as holidaymakers made their way towards Newcastle upon Tyne. He was planning to settle there for the summer. It was a perfect place, as he knew no one and he could get some odd-job work until he could get his head around what had happened.

Finding work was easier than he had expected since he had fled London three months earlier. He had found work in Cambridge as a pot washer at a busy café and painting some of the punts on the River Cam for summer. But Cambridge was where his ex-girlfriend Anika went to college and he hadn't wanted to bump into any of her old friends if they were still there, so he was on the road again quite quickly. He went to Cornwall and painted boats for a while and rented a room from an old man who had too many cats and a drinking problem. That ended when the man's daughter came and put him in a nursing home and surrendered the cats to the local pet shelter. Simon needed to stay still for a while and gather his thoughts but he had the feeling that wherever he went, the shame and humiliation was in his emotional sidecar.

The motorbike was his first purchase when the investment company had taken off. Charlie had the contacts and Simon had the knack of picking great stocks, based on the software he had created that analysed stocks and determined if they were a good investment for long or short term. Soon he and Charlie had more money than sense. He had paid for the motorbike in cash, and Anika had taken photos of him next to it, looking flash and successful. He cringed to think of it now. Those pictures would haunt him for as long as they existed on the cloud somewhere. He looked like a complete wanker, the young rich man with his toys. He wished he could access the photos now but Anika had changed all the passwords before he knew anything of the bomb that was about to blow up his life.

Simon realised there was something worse than death… and that was humiliation.

He tried to stay focused as he rode the motorbike but his mind kept replaying the day of the wedding. Still, after all these months.

Apparently, the affair had been going on for a year. *A year?* he had yelled from the side room of the church.

There had been a rustling from the restless guests outside.

A year – he still couldn't understand it.

A year of Anika choosing flowers and canapés and the band for the wedding. A year of toasts and invitations and table plans.

A year of betrayal.

Concentrate, Simon, he reminded himself.

The trip to Newcastle was about four hours, give or take. He had worked it out on the map, and he had planned to stop somewhere for lunch but when it was lunchtime, he wasn't hungry. He couldn't remember the last time he was hungry. Anxiety is one hell of a diet, he'd told his mum, but she told him he needed to eat anyway – just a little, she had encouraged. Now he ate because he was supposed to but not because he wanted to, enough to get through the day but not enough that he had any fat left on him.

Simon twisted the throttle on the powerful bike and took off towards his destination. The sooner he could get to Newcastle the sooner he could look around the area for a small village to settle. He could find a cheap rental room and look for work and try and forget about everything for a while.

Sometimes it made him laugh to think that just three months ago he was living in Kensington, renting a beautiful house and living with Anika who was the new weekend weather girl on ITV.

As he passed an Aldi truck, he gave a little laugh to himself.

Once he was Simon Herald, the King of Investments and now he was Simon Herald, the odd-job man, flat skint and whose girlfriend left him for his business partner.

Oh, how the mighty have fallen.

He wondered if the people in the cars he passed knew his fiancée had left him at the altar. Did they know he stood like an idiot in a suit with his shoes polished, nervously looking up the aisle waiting for Anika to emerge in a cloud of white on her father John's arm?

Did they know that her father had rushed up the aisle,

his normally ruddy face now redder than a cricket ball, beckoning to Simon to come with him?

An accident? he had asked.

No. Not that, thank goodness.

Instead it was public shaming like nothing he had ever imagined.

He didn't even miss Anika now. How could he after such deception? He just wanted to disappear and never matter to anyone or have anyone matter to him ever again.

Foxfield village was perfect for his stay, Simon decided. He had arrived in Newcastle and had asked the woman at the library if she knew of any villages where people might need some odd jobs done before the summer rush.

The woman had given him the names of three village and he had chosen Foxfield because he liked the name.

Simon always checked in at libraries when he was on the road. The librarians were always helpful and knew about much more than the Dewey decimal system. It made sense – all those people coming and going. A library was a sanctuary for many and had replaced the church in the community. Anyone could enter a library and have access to the internet, books, company, a place to learn, a place to chat and explore other worlds. Foxfield was only ten miles from Newcastle and it was close to the sea but not on the shore. It was the perfect distance between everything, he decided as he rode his motorbike towards the village.

The roads became narrower and there were hedges on either side before he entered the village. He rode his bike over the river that ran towards the sea and passed houses with lovely gardens protected by stone fences. There were hedges and a mix of Tudor and stone houses set back from the streets. As he went deeper into the village, the houses came closer to the footpaths, as though eavesdropping on those who passed. There were flower boxes outside windows with small flowers in them as though recently planted.

He passed the pub with the satisfying name of the Sinking Ship Inn, which he thought was apt for how he was feeling, but he rode onwards. Though he would have loved a beer, he was afraid if he started to drink during the day, that was another slippery slope he would have to climb up again, and he didn't have the energy to cope with another issue right now.

The village was smaller than he had thought but it had everything he needed, including a well-stocked store for necessities. He could get the bus into the bigger town for the larger shops if he needed them. There was a post office and some tearooms that Anika would have adored, judging from the very frilly interiors as he passed the lace curtains in the window.

He paused as a woman came out to a table and set down a large basket of scones, which he had to admit were of an excellent height. A flash of memory came back to him of making scones as a child with his grandmother. She would handle the dough firmly but gently, like a midwife handling a newborn baby. Confident and with knowledge.

His job was to lay them carefully out on the tray, sprinkling some flour on top before they went into the hot oven.

Life was so simple then.

He went through the village and then down a hill,

realising he had been heading towards the sea. There was an expanse of green grass on one side of the road and the sea on the other and, as he came around the curve of the road, he nearly lost control of the motorbike.

Because there was the most beautiful house he had ever seen. A Georgian manor with a wild, tumbled garden and a round gate with some sort of plant growing around it. There was a fence but it was only waist height, probably to avoid hindering the view of the sea from the house.

He pulled off the road, got off his bike and lifted the visor of his helmet to get a better look at the beauty before him.

He could see cars slowing down slightly as they passed the house and he didn't blame them. It was a doll's house, something out of a fairy tale, a vision in a somewhat bleak landscape facing the dull sea.

'You seem quite taken with her,' said a voice and he turned to see an older woman with a walking stick and a dog on a lead. She couldn't be more than eighty, he thought, but she seemed frail. She was well turned out, as his mother would say, with a tweed blazer and matching skirt. There was a silver brooch of a small thistle on her blazer lapel and what he noticed was an Hermès scarf. He knew that logo after watching Anika spend so much of his money there while they were together.

'It's a beautiful house. Do you live there?' he asked politely, taking off his helmet.

'I used to, but it's too big for me now. I've moved to the gatehouse, which is just as nice but more suitable for the old knees,' she said.

Simon smiled at her. 'So it's empty?' he asked.

'Not for long, we have someone moving in soon. Don't

we, Trotsky,' she said to the terrier whose overbite gave him a distinctly Winston Churchill energy.

'Lucky them,' said Simon. 'But the garden is a lot of work.'

'Yes, it is. Do you know anyone who might like to help?' she asked. 'I only ask because there aren't many young people in Foxfield who want to do this sort of work. Perhaps you have some friends who might like to do some labouring in the garden?'

Simon had known Foxfield was a good idea the minute the librarian had mentioned it to him in Newcastle. This proved it.

'I do, actually – I mean, I don't know anyone around here, but I'm looking for work,' he said.

'How long will you be in Foxfield for?' asked the woman, as the pug dog huffed beside her legs.

Simon shrugged. 'At least a month or two.'

The woman made a face and tipped her head to one side. 'I would need someone longer – it's an enormous amount of work.'

Simon looked at the house and the garden in front of them, pondering if he could stay longer than he usually did in one place.

'There is a small cottage at the back of the property,' said the woman. 'It's the gardener's cottage; hasn't been used in years but it's dry, and we can take a few things from the house to make you comfortable. It has all the amenities and power, if you want to use it while you're here.'

Simon was silent, thinking about his options.

'The payment is two thousand a month for three months with your own private accommodation.'

The appeal of staying put for a while and having some

money overcame any other reservations he had and he threw his head back and groaned. 'You are making it impossible to say no,' he said to her and he offered his hand in agreement.

'Simon Herald, your new gardener for the summer, at your service.'

'Diana Graybrook-Moore, your new boss until the new owner of Moongate Manor comes to our shores.'

'Moongate Manor? Is that the name of the place?'

'Indeed it us. The house faces the moon when it's full. It's quite a view.'

'When is the new owner coming?' he asked, curious about who would choose to live so far from anything.

Diana looked up at the house and he saw a small smile playing at the corners of her mouth.

'Any day now,' she said. 'I just have to pick the winner.'

'The winner?' Oh his interest was truly piqued now.

'Come and see me tomorrow and I can make sure you're all set up. As I said, I'm at the gatehouse. When you turn left at the driveway, you'll see it. I'll leave the gate open for you.' And then she walked away, leaving Simon standing outside Moongate Manor, mouth agape and with an unfamiliar feeling of things working out for the first time in a very long time.

3

Diana

Diana had seen the man standing in front of Moongate with the familiar body language of awe anyone got when they looked at the house and its enviable position. Of course the passers-by knew nothing of the time and energy it took to run an old home like Moongate Manor.

Diana was older now, ready to live a smaller life, not that her life had been overwhelmingly busy before she decided to move from the manor to the gatehouse. Unmarried women didn't get invited many places, unless it was to philanthropic events, which she had never been eager to attend. Why let the right hand know what the left hand is doing, she always said when someone invited her to a fundraiser for a hospital or for research into a disease. She didn't need people to see her in a smart outfit handing over a cheque. Why not just post the money and be done with it? But in truth, Diana's finances were running low and she didn't have much left, not enough to hire a full-time gardening team to reinvigorate the garden beds and lawns at Moongate. But she did have enough to pay one gardener to work over the summer, along with offering subsidised rent.

The house needed new blood now, new ideas and someone who would bring the energy she lacked back into the home.

But life has a funny way of catching up with you and recently her local doctor, who she saw in Newcastle once a year, had told her that her arthritis was beyond anything he could help with now and she needed to see a specialist.

The medication the specialist had prescribed made her tired and she was having other health issues from the side effects. The manor with all its stairs and slippery pathways were proving too much to handle, so she used the last of her savings and hired three men to come and paint the inside of gatehouse. Once she had new heating installed and the little kitchen and bathroom were upgraded, she was finally ready to move in.

The single-level house was much easier to manage than Moongate and she could access the garden whenever she liked, which was often and every day.

Choosing what to take from Moongate was harder than she had expected. There was her bed, and her chaise longue and a nice armchair that her mother had sat in to read when she and Diana had watched television, but the other furniture was too big and cumbersome for the pretty gatehouse. She had some movers come and walk it down the driveway using their trolleys and brute strength, but finally she had enough in the gatehouse to call it home.

The pretty Meissen tea set with the black rose pattern had come with her and the portrait of her mother by Leonard John Fuller was now above the fireplace. She had also taken some books of Mother's and sentimental silver and glass but not much else.

Diana didn't have time for sentimentality about material objects. If she did, she would have stayed in the house and eventually fallen down the stairs and broken a hip and stayed there for days until Mrs West came up from Foxfield village to clean and drop some groceries off.

It was Diana's father, Edward Graybrook-Moore, who cared about material items and reputation. Diana didn't like to reflect on her father if possible but she looked back on her mother with some understanding of how little agency she had in her life, married to a man like Edward.

Lillian Graybrook-Moore was well loved in Foxfield, donating large flower arrangement to the church at Easter and Christmas and always having the village at Moongate for the festival. It was often said by the locals – as Moongate had long been a source of village gossip – that if only Diana had Lillian's patience and grace then she wouldn't be a spinster, with no heir for Moongate Manor. Everyone in Foxfield agreed it would be sad that it wouldn't remain in the family after being passed down through the Graybrook-Moore lineage for hundreds of years.

While she might not have had her mother's patience or grace for people, Diana did offer both virtues to her garden, which was why, when she saw the man staring at it with such wonder, she had a feeling there was a gardener inside him. Not everyone had one inside them, she would explain if you asked, but Diana knew one when she saw it.

Some people could walk past a garden and not notice it at all, even if it was the most beautiful space in the world. Then there were those who admired the order or commented on the hard work it must take to keep the weeds from the borders. They weren't gardeners. One pot of pansies does not make someone a true gardener, she always thought. No, a gardener is someone who can see where the colour should be, like an artist.

Was this young man an artist? Perhaps, but the primary decider for Diana was the fact that he seemed to have a sense of wanting to belong somewhere. He seemed lost, out of place, like an outsider at a party, watching all the guests dance and laugh and chat, as though wishing someone would invite him in. Perhaps Moongate could be a place to for him to settle for a while and gather his thoughts, which she was sure she could see tumbling around his head, and she, in turn, could get some of the garden cleared. It was mutually beneficial, which Diana liked.

And she had organised the gardener's shed at the same time as her house, so there really wasn't much to do for him to be able to move in for the summer.

All Diana had to do now was send the letter. Typed up by her lawyers and ready to go once she had signed the thick paper.

It was time, she thought as she went back to the gatehouse after meeting Simon. He was the first sign that things where underway, and the added bonus was that her dog Trotsky hadn't tried to bite his shins. Trotsky had a low tolerance for fakery, so Diana always took his advice on the calibre of other people. He looked like a perfect Highland terrier that you might see in a calendar or on the tin of Scottish shortbreads, but he had the temperament of Leon Trotsky, who made enemies easily and trusted very few. He was a perfect dog in Diana's eyes.

She remembered the garden when it was beautiful. When it was strung with lanterns, and music filled the night.

When the scent of the jasmine promised love and possibilities. Perhaps it could come back to its former glory with some work? With some nurturing of the soil and caring for the existing plants, she didn't think it would require a huge amount of funds to at least get the garden back to some order.

Diana sat at the small desk in the living room at the gatehouse and took the letter from the manila folder sent by the lawyer.

She ran her eye over it and then picked up her fountain pen and signed her name.

Once the recipient received this letter, Moongate Manor would no longer hers.

4

Diana

1960s

The band in the garden was warming up. Diana Graybrook-Moore could hear them playing the recent hit, 'Sailor', by Petula Clark, as she turned slowly in her new dress, humming along to the song. The dress was perfect for her party. Pale peach georgette with an asymmetrical strap over one shoulder that tied in a lazy, elegant bow or could also be tied around her neck as a scarf. It was fully lined and the delicate silk overlay clung to her lithe figure, and with the Bardot neckline, her skin – slightly tanned from the summer – glowed.

'You look beautiful, dear,' said her mother, Lillian, whose own grey Hartnell dress was plain in comparison, even with its lace bodice.

'Thank you, Mother, and thank you for taking me to London to pick the dress,' Diana said and she kissed her mother's cheek in a rare display of affection.

Lillian seemed to grimace at the touch of her daughter's lips on her powdery cheek but Diana didn't take it personally. Her mother and father didn't understand Diana's need to show affection. It was a given that they thought fondly of each other, her father said to her when she once tried to hug him.

Edward Graybrook-Moore was as stiff and upright as any man of his background and class should be – not an emotional man. He had only felt like weeping once, when Lillian had had Diana when she was forty-three years old and he was close to fifty. There were ten years of miscarriages before Diana and the idea that Moongate Manor would not continue in the family had pained him more than he had told his wife. When Lillian learned she was with child again, Edward had made Lillian lie in bed from the start till the end, with her legs held up in a contraption he had made himself that resembled a quarter-sized hammock. Lillian had not argued with her husband because she couldn't bear to see the spotting again and she had so hoped it would work and keep the baby inside her.

When she had passed the date for the previous miscarriages, Edward had allowed her to have a few hours out of bed where she could sit and do gentle stretches but nothing more.

The day Diana was born was a full moon, so it was natural they would name her after the Roman goddess of the hunt, and now, they were hunting for a husband for Diana. She was eighteen, and Edward and Lillian didn't want her to face the same challenges they did of getting married later and then facing so many troubles in having a family.

Lillian and Edward were married when she was thirty-five, and she had thought her time was up. She wasn't a beautiful woman and she was shy, which meant she wasn't the most popular of the debutantes and – without suitors

– she was considered a spinster by the time she was twenty-five years old. Ten years on from that, she was presumed unmarriable, until Edward Graybrook-Moore, who had been living in India for some time, came back to England looking for a wife who wasn't silly or frivolous and who was still of childbearing age. He didn't suffer fools, and some even said his arrogance announced itself twenty paces before he came into a room. But Lillian – already living with an overbeating father and insipid mother – assumed this was the normal dynamic of a marriage.

When Lillian and Edward married, Moongate Manor was unoccupied but she took it over with the zest of a woman who could finally make her own decisions. It was a well-run home and when Diana finally came into their lives, Lillian was as content as she could be – more in fact, she often told herself. She forgave Edward all his moods and abrupt words, because she had a baby girl and a house that looked down over the sea.

Now, Diana's eighteenth birthday party was about to start in the gardens of Moongate.

There were Chinese lanterns hanging from the trees, a dance floor and a small orchestra that had been instructed to play nothing faster than a social foxtrot for the guests and waiters with fresh oysters from Holy Island.

There was a table of cold meats and salads and a dessert table of all of Diana's favourite pudding including raspberry jelly and ice cream, custard tarts and coconut pie.

It was going to be perfect, except for the choice of band and lack of modern dancing at the event.

Diana had tried to argue but her father said he had invited Princess Margaret and she might come with her new husband. Diana had thought that no one would have liked to have had a little swing on the dance floor more than Princess Margaret, but she knew better than to argue with her father. He always got his way.

At precisely seven, Diana went downstairs where her father presented her with the Moongate pearls. They had been in the family since the house was built, strung for Eliza, the first Lady of Moongate: 140 Tahitian pearls around a sapphire from Kashmir, embedded into a gold pendant.

It was an extraordinary necklace, probably too much to wear with a dress from Harrods, thought Diana as her father fastened it around her neck, but it was tradition and Diana had grown up with the pressure of expectation around her until she formed into her own society diamond.

The band had started and the sound of people's voice was drifting in from the garden towards the house.

'Happy birthday, Diana. We hope you have a lovely evening,' said her father, formally, his hands behind his back.

Her mother nodded. 'Hear, hear.' And in a rare turn of events, she leaned over and kissed her husband's cheek and then Diana's.

'Let's all go and have a glass of champagne. It will be Diana's first,' she said as they walked through the doors from the formal living room onto the steps down to the garden.

Diana gave a smile as her eyes became used to the darkness.

How little her mother knew of her, she thought, and she stepped down into the garden, determined to get drunk and lose her virginity.

5

Amanda

'The move is forcing me to sort all the stuff in the apartment,' Amanda said as she tried to look at the bright side of such a dark time.

Lainie sat on the bed, drinking an energy drink and looking at the chaos surrounding them both. If Amanda's best friend came back as an animal in another life, she would be a zebra. Besides the colours matching the scheme of her wardrobe, Lainie was courageous and untameable and she was the most black-and-white thinker Amanda had ever met. To Lainie, nuance was a foreign concept, like eating soup with chopsticks. Why would you even try?

'I don't know why you want to keep all of this stuff; I know your mom would tell you it's dumb.'

Amanda knew she was right but where would she put everything that had belonged to her mother? The clothes, the cheap jewellery she loved so much. Her mother had a collection of brooches, which were no longer fashionable, but Amanda swore she could remember a time when her mother wore each of them during her childhood. She looked at them in the wooden jewellery box. None of them were worth anything but how could she let them go?

She picked up one of a parrot in shiny green and blue metal. She remembered her mother wearing this to her college graduation. The Lucky Parrot, she'd called the brooch. Amanda couldn't face letting it go when it held such a beautiful memory. She remembered her mother's proud face and her cheering as she walked to accept her degree. No, the parrot would stay. She placed it carefully in the box again and looked around.

The books... so many books. What her mother lacked in reaching her writing goals, she made up for in buying books, particularly children's picture books.

'I just feel awful about getting rid of anything.' Amanda picked up a picture book about a girl with red curly hair that couldn't be brushed.

'She used to read me this one all the time.' She showed Lainie the book.

'Looks like an autobiography.' Lainie laughed.

Amanda's hair was the bane of her life. It was long and curled into ringlets, and if she brushed it, it went frizzy. If she cut it short, it turned into a red fuzzy helmet.

Mostly she kept it in a bun on top of her head and no matter how hard she tried to smooth it now, little sprigs of hair popped out to see their surroundings.

'I'm going to keep this one.' She put it onto the keeping pile, which was looking suspiciously taller than the throw-out pile.

'Did you meet the other roommate yet?' Lainie asked, adjusting one of the pillows on the bed and leaning back.

'Not yet,' Amanda answered.

She was moving into a shared apartment with two students from the art school she had graduated from two years earlier. It wasn't ideal but it was cheap until she could find a new job.

'You could move in with me,' Lainie reminded her for the umpteenth time.

'I love you, but I don't think our friendship would survive cohabiting.'

Lainie was a minimalist who loved black-and-white photography and turned her book spines backwards so you couldn't tell what was on the shelf. It was a design choice more than a process decision, she said when Amanda questioned how she searched for a book.

Lainie worked in a gallery while also trying to grow her career as a photographer, and had enjoyed infinitely more success since leaving art school than Amanda, whose cute drawings of animals didn't have quite the same reach as Lainie's moody black-and-white images.

Even though Amanda was upset about the eviction she also knew she couldn't have kept on paying the rent.

She had hinted to Mike – her on-and-off-again boyfriend – that she needed a place to live, and he had sent her a link to apartments to share on Craigslist. Not subtle. She wasn't sure why she'd even texted Mike. He had been missing in action since her mom had died and was barely around when she was sick. But Amanda couldn't face more loss, so instead of breaking up with her boyfriend of two years at the same time, she had ignored that he was unreliable, unsupportive and a total prick. He was a lawyer and behaved like he was in an episode of *Suits*, when he was really just a junior patent attorney whose student loan was crippling, just like Amanda's was from art school.

Amanda didn't want to think about Mike or money.

Her mother's savings had gone on the rent and bills. It was only thanks to a fundraiser to keep Wendy at home for the end of her life that they were able to stay until then, but it was inevitable that she would have to leave eventually. Eventually everything changed, especially in New York, no matter how hard you wished it would stay the same.

Part of Amanda was surprised at the financial situation they found themselves in at the end of her mother's life. She was sure her mother had more savings, but felt she couldn't ask because she didn't want to sound greedy and selfish when it was her mother who was losing the most.

Heaving another box to the table, Amanda opened it and saw all her artwork that her mother had saved over the years.

She hadn't had been able to draw since her mom was diagnosed. Nothing had inspired her during the past year. If she was asked how she saw the world before and after, it was as though she had gone from technicolour to monochrome. Everything felt like a shadow, and nothing was sharp.

'Jesus, this whole task is brutal,' Amanda said and closed the box again.

'Why don't you just put it all in storage and think about it in a year? If there is anything you really want or miss you can take it out of storage and if, after a year, you don't want it you can just piff it out.' Lainie was, as ever, the voice of reason. Her lens of seeing things through black and white was sometimes very helpful.

'I think you're right,' agreed Amanda, mostly because she simply didn't want to have to sort through the things now or ever.

'Let's go and get a drink somewhere and I can call someone tomorrow.'

But Lainie shook her head. 'No, you'll just put it off again. Do it now. I'll look for a place on my phone and give you the number.'

Lainie scrolled while Amanda frowned, knowing her friend was right. She did procrastinate as an avoidance tactic. It was her toxic trait, she had once told her mom. *No, it's not a toxic trait, it's a coping mechanism*, Wendy had corrected her. *You worry so much about the outcome that you end up collapsing under the weight of your own expectations.*

Lainie texted Amanda the number of a storage company and then looked at the pile of mail on the nightstand.

'What do you want to do with these?'

Amanda glanced at them.

'They're all junk. Mom was going through and signing up for all sorts of random things when the brain tumour started to grow. I thought it was dementia. I think she's signed up for every woman's catalogue there is, which is a lot. And she'd been entering competitions. So far, I have won a lifetime of dog food for the dog I don't have. So, I gave it to the Lost Dogs' Home. They were thrilled.'

'You didn't tell me that!' Lainie exclaimed.

'No, because it's sad and though hopefully one day I can see something good in it, right now, it's depressing.' She looked at the mail. 'You can go through them if you want. It would be a big help if you want real insight into the brain when it has a golf ball growing inside it.'

Amanda dialled the number of the storage company Lainie had sent her and went into the living room and spoke to the gruff man whose tone changed when she said her mom had died. He was, in fact, so kind that she felt her eyes becoming stingy and hot, and she had to brush away and a tear with the corner of her sleeve.

'Mands... Mands, Amanda!' Lainie called from the bedroom, and she finished the call and rushed in to see her friend standing on the bed.

'Your mother might have had a tumour but goddammit she had foresight.'

She waved a letter at her.

'What now? Cat food?' Amanda snorted.

'You won a house,' Lainie yelled and waved her arms around wildly.

'What? Stop talking crazy, and stop waving your arms. You look like Kermit when he's excited about something,' said Amanda, snatching the letter from Lainie.

'I am Kermit and I'm excited.' Lainie was jumping up and down like a child.

Amanda scanned the letter.

Dear Ms Amanda Cox,

We are delighted to inform you that you are the lucky winner of our first-ever raffle by the British Society for Preservation of Significant Houses. Your ticket, number 4561, was the lucky one chosen and you have been bequeathed a beautiful home called Moongate Manor.

Amanda looked at Lainie who was now clapping and jumping.

'The British Society for Preservation of Significant Houses? Moongate Manor? Really?'

'What? It's British. They do everything properly, including naming houses and organisations.'

'It sounds like something from Harry Potter,' she scoffed. 'Next thing they'll tell me I have to run into a wall to magic my way there.'

'Keep reading,' Lainie insisted.

However, with great success comes great responsibility. It is hoped that you will ensure the house is maintained to the standards it is in when you arrive and you are to bring the gardens back to their once-renowned status.

Amanda looked up. 'I can't garden anything.'

'What about those? They look in great condition.' She pointed to the potted palms in the corner of the bedroom.

'Plastic,' she said and went on reading.

'The house is located in a small village called Foxfield, outside of Newcastle upon Tyne in Northumberland, and is a well-loved part of the community, who are thrilled to know there is new life coming to Moongate Manor.'

'That sounds exciting,' Lainie enthused.

'It sounds terrifying.' Amanda finished reading the letter.

If you wish to redeem this winning ticket, please contact Mr William Smith to arrange the final details. Signed, the Honourable Diana Graybrook-Moore.

She paused. 'Forget it, I don't want it,' she said.

'Let's call this William dude,' said Lainie.

'Forget it, I don't want it,' Amanda repeated. 'It has to

be dodgy. Also, I never win anything, ever. So why would I start being lucky now?'

Lainie took back the letter and dialled the number.

'It's ringing,' she whispered.

'Why are we whispering?'

'I don't know, but we are,' Lainie stated and then changed gears into her normal voice. 'Oh hi, I'm ringing on behalf of Amanda Cox, daughter of Wendy Cox, the winner of the Moongate house thing? We got a letter.' She paused. 'Oh wonderful, excellent, of course.'

She put the call on mute. 'They sound legit, like super posh. They're getting Mr Smith. He's probably outside riding his pony.'

Amanda felt fury coming from inside her belly that went up to her throat and into her ears. She remembered the frustration at her mother's decisions before she was diagnosed and how touchy her mother was when she mentioned the rate of competitions her mother was entering and Wendy's reckless spending.

Lainie waved at her to take the phone. 'No, this isn't Amanda – I'll get her. This is her best friend, Lainie. Hang on.'

Amanda took the phone from Lainie and, scowling at her friend, she spoke. 'Hello?'

'Ms Cox, congratulations,' a man's voice said.

'For what?' she asked.

'Your mother, Wendy Cox, bought a ticket in our raffle and put you down as the recipient if the ticket won. We have tried contacting her.'

'A bit hard unless you have a Ouija board.' Amanda

couldn't help the tone that came out. 'I'm sorry, she passed away not long ago.'

The lawyer was speaking again. 'I am very sorry to hear that but yes, she bought a ticket in your name in September last year, it states here.'

'That makes sense,' Amanda said, thinking it was at the height of Wendy entering competitions.

'I can assure you this is a legitimate offer and you can live at Moongate Manor for as long as you wish.'

'And do what? I don't really know what to do with a house in England.'

'Why don't you just come and see what it's like, meet the previous owner, see the house.'

'I can't afford to do that, sorry. I've just lost my job and my mom's dead, and I have to move into a shared house, so you know, I'm really living my best life here. Why would I want to leave? I mean, everything is coming up roses.'

Amanda heard herself give a hysterical laugh and she wondered if she had finally lost the plot.

She handed the phone back to Lainie. 'I can't go. Explain it to him.'

Lainie took the phone and went into the hallway to speak to the man.

Amanda lay on the bed and looked at the ceiling.

What the hell was happening? Why didn't her mom enter to win a duplex in Tribeca? England was so foreign to her, and her mom had never wanted to go back there but she had made sure Amanda had a British passport, albeit so far unused.

Her mom had said her life was in America – well, New York to be exact – but now that life was over. Did that mean it was over for Amanda as well?

The door opened and Lainie came back into the apartment.

'All sorted,' she said and threw the phone on the bed next to Amanda, where it hit her elbow.

'Ouch,' said Amanda, but Lainie ignored her.

'You can go whenever you want. They will fund your ticket as part of the prize.'

Amanda sat up. 'What?'

'What?' said Lainie, her hands on her hips. 'It's not like you have so many amazing options here. Go and see the house, meet some people, get out of New York. This city is filled with rats and rodents. The rats being the shitty men we date.'

Amanda nodded. 'Yeah, I got that, but you can't be serious about this. What if I'm being trafficked?'

Lainie took out her phone and typed and then showed Amanda the screen. 'It's a real house.'

Amanda peered at the screen. 'God, it's gorgeous.'

'And it's yours,' said Lainie. 'You really want to live in a shared house when you could live here?'

Amanda looked at the boxes around her. She thought about sharing a tiny apartment with one bathroom with two strangers. Trying to find a job in a city that she was falling out of love with, and now her mom was gone there was nothing keeping her here.

'So you think it's a real thing?' Amanda asked. 'You think I should go?'

'What's the worst that can happen?' Lainie asked. 'It's not like things are set in stone here. Take a break, see the house, pull some weeds, take some time to think and mourn your mom.'

Amanda thought for a long moment. 'You're right,' she said eventually.

'Are you serious? Don't mess with me.' Lainie fist-pumped the air and danced on the bed again. 'This is the most exciting thing to happen since…' She paused as though trying to think of a comparable time. 'Since ever.'

Amanda looked around the piles of mess and thought about trying to find a job, living with strangers and seeing the ghost of her mom on every street corner. The idea of it all made her feel physically ill.

'Maybe I should just go and see what I can find out,' she said, barely believing she was saying the words.

'You have to try. It's the last thing your mom ever gave you, and you can't give it back; that would be rude. Besides, I think you're too good for this city. You're so kind and gentle and sweet and caring. This city eats people like you for breakfast.'

Amanda gave a small laugh and looked at the photo of her and her mom on the nightstand.

'Well, I would never be rude to my mother, I was too well raised,' she said in a British accent and Lainie jumped off the bed and pulled her into a hug.

'It's all going to be okay. Your mom is looking after you, I promise.'

If Amanda held her eyes closed tightly enough, she just might believe it.

6

Simon

Simon stayed one night in the Sinking Ship Inn pub, paying for a small room that had a double bed, an old cupboard for his clothes and a folding chair. His feet hung off the bed and he had nightmares all night that Anika and Charlie were under the bed, planning to cut off his toes.

In the morning, he tied his boots extra tight, paid his bill and headed over to Moongate Manor.

He wasn't sure why he agreed to stay for the summer. Maybe he was tired of running, maybe he needed to rest for a while and gather his thoughts. He couldn't keep on riding his motorbike through Britain pretending nothing had happened.

But Diana had almost told him he was staying, or had she? He wasn't sure. All he knew was he had agreed and now he was going to live in a shed for three months and pull an overgrown garden apart. He wasn't a gardener; he wasn't anything anymore. But had he even ever wanted to work in finance? He didn't particularly like the job but he liked the monetary rewards. His mother always told him he liked being outside as a child, and to find a job that honoured that. Instead he had stared at a screen all day. His only break was taking a holiday where he would then stare at his phone. He was so tired of technology. He was tired of trying to know everything, of the constant communication and endless scrolling. He thought of scrolling the internet or on his phone like galaxies within galaxies. He would never know it all and there was no ending. The content was being repeatedly updated and he was exhausted.

Now he had no reason to scroll and no reason to stay up-to-date.

Simon wasn't one to have regrets in life, except when it came to letting his business partner Charlie take control of the finances for their company. Charlie had told him he had it all under control, but he'd been siphoning it off for himself.

And Simon had trusted him, signing documents whenever Charlie asked and not inquiring after his own money. All while Charlie had been cheating with Anika behind Simon's back. God, he felt like a fool. How could he ever show his face in London again? He was an embarrassment. The poster boy of idiots.

As he rode towards the old house, he wondered if he should keep on riding, pretend he had never stopped there in the first place, but Simon was a man of his word, despite his need to run away from his life. That was his virtue and his downfall, his mother had always told him. He needed to find balance but how?

When he arrived at Moongate, he went to the gatehouse as Diana had directed him. All he had on him was his backpack holding a few changes of work clothes, toiletries and a pair of sneakers, and the boots he was wearing. Not exactly gardening wear but he could look into that later, he thought as he waited outside the house. The air was cold for early June and he wondered when Summer would arrive in Northumberland. Perhaps he should have headed down to Cornwall.

The door to the gatehouse opened and Diana stepped out in a green tweed suit and sturdy walking shoes, holding a dark wood stick with a silver rabbit on top of it and her dog on a tartan lead.

'Good morning, Simon, I'm so pleased you didn't decide to give in to instinct and keep riding past the house.' She smiled at him and he frowned.

'Me? Not keep my word? Never,' he half joked.

How did she know he had been unsure?

'If I were you, I would have gone past this mess of a garden.' She pointed her stick at some roses that looked like they were grasping for prisoners to wrap their thorns into. 'Come along and I will show you the shed.'

They walked along the driveway and then left of the house, the garden becoming more unruly as they went.

There was a dark wooded area, which Simon was careful to watch Diana walk over, as some of the pathway was mossy and slippery. He made a mental note to clean that up as soon as he could.

The light became brighter and then they came to a clearing where a small wooden cottage stood amongst what looked to be grassy meadow.

'This is the wildflower meadow,' said Diana. 'I used to catch all manner of insects here as a child, especially butterflies.' She handed him a key. 'It's all set up for you,' she said, gesturing to the cottage.

'I thought you said it was a shed,' he murmured.

'It is a shed, but we made it a liveable shed.' She smiled at him, her brown eyes twinkling.

'I don't believe anything should be on display that isn't lovely and the gardener needs something nice to live in. I had someone come by who gave it a spit and polish and put all the necessities out for you.'

She pulled at the dog's lead. 'Come on, Trotsky, we have to take our walk.' She then turned right and walked along a small path, pressed down in the grass from years of feet tramping through the meadow.

Simon stepped over the grasses towards the house. There was a path underneath, he could feel it, but for now he was knee-deep in plants and wild waving grass.

The key was old, iron and simple. It felt rough in his hand and wasn't attached to anything. He liked how it felt, the weight and the age, he thought as he came to the front door. He dropped his backpack at his feet, put the key in the lock and twisted.

It opened easily, and he could smell the cleaning supplies when he opened the door.

His eyes adjusted to the light and he saw a lovely, simple room – a small kitchenette with a microwave still in its box, a kettle, a toaster oven, and some bench seating with red striped covers on the cushions.

There was a bed, a double with plain bedding and a red mohair rug at the end of it for colder nights. Panel heating was more than enough for the small space and there was an armchair and a desk and seat.

He carried his backpack inside and opened a door, finding a bathroom that was small but perfectly functional.

This was certainly more than a shed, he thought as he walked around and opened cupboards and drawers. There was everything he needed and more. Perhaps his summer here would be more tolerable than he thought?

But where were the gardening tools?

Simon pulled a cap from his backpack to keep the sun from his eyes and he left the cottage. He needed to bring his bike up here and then he would have a good look around.

Soon he was walking round the house, trying to get an understanding of the land and the gardens.

There was a sense of order under the chaos – he could see paths and walls – but so much was overgrown and messy. He wished he could have seen what they used to be like before they became wild and chaotic.

He would have asked Diana but she was nowhere to be seen, so he peered through one of the ground floor windows of the house. There was a dining room, with a large marble fireplace and a painting in a gilt frame of the bay of Moongate with a full moon hanging over it. It was an enormous painting and would have required at least four men to carry it, if they were willing to risk their back health. The room was also furnished with rugs and old furniture that would have been elegant in the 1920s but now seemed old-fashioned and uncomfortable.

But as far as he could see it was clean and orderly. Anika would love to live in something as grand as this, he thought, but he pushed her memory away. She had made her choice, and she'd chosen Charlie over him.

Simon walked the rough outlines of pathways and felt stone walls under the vines that seemed to grow everywhere.

He wished he knew the names of some of the plants so he could care for them properly. He could have rung his mother and asked, maybe even taken photos of them to send to her, but then she would ask questions and tell him all about what happened after he left the non-event wedding, as he called it in his mind. He loved his mother but she loved to gossip and if he spoke to her the news of his whereabouts would move faster than Anika at a Selfridges sale.

No, he would just have to see if Diana had any gardening books, as he was fairly sure he wouldn't have internet access in the gardener's cottage.

As though he had summoned her, Diana rounded the corner with her dog, right by an empty pond.

'I was just thinking about you,' he said.

'Of course you were.' She didn't seem pleased or displeased at this news.

'I was wondering if you have any gardening books. I don't think you have internet here?'

'I do at the gatehouse. I like the *New York Times* Wordle. I'm on a seventy-four-day streak,' she stated proudly.

'Okay,' said Simon. 'Well done, I guess.' Was he supposed to celebrate this? It was hard to know with Diana. He couldn't read her.

Diana kept walking, clearly expecting him to keep up.

'Come to the house. I'll give you some of the original plans for the garden from William Robinson.'

'Who is that?'

'The garden designer, Robinson – do you not know his work?' Diana seemed disappointed in him, as though this was a name that should be instantly recognizable when one thought of garden design.

'No, I don't. Sorry, I don't know much about gardens,' he admitted. 'But it's nothing I can't learn.'

'I have a book on him also, so I will share that with you so you can understand his thought process and approach to gardens.'

Bees and other insects seemed to be everywhere, feeding off the flowers that remained, and as they walked to the house Diana pointed out some butterflies.

'Tortoiseshells there. That's a comma. The ones on the bluebells are orange tips. If we're lucky we might see a holly blue as they come in spring but we will get a second generation in summer.'

Simon looked at her amazed. 'Are you a butterfly collector? I can't remember the proper name for them.'

'A lepidopterist,' she said.

'Yes, one of those.' He nodded.

'No, I am nothing really – not an expert in anything except knowing what is in this garden. The plants, the flowers, the bulbs and the bees, birds and butterflies.'

Simon smiled at her. 'Then you're a Moongate-ologist,' he said and Diana laughed harder than he expected her to.

'I like that. Yes, I am, but I'm hoping to hand it to someone who also wants to be a Moongate-ologist.'

'What are all the vines?' he asked as they passed the plants in question. The stems seemed to have many leaves, with long thin tendrils reaching out for support.

'It's all wisteria,' she said. 'Purple, pink and white but the pink and white are not as greedy as the purple. Her fingers are everywhere. The thin tendrils are whips. I cut them off – they're so demanding.'

'Is the wisteria a problem?' he asked.

'Do you mean should you pull it out?' She kept walking towards the manor.

'Yes, I guess so.'

'I wouldn't. Some people believe that wisteria over a gateway is a portal to another world, which is why it's mixed with the roses over the moon gate. Also it's lovely. It just needs some diversion and controlling guidance.'

Simon was intrigued. 'Why did you plant the wisteria with the roses? From a meaning perspective?'

'Well, roses are planted near graves to protect the souls from evils spirits. So if you're planning to enter a portal to another world, it's probably best you don't have any evil hitch-hikers.' Diana laughed.

Simon joined in as he looked back at the moon gate in the distance.

'It is a bit like being in another world here,' he said. 'My mother is a historian. She loves symbology and meaning in nature and so on. She would love all of this.'

'You should invite her to visit,' said Diana. 'There is so much history here.'

Simon pondered the thought, wondering how his eccentric mother would manage at Moongate, but he knew it would never happen. He wasn't staying; he was only here for the summer.

They came to the front door and Diana turned to survey the garden and the distant view of the sea.

'It is very special,' she said. 'But I'm getting older and I need to find the next generation to take it on. It's a huge job for someone.'

'You said you were choosing a winner for the house?

Does that mean you don't have family?' Simon asked, hoping he wasn't prying. He couldn't help it though; Diana Graybrook-Moore was fascinating in every way.

'No family,' she said as she put the key in the door, turned it and stepped inside. 'Just me now, and I'm not sure for how much longer either.'

Simon didn't want to ask if she was unwell. She seemed fit, but there was a sense of melancholy about her. It must be lonely here, he thought as he followed her inside the house.

And he wondered where her friends were – she couldn't have no one, could she? Everyone had someone. And then he thought of his own life lately. Perhaps she had chosen to be alone. That, he could understand.

Perhaps he would try and be some company to her while he was here for the summer and until the new owner had settled into the house. It wasn't too much to do, not if you were a decent person, which he hoped he was. Bad things might have happened to him but it didn't mean he had to be a bad person in return.

Diana looked at him as she stood in a doorway to a room that looked to be lined with bookshelves.

'Daydreamer, are you coming?' she asked, banging her stick on the floor a few times like the Serjeant at Arms in Parliament.

'Yes, here, present,' he said.

'Good, pay attention, you have much to learn.'

'Agreed,' said Simon with a smile.

It was going to be an interesting summer.

*

Diana – 1960s

'These shoes are killing me,' Diana complained to her best friend, Helen, as they crossed the road towards the hottest club in Newcastle in the 1960s: La Dolce Vita.

Diana had borrowed Helen's very narrow patent leather heels with a pointed toe. Her toes were crushed in the end of the shoe and she wondered if she would even be able to walk inside the place, let alone dance the night away.

It was two weeks after her eighteenth birthday party and while she'd had a wonderful time, it was, she realised, a party for her parents. There'd been so many older people who she smiled at and danced with, but she'd noticed her friends had looked bored. The alcohol had also been carefully distributed and so her plans to be drunk and carefree with her virginity were thwarted, which was disappointing. At this point, she felt like a silly little girl who couldn't make a man interested.

Helen had done it three times – all with Joe, she told Diana, but she was considering branching out to a man she had met on the bus on her way to her job at Wegners department store.

Diana was in awe of Helen. She had the best clothes, courtesy of her job as a sales assistant to fancy ladies in Newcastle, and she was a modern woman. She smoked cigarettes and she had her own money she could do what she pleased with.

Diana was still getting an allowance from her father and was not allowed to wear shoes that had a toe like the ones she had on now. Perhaps he was on to something though, she thought as they stood in line for the club.

Truth be told, her parents didn't like Helen. They said she wasn't someone that Diana would stay close with over the years ahead, but Diana knew this was code for Helen wasn't of their class. Her father was the gardener at Moongate, and Diana and Helen had been friends since they could remember. The first time Helen came to Moongate was when she was six and her mum was having another baby, so Helen had been sent to work with her dad for the day.

Diana remembered them eyeing each other up and then stepping forward and asking Helen whether she would like to come and look at the fish in the pond.

Helen asked if they could catch them and Diana had thought about it for a moment and then shook her head.

'No, but we can give them names.'

'Can I call one Roger?' asked Helen.

'I think so,' Diana had answered, and a friendship was born.

Helen came to Moongate every Saturday after that, even though her father didn't work on a Saturday. Diana's mother had encouraged the friendship initially because then she didn't have to entertain Diana, who she believed had far too much energy for a child. Lillian had told Helen that she didn't remember having ever said, 'I'm bored,' when she was a child, the way Diana used to do before Helen came to play.

It didn't matter that Helen went to the local prep school and Diana was sent to Dame Allan's in Newcastle and then to Mowden Hall for boarding in secondary school; Diana and Helen picked up every weekend and holiday and kept in touch through letters in the meantime.

Helen was the very stylish and modern sister Diana had never had.

'All right?' asked the men outside the club as they passed Diana and Helen to go to the end of the line.

Helen rolled her eyes or ignored them but Diana, ever her mother's daughter, said hello to each and every one.

'You sound a bit posh,' said one young man with a quiff with peaks that would rival any meringue about to go into the oven. 'You not from round 'ere?'

'Piss off,' said Helen.

Diana smiled at him apologetically and as he stepped away, she saw a young man behind him, with a nice suit and tie on and his copper hair smoothed back from his face.

He was taller than her but not so tall that he felt he needed to boast about it. Height wasn't a personality trait, she often told tall boys who lorded it over shorter men.

He looked nervous as he followed his mouthy friend with the meringue hair to the back of the line. She turned to watch him walk away and he turned at the same time.

She couldn't help herself smiling and giving a little wave. His hand lifted from his trouser pocket and he returned her wave with a small movement, which no one else saw. It was just for her and this pleased Diana. Sometimes secrets were good to hold, as long as they didn't hurt anyone, she told herself.

The doors to the club opened and they streamed inside.

The band were playing a song that Diana didn't know but Helen was already singing and swinging her hips in her wiggle skirt and soon they had a Babycham each, planning to nurse that until a young man bought them another one.

Diana felt out of place in her simple pink silk dress and matching bow in her hair. The shoes were the most modern thing she was wearing. She and Helen had completely different figures but even if she could fit in Helen's clothes, she would have felt uncomfortable with those tight-fitting dresses. On Helen, with her Jayne Mansfield shape, they looked amazing.

Soon Helen was dancing and Diana laughed as she saw the way the men looked at her friend. A complete bombshell, she thought.

'Hello,' she heard behind her.

Please don't ask me to dance, not in these shoes, she thought, and she turned to see the man in the suit with the copper hair.

'I'd ask you to dance but I don't know that I like it very much,' he said. 'Can I buy you a drink and we can have a seat and chat?'

His accent was Scottish – Edinburgh, not Glasgow, she thought – and he was nervous. She could tell by the way he blinked and swallowed more than necessary.

The thought of a chair made her knees almost buckle. These shoes were the silliest idea she had had all month.

'Another Babycham?' he asked.

Diana looked at her drink. 'I don't like it very much. Can I have an orangeade?'

'That's my favourite too,' he said, looking relieved.

He bought their drinks and she followed him to the back of the room where there were tables and chairs.

Diana sat down with a sigh of relief.

'You all right?' he asked.

'My feet are killing me,' she said. 'I don't think I'm

designed for fashionable shoes.' She put out her hand. 'Diana,' she said.

He took her hand and shook it firmly. She liked him immediately. Some men were afraid to shake women's hands like equals.

'Douglas,' he said. 'Douglas McKay.'

She smiled at him and took a sip of her soft drink.

'Why are you in Newcastle, Douglas?' she asked.

'I'm on a motorbike ride actually,' he said. 'I'm going to ride down to Cornwall and then get the ferry to France and then ride through Europe.'

Diana leaned forward. 'And then what?'

'Then what, what?' he asked.

'What will you do when you've done that?'

'I might try and ride my motorbike through Canada or America,' he answered.

Diana sat back in her chair. 'So just for adventure?'

He nodded and took a long drink until it was nearly finished. 'Adventure is exactly it,' he said and he smiled, his blue eyes bright. 'Seeing other countries and people and how they live and eating new foods and hearing new languages and music... What a grand thing it will be.'

Diana hadn't ever imagined she would travel unless it was with a husband and yet here was this young man about to head off alone, on a motorbike.

'Do you have money?' she asked, thinking of all the practicalities.

'A little, but I'll find work,' he said.

'And when the adventure is done, what then? Will you be married or get a job in Scotland?'

Douglas laughed. 'The adventure never stops,' he said.

'We're not meant to be doing one thing forever, staying in one spot. We need to keep learning and evolving; that's the way to really live your life. For you, not for anyone else.'

His words lit her up inside. Imagining the places she could go and see and the things she could do.

'I want to see the waterfalls of Norway,' he said. 'And ride through the alpine passes in Austria, and feel the air in the Black Forest in Germany, and the warmth of the sun on the coast along Sardinia. There is so much to see.'

Diana had never thought about many places to see like Douglas had. He could rattle off countries like a geography teacher and spoke with a passion that she had never had for anything in her life.

'What about you?' he asked. 'What great adventures do you have planned?'

Diana looked down at her hands, ringless, fine-boned, without a scar or a callous.

'I don't know,' she said with a shrug. 'But I'm only eighteen. I have time to find out.'

Douglas laughed. 'Aye, you do that.'

The sat in silence watching people dance. Helen was close with a new guy Diana hadn't seen before. He looked handsome and Helen was gorgeous. They made quite a pair as they danced together.

'You hungry?' Douglas asked.

'They don't have food here,' said Diana. 'Only drinks.'

'I know, but there's a chippy up the road,' said Douglas. 'I could murder a cod and chips.'

Diana looked around for Helen. She was still dancing and laughing. She was fine.

'Okay,' she said quickly, before she could change her mind.

She waved at Helen and pointed to Douglas. Helen made a silly face as though she was kissing the air and then waved goodbye to Diana.

They walked out of the club and down the street. Diana winced as the shoes pinched her feet, occasionally stopping to get her balance.

'Those shoes are ridiculous,' said Douglas, looking at her feet.

'I know, they're Helen's. I thought they made me look interesting and modern,' she said.

'They do, if you think modern if a woman saying "ow" as she hobbles down the street,' he said with a gentle laugh. Suddenly he stopped and took off each of his shoes and pushed them towards Diana.

'There you go,' he said.

She could see a small hole in one of his socks near the big toe.

'What are you doing?' She looked around to see if anyone had noticed but the streets were empty.

'I want chips and you can't walk, so I can walk in my socks and you can wear my shoes and carry those torture instruments you thought were modern and interesting.'

Diana took a moment to decide and then kicked off the heels and slipped her feet into his shoes, sighing with relief as she did. They were warm inside and her feet relaxed at once.

Douglas leaned down and picked up her heels and put one in each pocket of his suit jacket.

'Come on then. I'll buy you a cup of tea and I'm going to ask you all about yourself – instead of me talking about myself.'

7

Amanda

Amanda arrived in London to pick up the key to Moongate Manor from the lawyer's office. She didn't have time to sightsee, nor did she have the money, but she couldn't help but feel a thrill as the taxi drove past Buckingham Palace and over London Bridge.

As soon as she was settled in Foxfield, she promised herself she would return to London and look at everything properly.

Amanda's appointment at the legal office in Chancery Lane was in the afternoon, and then she planned to stay the night in a hostel and head to Foxfield on the train in the morning. It would be a three-hour train trip and then she would get a bus for the last stretch. She had it all planned in her head, but it still felt surreal.

She had put her bags in the hostel, showered to get rid of the travel grime and changed into what she hoped looked respectful and respectable for a twenty-six-year-old woman about to be entrusted with an old home with no caveats other than a hope she would maintain the house and returning the garden to its former glory.

A simple pink dress, cream sandals and her hair pulled

into a bun would suffice. Some people said redheads shouldn't wear pink but she couldn't ever imagine not wearing pink. It made her happy and she needed that right now. She didn't need to pretend she was anything other than what she was.

And with that resonating in her heart and head, Amanda went to her appointment to pick up the key.

Lainie rang Amanda's phone as she was leaving the appointment.

'How was it? Did they gift you with a large key to the house and present it on a red velvet cushion?'

Amanda stood outside on the street and looked up at the building.

'You know, it was sort of anticlimactic. They gave me a bunch of papers to read and return to them in the mail, and a key in a yellow business envelope with my name scrawled across the front. I literally turned up at reception and they handed it to me.'

'That's it?' asked Lainie.

'That's it,' said Amanda as she began walking.

'So what now?'

'I'll head up there tomorrow and see what it's like. I have to meet the old owner – some woman called Diana something-something, one of those fancy two-surname people. Apparently, she'll show me around and then it's mine. My main task is to fix up the garden, which is a bit overgrown.'

'Amazing! It all sounds so easy and we love it when things are easy. Let me know how it is. FaceTime me,' said Lainie.

'You're right, it feels too easy,' said Amanda. 'Like there's a trap of some sort that I'm not aware of.'

'Why so suspicious? Maybe it's just an amazing thing that's happened for you?'

'Maybe, but it all feels very unrealistic and kind of unreal.'

Lainie sighed. 'You're feeling tender because your mom died and you lost your job and your apartment, and now something great has happened to you and you can't believe it's real. You're waiting for something terrible to happen because that has been your experience in the last year.'

'Maybe you're right,' Amanda admitted as a bus went past.

'I just saw a double-decker red bus,' she said. 'In the wild.'

Lainie laughed. 'Wow, love that for you. Did you hear anything I said?'

'I did, I promise. I do feel a bit tender,' she admitted.

'Then stop pushing the emotional bruise. Let this experience heal you. Your mom bought you a ticket and it won. I mean, what's not to love about that parting gift? All you have to do is pull some weeds at this house and plant some flowers, right?'

'Yes, you're right. I promise to stop pushing the bruise.'

'Good. Call me when you get to the house. I can't wait to hear everything and see photos.'

'Okay, speak tomorrow,' said Amanda.

Lainie was right. All she had to do was move in and start pulling out the weeds and planting some pretty flowers in the garden. That didn't sound so hard. It was going to be a fun summer.

*

After a train trip and two bus changes, Amanda had finally succumbed and called a taxi to get her the last few miles to the house. She was tired and grimy and ready for a shower and to call Lainie.

'Oh,' said Amanda, looking out the window when the taxi pulled up outside the house.

'You're staying here?' asked the taxi driver.

'I was planning on it,' she said.

'It looks abandoned,' said the man, winding down the window.

But Amanda didn't see it. It was just the garden that was neglected. The house was beautiful – old, but not ostentatious – and if the garden was cared for, then the beauty of the house would be easier to see.

She opened the door and the driver brought around her suitcases from the trunk of the car.

'Thanks,' she said, using her card to pay. Once the taxi had driven away, Amanda assessed the house and the best way to get inside. There was a round gate at the front but she walked to the left and found a driveway that led to the side of the house. With determination despite her tiredness, she set off walking up the drive.

'Miss Cox?' She heard her name and turned to see an older woman with a small dog next to her.

'Call me Amanda, please,' she said, walking to meet the woman halfway.

'Diana Graybrook-Moore,' she said. 'And this is Trotsky.'

'Hey there, Trotsky,' said Amanda to the dog and then smiled at Diana. 'Nice to meet you. Thank you for choosing my mom's ticket. I have to tell you, this is the craziest thing that's ever happened to me.'

Diana raised her eyebrows. 'Then you're very lucky. I've had too many crazy things happen to me.' As she said the word 'crazy', she made quotation marks in the air and then smiled.

Amanda nodded. 'You're right. I am lucky.' She looked at the house. 'It's really beautiful. Who lived here before me?'

Diana pulled Trotsky away from sniffing an empty drink can on the ground.

'Me… and generations of my family before me.'

'Gosh and you're giving it to someone outside of the family? That's intense. I mean, I don't want to pry, but don't you have any family left?' Amanda asked. She couldn't help herself. She needed to understand why she was here and why this woman didn't have even a distant cousin to leave the house to when she died.

'No, no family,' Diana said quickly. 'Now, come and put your bags in my gatehouse and then I can show you around starting from the moon gate.'

'The moon gate? You mean the circle thing?'

Diana sighed. 'Don't be so reductive. It's a moon gate. Come and I will show you.'

Amanda left her suitcases and followed the woman to the front gate. The gate was unlike any she had seen before, being set within a circle, and was not wide enough for a car to drive through yet bigger than an ordinary gate.

The circular gateway was made of stone and brick and the iron gates were rusted, yet still quite sturdy. Some sort of rose and a purple vine was tangled around it, bees buzzing almost angrily, she noticed. As though her presence was disturbing them.

'I'm sorry, bees,' Diana said to the insects. 'But Amanda

lives here now and I think you will have to get along for everyone's sakes. Isn't that right, Amanda?'

Amanda nodded, unsure if she was supposed to speak to the bees or not but Diana didn't wait for her answer.

'Now, this is a moon gate, as you can see. It is both a gateway and it is also a traditional architectural element that you can find in Chinese gardens. The second generation of Graybrooks added this as my family was in exports and shipping, and we assume my ancestor saw it in a Chinese garden on one of trips. He also brought back the wisteria you see here. Now, you can tell this is Chinese wisteria because the vines twist anticlockwise, whereas Japanese wisteria turned clockwise.'

'That's so cool,' said Amanda, touching the vine.

'And the moon gate is designed to look as though it is rising from the ground like the moon. When you stand at the top of the house, you can see through it to the sea, with the gate forming a frame, and when the moon is full, the reflection on the sea looks like stairs to the moon, through the gate.'

Amanda gasped. 'That sounds amazing. I can't wait to see it,' she said.

'The next full moon is in two weeks. I will let you know in advance and you can watch it from the top of the garden.'

Amanda turned to Diana. 'Thank you. Perhaps you'd like to watch it with me?'

Diana paused, as though taken by surprise. 'I can if you like. The symbolism of the moon gate is of birth, new life, renewal and entering another world.'

Amanda looked around. 'It does feel like I've entered another world. This is so different from New York.

Have you ever been to New York?' she asked the older woman.

'Once, a long time ago. I didn't like it. Dirty, noisy, and full of rude people. Now, come along. Say goodbye to the bees,' Diana said and Amanda wondered why she felt she had been told off as though she was solely responsible for the culture of New York.

Perhaps she was jet-lagged and overwhelmed, and as for talking to bees, she couldn't remember the last time she had even seen a bee in New York. The bees' buzzing seemed to drop to a low hum as they walked past them.

'Bye, bees,' Amanda said, feeling stupid.

'Farewell, bees, see you soon,' Diana said in a cheery voice. 'They're happier now. All you have to do is keep them informed of what you're up to and they will be contented. Bees are nature's gossips. The more they know the more important they feel.'

'Good to know,' said Amanda, wishing Lainie was here to witness the situation. Amanda hadn't just walked through the moon gate to a new world, she had entered a portal to a new dimension.

They walked along a very overgrown driveway, framed by trees and shrubs and flowers she didn't recognize. *Mom would know what they are*, she thought, and she stopped briefly and held a white bell-shaped flower in her hand.

'My mom would have loved this. She adored flowers,' she said.

Diana stopped and turned slowly. 'Did she have a garden? Your mother?'

'No, we lived in an apartment that didn't even have a balcony, but she was volunteering at the community garden before she became sick. She loved to show the little kids from the high rises how things grew and stuff like that...'

Amanda heard her voice trail off. How many times had her mom asked her to go to the garden to help out and she had said no, she was too busy? She would do anything to spend some time gardening with her mother now.

Amanda was slowed down by the suitcases but kept pace with Diana who walked towards her gatehouse much slower than expected. Perhaps she was ill, Amanda thought.

'This is my little place,' said Diana, the pride evident in her voice.

The gatehouse was a smaller version of the main house but single level and with a lovely stone wall around the small garden at the front.

That garden was in better shape than the one out the front of Moongate Manor, but it still needed some tidying. Was Amanda supposed to help with that also?

Diana opened the gate and ushered the dog through and then opened the door for Amanda.

'Pop the cases in here and then I can take you to see the house.'

Amanda placed the suitcases out of the way, noticing the neat, orderly and very elegant house interior.

'This is a gorgeous home,' she said to Diana.

'Thank you. I'm very happy here.'

Diana didn't offer to show Amanda around, nor did she offer her a drink or to use the bathroom, and Amanda didn't ask although she could have done with all of those options.

'Do you miss living in the other house?'

Diana laughed. 'Not at all. It's too big for me and requires all that dusting.'

'You don't have a cleaner or anyone to help you?' Amanda asked.

'No money for that. I wore the rubber gloves in the house for many years. It's your turn now, unless you plan on hiring a cleaner?'

It was Amanda's turn to laugh. 'No, I'm poor. I have nothing – nada,' she said, thinking about where she could get a job that would at least pay for food and bills until she could work out how to make house sustainable and pay for itself.

Trotsky settled in his bed for his nap and the two women walked towards the main house. Nerves filled Amanda's stomach as they approached. It looked like a doll's house. A very old doll's house. There wasn't much decoration on the front of the house but it didn't need it; the garden did all the work. There was wisteria with the same purple flower growing up the front of the house, spreading out like veins in an old lady's hand. She remembered her mother's papery hands at the end, the veins no longer healthy, collapsing from the medication and saline drip.

The roses she recognised but there were so many different types of flowers she had no idea where to begin identifying them. Was she expected to know the names? Would Diana test her progress on learning the names of the flowers? Maybe there would be a quiz? God, she was never good at school. Art was the only thing she ever got an A for during her education.

It wasn't that Amanda wasn't bright, she just found it hard to focus and learn about things she didn't think she would ever use again in everyday life.

And she liked to daydream. Her mother used to say that

if daydreaming was a subject, then she would be the dux of the class. And when daydreaming turned into the images in her drawings, then she was in her element.

The house looked in better condition than she had imagined when she first saw it. It was apparently Georgian, which again she knew nothing about and would have to learn about soon. There were five windows across the top floor and two either side of the wide front door.

Diana stood at the front of the house looking up at it with an expression that Amanda couldn't quite decipher.

'This house was built in 1804 by my grandfather – many times removed – for his wife upon their engagement. He was a sea merchant and a very successful one. Their names were Samuel Graybrook and Eliza Moore and they were so in love they took each other's names when they married, which was unheard of in those times.'

'Still is, mostly,' said Amanda.

'Then tragedy struck when Samuel sailed to Africa and didn't return. Eliza had a widow's walk made for the top of the house where she would spend most days looking out for Samuel.'

'Oh that's so sad.' Amanda peered up at the house, seeing the small cupola at the top of the roof.

'Yes, it was very sad. Eliza was pursued by many men, both because of her beauty but also because of her wealth, as Samuel's company was very successful, despite him going missing at sea.'

'Did she marry again?' asked Amanda.

'No. Her son took over the business and then he married, but his wife died in childbirth. The child survived though and he married a second time, to a woman named Susannah. But she died from consumption after her first child was born.'

'Gosh,' said Amanda. 'Times were hard, weren't they?'

'Very,' agreed Diana and she turned to Amanda. 'Every heir to this house has been an only child and male. It wasn't until I was born that it would be handed to a female but, sadly, I never had a child to hand Moongate to.'

Amanda was silent for a moment. 'It's not lost on me how enormous this responsibility is and I will do my best to not let you down.'

'Good woman. Now, let's look inside. I think you will be very happy. I have had it cleaned so you can stay ahead of the dusting.'

As they walked towards the house, a man with a wheelbarrow came through the messy garden.

'Simon, excellent – you're here.'

The man was older than Amanda – in his early thirties, she thought. He had unruly brown curls that looked to be in the process of growing out of a previously sensible haircut, and he was slim, but in an underfed sort of a way. She knew that physical look. It was a physique that came from pain, or sadness, or emotional loss. She had only just started to put back on the weight from when her mother died. The combination of caring for someone and grieving meant she was never hungry or never finished anything, not even a coffee.

Amanda gave the man a friendly smile and he returned it with a nod.

'Amanda, this is Simon, who is here to help you clear the

garden. I expect you two will be working closely together to get Moongate back into shape for autumn when we have the Moongate Festival.'

'The Moongate Festival?' asked Amanda.

'Yes, when the village comes to celebrate the full moon before winter. We have bonfires and entertainment and music, and then we watch the full moon create steps across the water. We haven't had it here in forty years, but it's time now and I know you two will be the perfect pair to bring Moongate Manor back to its purpose and beauty.'

'Okay, that seems like a big task,' Amanda said to Simon. 'We'd better get started.'

Simon looked at her and frowned. 'No, I'm only here for the summer, so I'll be gone before the festival. I'm sure Diana will be more use than me.'

And with that, Simon lifted up the wheelbarrow and walked past them both.

What a rude guy, thought Amanda. If he was the person she had to work with, then she doubted Diana's dream would come true.

'Never mind him,' said Diana after he left. 'He's sad and angry, but he will warm up. He runs a bit hot and cold, but hurt people always do.'

Amanda shook her head and rolled her eyes. 'Interesting guy,' she said.

'I think he is,' said Diana.

'Why is he so grumpy?'

'Life has been a little tricky for him lately.'

'Join the club. Doesn't mean he gets to be rude.'

Diana laughed. 'You two will have to work something out, otherwise Moongate Manor garden will get even worse. It's the start of summer and it grows wild without some sort of regime.'

Amanda looked around at the plants, not knowing which ones were weeds and which were flowers, and at the dried branches and old gravel, and she wondered where she would even start.

Lainie was wrong, this was much more than pulling a few weeds. It was starting again from scratch.

8

Amanda

Diana opened the door to the house and stepped inside. Every house had its own particular smell and Moongate Manor was no different.

It smelled of beeswax polish, wood and was maybe a little musty.

But it was the interior that Amanda found fascinating. It was as though time had stopped. Everything was working but old, older than anything Amanda had ever owned.

Amanda wondered how long Diana had been out of the house, since there was nothing there that was remotely modern and she seemed very settled in the gatehouse.

The foyer was oval-shaped, which Amanda wasn't expecting, with a series of doors leading into different rooms and one coat cupboard.

'You will learn what is what eventually,' said Diana, turning a circle in the space. There was a round wooden table in the centre of the foyer with a blue and white vase on top of it that was begging for flowers.

'My mother always had white hydrangeas in that vase but I never put anything in it after she died. You can fill it with whatever you like now that you're the lady of Moongate.'

Amanda smiled. 'The lady of Moongate – that just seems so crazy to me. I don't know anything about England. My mom was born in the UK but she left at twenty and never came back to visit. Not even to see her parents.' Amanda looked around at all the doors. 'I would have liked to have known my grandparents but she wouldn't even talk about them, let alone have me meet them. She did get me a UK passport though, which was helpful.'

'Oh why was that?' asked Diana.

'Why was what?' Amanda asked.

'Why did she dislike her parents?'

'She didn't dislike them,' Amanda corrected. 'She hated them. When she talked about them, her face changed, like a cloud had come over her – you know what I mean?'

Diana nodded. 'I think so.'

'I used to ask Mom about them when I was little. I would read books and there would sometimes be grandparents in them, with warm cocoa and nice cosy moments and I wanted that so badly. But Mom would get cross with me for asking, so I stopped. She didn't like to talk about the past, but she did admit that her parents were pretty abusive.'

Diana's stick slipped and Amanda rushed to her side and held her elbow.

'Are you okay? Which door leads to somewhere you can sit down?' She looked around.

Diana stood up straight. 'It's fine, just a little bit of arthritis; too much gardening back in the day,' she said. She straightened herself and walked to the first door and opened it. 'This leads to the morning room. It gets beautiful light and has doors out onto the stone terrace, which is not in great shape, I'm afraid.'

'I'll put it on my list of things to tackle,' said Amanda with a laugh.

Diana moved to the next door. 'I have some funds for the house, not enough for a full renovation, but there should be enough to get things up to scratch where you see fit.'

She pointed at another door. 'This one leads to the kitchen and the breakfast nook.' She opened it for Amanda to peer in and see a clean but very old-fashioned kitchen.

'I didn't spend much time in here. I was a toast and tomato soup sort of a lass, would rather be gardening than cooking.'

Amanda laughed. 'You sound like my mom. She always said she was very good at heating things up.'

Diana smiled and moved to the last door.

'And this is the living area and dining room.' She opened the door wide and Amanda stepped through and onto a deep rug with a pattern of roses and crested moons in pale pink and cream.

The walls were also cream but they looked to be fabric, not wallpaper. Amanda moved to the side of the ornate marble fireplace and touched the wall.

'Silk damask,' Diana said. 'Nothing has changed here since my mother died. This was her favourite room.' She pointed with her stick to the painting hanging over the mantel. 'That's Lillian, in the pearls,' she said.

'The pearls?' Amanda asked.

'The Moongate pearls. And this is me wearing them on my eighteenth birthday.' She pointed to a painting on the other side of the wall of a young Diana in evening dress with the pearls around her neck.

'A family heirloom. That's cool,' said Amanda, looking

closely at the painting of Diana. 'I don't have much of jewellery collection but I do have my mother's brooches, which I love.'

'I like brooches too,' said Diana pointing to her chest where a small, jewelled bird sat on one side of her blouse.

Amanda looked at the jewel on Diana's clothing and smiled. 'My mom would have loved that.'

She turned her attention to the painting and Diana was silent as she studied the artwork.

'These brushstrokes are so deliberate. It's very carefully painted; the artist was very good.'

'He was the person to have your portrait done by when I was young. Now everyone takes photos on their phones.'

Amanda laughed. 'Guilty as charged, but I do paint as well. I went to art school.'

Diana nodded as though she knew but Amanda couldn't imagine how. 'You must show me your work.'

Amanda shrugged. 'It's probably too childish for your tastes. I mean, I draw a lot of animals but doing human things.'

'Oh?' Diana moved to one of the large sofas. Overstuffed with tassels around the bottom hem, they looked very comfortable. 'What sort of things do these animals do?'

Amanda realised Diana was waiting for an invitation to sit down. 'Let's sit, please, I'm tired,' she said to the older woman.

'Tell me about your anthropomorphic animals,' said Diana, placing her stick beside her.

Amanda put her head in her hands. 'It sounds crazy when I try and describe it to people.'

'Try,' said Diana, and Amanda knew this was an instruction not an encouragement.

'I see people as animals, and they have jobs. Like the man on the corner where I live in New York, Arnold. He makes me coffee and bagels and, to me, he's a badger. He has a streak of grey in his hair and he's kind of portly and he's very kind. Badgers look kind, you know?'

Diana laughed. 'I have never thought about it but I suppose they do, yes. So what was your mother?'

Amanda threw her hands up. 'My mother, she was easy. She was an orangutan – you know the ones with a baby on their back, being regal and beautiful in their red-headed glory? That was my mom. She was the mother superior and the best mother of all time.'

Diana swallowed. 'She sounds lovely.'

Amanda nodded. 'She was, she really was. The funniest, most adventurous person. I mean, she was really creative also. I had the best costumes for dress-up days and she always gave me these really cool birthday parties. One year she did a sleepover in our tiny apartment for five girls and me, and she set it all up like we were in the Elizabeth Arden Day Spa. She did manicures and facials with cucumber on our eyes, which we thought was so glamorous. And we all got these cute robes from the discount store and she sent the guests home with little bags of nail polish and hand cream. It was considered the best party ever.'

'That does sound fun.' Diana smiled and then she put her hands in her lap and tilted her head to one side. 'So how do you see me? Which animal do you see when you look at me?'

Amanda stared at Diana for a long moment. 'You're not a land animal,' she said very slowly, and finally she squinted and then sat back on the sofa, leaning into the soft cushions. 'You remind me of a goldfinch. It's a bird I'm kind of obsessed with. Maybe that's why now I've met you, I feel like you're the goldfinch I was looking for.'

Amanda laughed but Diana looked shocked.

'Oh I'm sorry, no, gosh, I've offended you. I'm sorry.'

Diana stood up with some trouble using her stick to balance. 'You haven't offended me in the least,' she said. 'Now, let's do the rest of the tour of your new house.'

Amanda wondered what she had said wrong but knew she had already asked Diana too many personal questions. If she wanted to tell Amanda, she would.

They walked through the bottom level of the house, which was clean. It was warmish, and it had electricity and hot and cold running water. She couldn't complain about anything inside besides not having any internet but that could be arranged when she had time.

Upstairs were four bedrooms and a bathroom with a chain to flush the toilet and a huge bath with clawed feet.

The main bedroom looked out over the front garden and down to the sea. It had a four-poster bed and there was a mix of patterns and textures in the room, with old Persian rugs and a hand-blocked linen bedspread that was old but perfectly suited the space. The curtains were a mix of antique fabrics including silk and velvet and even ticking. An armchair and small round table sat by the window, inviting Amanda to sit and draw, and the marble mantelpiece framed a clean fireplace.

'Much of what is in this room has come from my family's travels from their time in business. The bedspread came from India. The silk curtains are from China, and the rugs on either side of the bed are from Azilal, in the Atlas Mountains in Morocco.'

Amanda thought Diana could have been speaking a foreign language the way she reeled off the names of the places her family had been. They brought back so many different parts of the world with them.

But when she looked around the room, she realised she wouldn't change a thing.

The other bedrooms where unadorned and simple with what Amanda assumed to be Diana's childhood room, with a single bed and a desk and bookshelf. But Diana seemed to skip over those rooms and encouraged Amanda to go outside to the garden again.

However, it was the garden that filled her with dread because of Simon the Sullen, as she had decided to call him, wandering about with his wheelbarrow of sorrows. She didn't feel entirely welcome around him.

'I am returning to the gatehouse now for a rest, as this is all very tiring, I'm sure you can understand. Take your time to explore and then you can settle in,' Diana said. 'But I will check on you later. If you have questions, write them down and we can go through them together.'

'Thank you, Diana,' Amanda said, and in a burst of sentimentality and relief, she leaned forward and gave the older woman a hug.

'Goodness,' said Diana, but when Amanda pulled away, she thought Diana looked more surprised than upset. They walked down to the gatehouse and Amanda took her cases and gave Trotsky a pat.

'Okay, see you soon,' she said.

Leaving Diana, Amanda made her way back to Moongate. Her new home.

9

Simon

Simon hadn't meant to be rude to Amanda, but he was in such a foul mood after the phone call he had received moments earlier, he thought he might tear the wisteria out from its roots.

The wedding caterer had called and said they still hadn't been paid even though the wedding didn't go ahead.

'Call Anika – she's the one who booked you and then didn't turn up. This isn't my issue,' he'd snapped into the phone.

'We did call her and she said you had to pay for it, as she is without funds.'

'Are you serious?' he said.

'We have given you a discount – the best we can offer – but everything was prepared, you see, and we have to pay for people's time, like the waitstaff and car staff. Also, there are three cases of Perrier-Jouët that you had already paid for and we need to deliver them somewhere, as we can't store them.'

The fury he felt made it hard to see straight.

'Leave it with me. I will speak to some people and get back to you.' He had hung up the phone and texted Anika.

Pay the caterer.

A text came whizzing back.

I can't. I'm broke.

I'm broke thanks to the man you cheated on me with. He can pay it. And have the champagne delivered to yours or it will be thrown out.

I can't. I'm in Santorini.

At this point, Simon had turned his phone off and put it in his pocket because the audacity of this woman to casually mention Santorini when she knew it was supposed to be their honeymoon spot was like a knife to the heart.

There was a certain sort of pain when you realised the worst betrayals didn't come from your enemies.

The two people he had most loved and admired had broken him.

And then he'd met Amanda with her freckled face and curly red hair and a cute smile, so innocent and so American. She looked like a doll and had an excitable energy and he knew he'd dampened it with his mood. He wasn't being fair but he also wanted to tell her that the world was an impossible place and there were people like Anika and Charlie, and she should try and stay alone and never share her heart with anyone. Instead he'd been a complete Eeyore.

He could find her and apologise, but then he would have

to tell her his sad story. No, he would just avoid her so she didn't get brought down by his mood and his failures.

That's all he could offer right now and until life changed, it's how he would stay.

10

Amanda

After Amanda left Diana at the gatehouse, she unpacked her cases and put her clothes away in the large free-standing wardrobes. She explored the house some more, trying to memorise the layout and deciding which room would be the one she painted in. She took lots of photos for Lainie and shared them with her.

Then she pulled on her Converse, some denim shorts and a T-shirt from her college days. She sprayed some bug spray on her legs and arms and applied a large amount of sunscreen and then she was ready to look at the garden.

Simon wasn't anywhere to be seen when she went outside, for which she was grateful. Diana was paying him to be there for the summer she had said, but Amanda wished it was someone jolly and personable. And what annoyed her the most was that she couldn't work out what animal Simon was. Nothing came to mind and that irked her more than she wanted to admit. Sometimes Amanda thought her labelling of people as animals was a superpower and she wondered if her mother's death had thieved her of her skill. She hadn't painted since then either, she reasoned, but she knew she had named Diana correctly, even if the old woman had responded strangely to the comparison.

Amanda walked along the paths until she found an empty pond with vines creeping into its depths.

She pulled at one but instead of giving, it cut her hand.

'You need gloves for that – it's wisteria. It's very hard to pull on; it needs to be cut and trained.' She turned and saw Simon behind her with his wheelbarrow, and his scowl.

'Okay, good to know,' she said, feeling embarrassed at his judgemental tone.

'There's a spare pair of gloves in the potting shed,' he said and then walked past her.

She followed him. 'Are you going to the potting shed?' she asked.

'I wasn't going to, but I can show you now, I suppose.'

She made a face at him behind his back. 'That would be great, thanks so much,' she said. Maybe if she was super nice to him, he might thaw out.

They walked in silence for a little, passing overgrown garden beds and walls with plants growing up them. They turned down a small pathway, which was filled with ferns and tropical-style plants.

'Oh this is gorgeous, I love ferns,' Amanda said.

Simon ignored her as he stopped.

'That's the potting shed,' he said, pointing towards the structure. 'There's all manner of things in there for you to start gardening.'

'Thanks so much,' she said.

'You don't need to thank me, it's your house now,' he said without any emotion, and he dropped the wheelbarrow to the side of the path and left her alone outside the shed.

He was a donkey, she decided. A sad, grumpy donkey, like the one from Winnie-the-Pooh, always bringing the mood down. She giggled to herself as she stepped into the shed and looked around. There were stacks of terracotta pots of all sizes, and pieces of trellis and a variety of stakes. It was filled to the brim with gardening tools, and bags of what looked to be some sort of soil.

There were a large number of spider webs but they didn't bother Amanda. Her mother had told her as child that spiders were her friends, confirmed by her favourite book as a child: *Charlotte's Web*. Instead she greeted them.

'Hello, spider friends, catching some nice bugs and flies today?' she asked as she opened a drawer and found the gloves Simon had mentioned. They were worn yellow leather with extra padding on the fingers and palm, and well loved, she thought, as she tuned them inside out to check for any further spider friends.

She turned them back to the right way and slipped her hands into them, feeling the softness of the leather that seemed to have been made just for her hands.

Keeping them on, Amanda moved some broken pots from the shed and put them outside the door. There were also some broken stakes and a plastic watering can with a split down the side.

Soon Amanda was busy making a pile of things to throw out and enjoying the process. It wasn't lost on her that she should have done this to her flat in New York, but it felt different doing it outside in her own little potting shed. Eventually she decided to clean out the potting shed completely and had a pile of items that were usable on one side of the path and another of broken items to have taken away.

As she moved things out of the shed, she found a broom and she swept the floor, coughing at the years of dust and dirt she was disrupting.

Next she decided to clean up the benches. One of them had been hidden behind the stack of pots and she noticed a wooden box with small drawers on the front. She opened a drawer carefully, just in case there was an unwanted surprise of a dead creature inside but instead there were small envelopes, the sort that held buttons on a new top when you bought it from a store. She picked up the first one and blew the dust from it.

Delphiniums – White, was written in neat handwriting with a little symbol next to it of a star.

Dahlia – Jomanda Pink, read the next with a different symbol of a triangle.

Amanda realised each drawer held seeds that were organised alphabetically and she picked up the box and carried it outside, placing it on top of the pile to be kept.

She would take that to Diana to talk about later, she thought.

It was an okay job, she thought as she stepped back and looked at her work.

'You've been busy,' she heard Simon say and she turned to him.

'Look at this; I found seeds!' she said and opened a drawer in the box.

Simon peered inside it and took out a packet and read aloud: '*Aster – Apricot Duchess.*'

Amanda sighed. 'I know so little about gardening. I need to learn quickly. Can you teach me?'

Simon gave a harsh-sounding laugh. 'I know about as much as you to be honest.'

'But you're the gardener here,' Amanda said.

'No, Diana hired me to clean the garden up and pull everything dead out and get it to a manageable state, which, to be honest, is too big a job for one person.'

He sounded defensive as he spoke and Amanda stepped back. 'I'm sorry, I didn't realise.'

Simon shook his head. 'It's fine, I'm just here for the summer to help her out.'

'And then where will you go?' Amanda asked.

'I don't know yet.' Simon was looking at the pile of tools that Amanda had leaned against the shed wall.

'These can be sharpened again. A lot of them are great quality,' he said, picking up a pair of shears.

'Do you know how to do that?' she asked, sceptical at the amount of rust on the blades.

'Nope, but I think I can learn,' he said. 'I'll go into Newcastle and use the library as there's no internet here and it will kill my data plan on my phone.'

'I need to get onto that,' said Amanda, looking around. 'There is so much to do and while it's amazing I won the house, I'm not sure I can afford it. I mean, all of these need to go to the junkyard or whatever you call it here.' She gestured to the pile of broken items. 'I need internet, food… I also have my student loan to pay. I have some money from leaving my job but that won't last long. God it's so depressing being poor.' Then she laughed it off. 'Sorry, you don't have to listen to my cost of living worries – I'm sure you have your own stuff to deal with.'

Simon gave a short laugh. 'We all do.' He paused and then looked at her, his face serious before it changed to a softer expression. 'Don't worry about money, just maybe get a job somewhere to pay for day-to-day stuff and I can work on the garden as much as I can since I'm being paid. You can point at things and tell me what to do when you're not working. It will all sort itself out.'

Amanda nodded slowly. 'You sound like my mom. Thank you. I needed that reality check. I need to be positive it will all work out, because as she used to say, it usually does.'

Simon loaded the tools into his wheelbarrow. 'I might look into getting these sharpened, if that's okay with you?'

Amanda shrugged. 'Go for it, please.'

She wasn't sure what had changed but he seemed a little less donkey-like.

Simon picked up the wheelbarrow and had started to walk away when he turned back to Amanda.

'Nice work on finding the seeds. We should chat to Diana and see what goes where and when.' He smiled at her and she nodded.

'Let's,' she said with a grin. 'And thanks again for the pep talk. I needed that.'

'Anytime,' he said as he walked away.

11

Simon

Simon almost believed his own words of positivity except he then remembered that he worried about money all the time. But he reasoned as he went back to his place to assess the tools, it didn't mean he wanted other people to worry about money. He pulled a chair outside and sat on it, looking at the state of the gardening equipment.

As though the world was conspiring against him, he turned on his phone and saw a text from Charlie for the first time since the wedding day.

> Si, we need to talk about work and the catering bill Anika told me about.

Simon turned the phone over and ignored the text. He didn't have anything to say to Charlie. He had ruined him financially and emotionally, and Simon had been a fool to believe anything Charlie said.

Simon picked up a pair of shears that were worn but the steel was quality, better than anything he had seen in the gardening store in Newcastle.

He picked up his phone again and deleted the message from Charlie and then looked up tool sharpening in his area.

There was a local man in the next village over, it said, and he looked up the address. He might as well get them sharpened, he thought – easier and more cost-friendly than replacing everything – but as he looked at the pile on top of the wheelbarrow he realised he couldn't take them on his bike. He would have to borrow a car from someone.

He piled the tools out the front of his little home for the time being and went inside to make tea. The books Diana had given him sat on the table but he hadn't opened them yet.

He picked up the first one, a thin volume with a photograph of Moongate Manor on the front.

The Gardens at Moongate, read the title, by Diana Graybrook-Moore and Peter Buckland.

Who was Peter Buckland? he wondered.

He flicked through it. There were photos throughout the book, if he could call it that, of various parts of the garden with old drawings, presumably from the original designer, and text describing the areas and the soil type and what liked to be planted where.

In the centre of the book were fold-out maps, on thin tracing paper, and as Simon read them, he saw they were corresponding planting guides to the seasons and the plants listed had little symbols next to them.

He frowned, trying to think where he had seen the symbols and then he jumped up and grabbed the book and ran to the gardening shed, where Amanda was just leaving, the drawers in hand.

'I have to show you something,' he said, puffing a little as he spoke.

'Okay, come to the house. I need to put the drawers down,' she said. 'They're heavy.'

'Here.' Simon put his hands out for the box. 'Swap.'

Amanda handed him the box and looked at the book. 'Oh wow, old Moongate Manor, and written by Diana – amazing.'

'That's not even the good bit,' Simon said as they walked to the house.

They walked through the back door into the kitchen area and Simon put the box down on the bench.

'Coffee?' Amanda asked.

'Tea?' he countered.

'Sure,' said Amanda and she filled up an old kettle, put it on the hob and turned the gas on.

'God, this is an old kitchen,' he said, looking around.

'Tell me about it.' Amanda laughed. 'But I don't mind – it's sort of cosy and cute.'

'But even I have a microwave,' said Simon, looking at the old fridge and sink.

'You have a microwave? God, you're living the life, aren't you.' Amanda laughed and Simon noticed how infectious her laugh was and he couldn't help but smile.

'So look at this,' he said, opening the book.

Amanda leaned on the bench with her elbows.

He opened the pages to the middle of the book and carefully unfolded the first map.

'This is summer at Moongate, and every bed is shown with the planting patterns.'

'Oh that's very cool,' said Amanda, her finger running over the map.

'But all of these beds have a symbol on them and...' He opened a drawer of the box and took out an envelope. 'Theses seeds are labelled with the corresponding symbol.'

'What? That's crazy,' said Amanda, looking at the symbol on the envelope and then looking at the legend on the first map.

She went to the next map and opened it and then the next.

'These are Canterbury bells. They are sown in June, it reads here,' she said triumphantly. 'God, this is amazing. What a find – well done,' Amanda said to Simon who shook his head.

'Diana gave me the book but I hadn't looked at it yet. But you found the seeds and cleaned out the shed. I should have done that.'

Amanda laughed. 'It doesn't matter who did it; it's found, and now we can start to plan. It's so exciting. I found nasturtium seeds. They were my mom's favourite flower. She just loved the way they fell from the community garden beds in our neighbourhood. I did a painting of them once for her. She loved it so much.'

Simon smiled. He had to admit he felt a small flicker of something resembling optimism, which was refreshing after so many months of gloom and going over what had happened every waking minute.

'So why are you here?' she asked him as she poured hot water into his mug.

'Just to have a break from the world. I've been riding around Britain, working odd jobs and so on.' He was deliberately vague in his answer. She didn't need to know too much since he wasn't going to be here in a few months.

'Where did you live before?'

Simon had a choice to make. He could be like Anika and Charlie and lie to her, tell her all sorts of untruths to keep her from knowing him… or he could tell the truth.

Whatever he was, he refused to be like them.

'I was in London,' he said.

Amanda nodded. 'I went there briefly to get the keys to this place and sign the papers but I didn't stay. I'd love to go back and see all the sights.'

'You should – it's a great city.'

Amanda handed him his tea and some milk from the fridge. 'I'll leave you to make your own the way you like it. Except I'm not sure I have sugar. I haven't really gone through the cupboards yet.'

Simon dipped the bag a few more times, then removed it and added a dash of milk.

'And what about you? You're from New York? That's all I know.'

Amanda sighed. 'Born and bred, but I sometimes wonder if New York was really in my blood, you know?'

'How do you mean?' he asked.

'Let's just say I have a deep inner world that doesn't look like New York.' She gestured to the house around her. 'I have hardly spent any time here and yet it feels more like home than New York ever did.'

'Maybe you're just one of those people who like the country,' he said.

Amanda nodded. 'Maybe. What about you? City or country mouse?'

'I'm a city mouse through and through,' he said. 'Born and bred in London and my mum's still there, although she hates it. She would love this.'

Amanda moved some hair out of her eyes that had sprung from her bun and she grinned at him. 'Does she like to garden? If she can identify a weed at thirty paces, then she can come and stay.'

Simon rolled his eyes. 'God, she would love that but no, let's leave her in London.'

He felt a pang of guilt as he spoke, knowing his mother would be worried about him, but he couldn't tell her where he was, because he didn't want Charlie and Anika to know.

Amanda moved to the table with the book. 'Can you bring the seeds over? I'm going to read this now and get my head around it. I need to visualise it.'

Simon nodded. 'Do you mind if I take this tea into the garden? I'll bring the mug back.'

Amanda nodded as well, already engaged in the book. 'Sure thing, I'll be here.'

Simon walked to the back door and opened it.

'Hey,' he heard her say and he turned around. She was sitting at the old-fashioned table, a pendant light from the 1960s above her, with yellow-painted walls surrounding her. A ribbon of light ran from the window across her.

'Your hair,' he said. 'It's copper, not red.'

She reached up and touched it, perhaps a little self-consciously. 'Yes, butterscotch my mom used to say.'

'I can see that,' he said with a smile.

'I wanted to say'—she seemed awkward—'I mean, I'm glad we spoke. It would be great if we could be friends. I don't know anyone here, so, you know, it'd be good to have a partner in the garden...' Her voice trailed off into nothing and he wondered if she was biting the inside of her lip.

'I was grumpy when we met earlier today.'

Amanda smiled at him. 'Yes, you were being a bit of a donkey,' she said.

Simon laughed. 'I know, I thought I was being like Eeyore.'

'That's his name, I was trying to remember,' Amanda said.

Simon laughed. 'I can't believe you called me a donkey – that's exactly what I was thinking.'

He had spent the last few months avoiding people. He rode alone, he lived alone, he worked alone as much as possible and now, he had his own bed, a commitment to a project, and a lovely girl asking to be his friend.

'Of course we can be friends,' he heard himself say. He was surprised at his answer but it would be hard to avoid talking to her and she would have to plan the garden with him since she was the owner.

'Great, I'm super excited,' she said.

'Well I better get on with it then,' he said, and he closed the door behind him, wondering what on earth he had just committed himself to.

*

Diana – 1960s

It was becoming tiresome to keep lying to her parents about where she was most days and nights.

Her mother must have known she wasn't with Helen every day as she claimed, but she seemed happy to turn a blind eye to Diana's comings and goings.

Perhaps her mother thought Diana needed to get her youthful exploits out of her system, as she had said about other girls Diana's age who went and did things that her mother considered outrageous such as learning to type and going to university.

But for Diana this was more than getting her youth out of her way – she was falling in love.

Douglas would meet her on his bike, around the bend from Moongate, and hand her his own helmet. He had painted a beautiful letter D on the back in black over the bright, fire-engine-red paint.

Diana would run down and meet him, her lies to her parents becoming less creative and embellished with details. She was off to see Helen, she said. She was having lunch with Christina from Mowden Hall. There was an exhibition she wanted to see at the Laing Art Gallery, or a new dress at Fenwicks she needed to try on.

Her father didn't take much interest in Diana's life before so she wasn't expecting him to care now, especially when he was so focused on developing a new line for the shipping company, but this time with aeroplanes.

Diana was free to come and go as she pleased as long as she didn't bring any shame upon the Graybrook-Moore name.

Douglas had postponed his trip twice now and she was madly hoping he would postpone it forever, she had told Helen when they had a discussion over coffee before Diana met Douglas for a picnic at Plessey Woods.

'You think he's going to stay?' Helen scoffed.

'Why wouldn't he?' asked Diana.

'Because there's no future for him here with your parents. They can barely stand that you're best friends with the gardener's daughter let alone seeing an unemployed Scottish boy on a motorbike.'

'He's going to come back and study when he's finished his adventure,' said Diana, which wasn't strictly true but he might, one day, he had said to her.

But Diana had no idea what he wanted to do if he did study. She had suggested business because in her fantasy he would marry her and then run the business with her father and everyone would be happy.

Douglas had laughed and said he would be no good at business and instead he might do something with his hands like become a mechanic or something.

Helen wasn't convinced about Douglas while Diana was head over heels for him.

'If you sleep with him, use a condom,' said Helen, pushing an envelope towards her across the table.

Diana gasped. 'Helen,' she said, but picked it and shoved it in her handbag nonetheless.

'You know you don't want anything unexpected,' Helen reminded her.

Diana was blushing as she took a large sip of her coffee and started to cough.

She and Douglas had made out, a lot. Heavy sessions

where she could feel how much he wanted her and he could feel her desire. But he was staying in a room above a pub in Newcastle and she hadn't imagined losing her virginity to the sound of music from downstairs and the smell of stale beer.

Helen went back to work after her break and Diana met Douglas outside, where he was sitting on his bike, her helmet in his hand, wearing jeans and boots and a large peacoat as the weather was getting cooler in the August days.

'Ready?' he asked, patting the rucksack tied to the back of the motorbike.

She smiled as she took the helmet and jumped on the back, her trousers making it easier for her to ride it than in her dresses, where she had to tuck the fabric under her legs so she didn't show off more than she wanted on the roads of Newcastle.

She put her arms around Douglas and he took off in the directions of the woods.

This would be the day, she decided. The feeling of making such an adult decision was freeing and for the first time she wondered if she might leave Moongate Manor and go on an adventure with Douglas. Once she lost her virginity she could do as she pleased – there was no holding back in her life now.

She squeezed Douglas tighter and she felt the bike pick up speed as they passed the hedges and trees. She was about to be a modern, independent woman, and nothing her mother or father said could change that fact.

12

Amanda

Amanda had spent two days reading the history of the garden at Moongate Manor in the slim volume that Simon had shown her, as well as researching the plants mentioned inside. While she wasn't familiar with the gardening terms and some of the more specific soil-testing procedures and how to store bulbs, the vision for the garden at Moongate was all there. Diana's work and the knowledge of her and her co-writer, Peter Buckland, were evident in every page.

But Amanda had to wonder why Diana had let the garden go completely to ruin when she had so clearly loved it beyond measure.

The garden was not formal or contained in strict structures or manicured hedges. It was an ode to nature with wild plantings and a mix of plants that were not usually paired together at the time the garden was designed.

As Amanda read the book, she took notes of the types of plants mentioned, and she made a list to look up in the flower books she had found in the library.

The books on planting and flowers were extensive and many of them older than Diana, but they had pictures of the plants inside them, which helped Amanda see how they would look in full bloom, but she was still struggling to imagine it complete.

There was only one thing that Amanda knew she could do to make the garden something she could see in her mind.

She went to her room upstairs and pulled out the suitcase that she had packed some art supplies in. She found her watercolours and paper, some brushes and pens and went downstairs and set them up on the kitchen table.

Drawing and painting had become something she viewed as an indulgence when her mother became ill, despite Wendy's protestations that Amanda should be drawing every day.

But she couldn't concentrate on anything but trying to help her mother and when the news came that the brain tumour was terminal, Amanda had put her art supplies away.

Now she opened the tin of her best French watercolours with the most intense hues and laid it carefully to the side.

She went to the cupboards and found a jam jar and put some water in it. She also found an old cloth; perhaps it was a dusting rag, she thought, as she took it from the drawer, as it was too frayed to be anything else.

She opened the book to the maps of the garden in season and then opened to a new page in her A3 sketchbook.

She carefully sketched out the layout of one of the beds along the driveway. While it wasn't an architectural masterpiece, it gave her an understanding of the parameters and boundaries of the stone walls and edging for the beds.

Looking up the plants recommended for summer she

marked the pages for each of the flowers mentioned and then set to work.

White hydrangeas sat happily besides pink cosmos daisies, and snapdragons and tall white and pink foxgloves. They were mixed with something called a hosta, which Amanda immediately loved for its verdant green leaves. The pink and white were a gorgeous combination, she thought, as she painted the layers of the water colours for the different shades of pink.

She started to shade the pathway but couldn't remember what the ground was like. Was it stones or crushed gravel there? she wondered. Taking her drawing pad and her pens with her, she walked to the part of the garden that she was drawing. The driveway passed Diana's house and she wondered if she should call on her but she was mindful not to bother the woman. She had a life outside of Moongate and didn't need Amanda asking her silly questions that she could probably find answers to herself.

Amanda scuffed the ground to see what the path was next to the bed along the driveway and saw it was gravel. She filled in some shading and then stood back and looked at the empty garden bed and then at her drawing.

If she could turn that into this, she thought, it would be a miracle.

'Doing a little sketching?'

Amanda turned at the sound of Diana's voice and saw her standing with her dog, who was off leash and sniffing about the ground.

Diana was in a simple pale green dress that looked very good quality, if not a little old-fashioned, and a light yellow cardigan and sensible lace-up flat shoes. She was also wearing tortoiseshell-style sunglasses, which seemed slightly incongruous with the rest of her look, but Amanda could hardly pass any style judgement while wearing purple Indian harem pants, no shoes, and her 'New York Baby' T-shirt tied at the waist.

'Hi,' Amanda said. 'Simon showed me that book you wrote. You're amazing!'

Diana laughed. 'It's not really a book and we only printed a few copies, but I thought it best I record what we did to bring it to its full glory in case anyone else wanted to restore it one day.' Diana looked at the pad that Amanda was holding. 'What did you sketch?'

Amanda looked down at the page. 'I was trying to imagine the flower beds, so I did this. I mean, it's not great, but I'm a visual learner,' she said, handing the pad to Diana.

Diana looked at the paper and then the garden bed and back again a few times.

'Remarkable,' she said. 'It's near perfect. You must have a strong knowledge of flowers to be able to replicate the ones on the legends of the maps.'

'Not really, I looked them up, but I found the drawer of seeds in the potting shed.'

'You didn't?' Diana gasped. 'I thought that had been mistakenly thrown out.'

'No, all there and they're all so neatly marked. The box is lined and was weather proof, so I think some of them might germinate, or at least I'm hoping. Even if some don't take, I at least have the names of everything now. The writing is so neat.' Amanda laughed. 'Neater than mine.'

'That was Pete's writing,' said Diana. 'He did all of that work.'

Diana looked back at the paper, her finger trailing over the artwork.

'This is exceptional,' she said to Amanda, who blushed.

'It's very rudimentary, but it helps me see what it was like.'

Diana nodded. 'Will do you do other seasons? I would very much like to see them.'

'Of course,' said Amanda. 'I can't wait to show you but I need to head to a bigger town or village or whatever you call them so I can get some more tracing paper and things. Is there a bus?'

Diana smiled. 'I can do better for you than a bus,' she said. 'Follow me.'

They walked slowly along the driveway, Amanda making sure she was keeping pace with Diana who, at times, winced with pain.

'Are you okay?' Amanda asked finally as they moved around the side of the house and along a path.

'I am fine but my knees are not – many years on them in the garden takes its toll.'

'You could have a replacement,' said Amanda. 'They're made of titanium and chrome now.'

Diana snorted as they walked over a cobblestoned courtyard and through a gate.

'Have you been out here yet?' asked Diana.

'I haven't,' admitted Amanda. 'I'm still trying to remember where my bedroom is in the house. It's bigger inside than I expected.'

'These were the stables,' said Diana, pointing with her stick. 'I wasn't much of a horse person – I preferred dogs.'

They walked through the stable, Amanda treading

carefully on the warm cobblestones, and came to a set of large stable doors.

'Can you open these?' Diana gestured at them.

Amanda lifted the latch, which moved easily, as though regularly oiled, and the doors pushed back and there, in the cool air of the stables, was a small car.

'This was my first and only car,' said Diana. 'It is yours now.'

'Mine? I can't take a car,' Amanda said.

'You took the house; what does it matter if you take the car as well?' Diana said impatiently. 'I don't drive anymore but it's been serviced and cared for since I've had it.'

Amanda couldn't argue with that and she walked to the car. 'When did you get it?' she asked.

'When I was eighteen. I paid for it myself,' she said proudly. 'I had to sell some jewellery and a watch because my parents wouldn't let me get a job, but driving this, alone, was the best feeling in the world.'

Amanda opened the car door and sat inside and looked around. Diana was correct in her statement that it was in top condition. The car had clearly been looked after with everything clean and shiny, albeit old.

That's what Amanda didn't understand about Moongate. The house was in good condition, the car was fine, everything had been cared for... except the garden, which Diana had obviously adored.

Amanda got out of the car. 'What a gorgeous car. Now I can drive you wherever you want to go,' she said to Diana.

But Diana shook her head. 'I don't really see anyone. I don't have friends.'

'You don't have friends?'

Dina shook her head as though she was shooing away flies.

'No, no time for them when I was in the garden.'

Amanda was silent, thinking about Lainie and how much she loved her best friend.

'I had a friend – Helen. She was the gardener's daughter, but then life happened and took us on different paths,' Diana said and Amanda saw her shoulders soften, almost droop – she wasn't sure why but she knew the older woman felt sad.

'That's not true about not having friends,' said Amanda brightly.

Diana looked up at her.

'We're friends, and Simon and I became friends the other day, so the three of us are friends now.'

'I'm too old to be your friend,' said Diana, but not convincingly.

'Are there rules for friendships? I didn't know that age differences matter when you're buddies.'

Diana frowned. 'Buddies,' she repeated and rolled her eyes at Amanda. 'So American.'

'As apple pie, buddy,' teased Amanda, and Diana laughed in spite of herself.

Amanda was serious for a moment. 'The only thing is, I haven't driven much. I mean, I have my licence, but we didn't have a car in New York, and over in America we drive on the other side of the road.'

Diana turned and started to walk back the way they had come.

'You can get Simon to teach you – he will know how. Now, come on to my house and I will make you tea.'

Amanda's phone buzzed in her pocket and she took it out and saw a message from Lainie.

Thanks for the photos. Love everything. FYI, I saw Mike out with a blonde. He's so gross.

Amanda sighed. Of course Mike had moved on quickly. Why on earth had she ever thought there was something more there? She was part-time, not a partner.

'Everything all right, dear?' asked Diana.

'Yes, my friend in New York told me she just saw my ex-boyfriend out with a blonde. He clearly isn't sad without me,' she said with a small laugh. But she felt okay about it, she realised. Mike was nothing more than company. She had mistaken physical connection for emotional understanding. Never again, she told herself. Whoever she was next in a relationship with, it had to be a connection at a soul level.

'A blonde?' Diana sniffed. 'His loss. Come on, I need tea.'

Amanda followed Diana, pushing her thoughts of Mike away for the last time. Instead she started to wonder how Simon would feel about teaching her to drive and why everyone in England seemed to only drink tea.

'Any hope of coffee?' she asked Diana.

'Not a chance.' Diana laughed. 'You're in England now. Our coffee is terrible but our tea is exceptional. You'll learn to love it.'

'Like Stockholm syndrome for beverages,' said Amanda as they came to the gatehouse.

'Exactly, dear,' said Diana.

13

Simon

Amanda sat in the car Diana had given her and turned the key.

It started without any protest and she turned to Simon sitting next to her.

'Diana was right. She said it was in good shape but I thought she was exaggerating.'

Simon shook his head. 'I don't think Diana would ever lie to anyone. She has that way about her, you know?'

'No, what do you mean?'

'I just think women like Diana... they're raised to be polite but also not to take any bullshit from anyone. I think she would tell you if you asked her opinion on something but the key to her is, you have to ask first. She isn't the sort to offer unsolicited opinions.'

Amanda laughed. 'I don't know. She's been pretty opinionated with me. But no wonder she said she didn't like New York when she went. You can't walk down the street without someone offering commentary on your look, walk, your inability to step sideways in time for someone in a hurry.'

She took off the handbrake and slowly drove from the garage and around the side of the house and onto the driveway.

Diana was standing by her gate with Trotsky next to her, watching how Amanda was getting on.

'God, this is terrifying,' Amanda said. 'Please don't let me crash the car.'

'You're not going to crash the car,' Simon said assuredly as she came to the front of the gatehouse.

'First drive – do you want to sit in the back seat?' she asked.

Diana waved her stick at her. 'No, thank you. Now get along with you both.'

Amanda smiled and gave the car horn a toot before driving on down to the road.

'Okay, tell me what I'm doing,' she said to Simon.

'You're turning right, so you will go out onto the other side of the road.'

A car passed them and Amanda turned on her indicator.

She looked both ways and then turned onto the road as Simon instructed.

'Oh my God, I'm driving on the other side of the road,' she said, gripping the steering wheel.

'That's what people from the UK say when they go to America and drive there,' Simon reminded her.

'True, but still, it's fun,' she said. 'Where will we go?'

'It's your car, so wherever you want,' he said.

'Let's go to the village. I haven't seen any of it yet. Have you?'

'I spent one night in the pub. I didn't really fit in or

probably I didn't try. I don't really have a lot of friends. Not because I don't like people but it feels like no one takes the time to know anyone anymore,' he said.

'Nice self-awareness there, old man,' said Amanda.

'You're one of those Americans who loves therapy, I bet.'

Amanda laughed. 'I have been in therapy since I was twelve, but stopped going when my mom got sick. I mean, you can't really make someone happy about their mom dying of cancer.'

'True,' agreed Simon.

They drove in silence for a while but it wasn't awkward, for which Simon was relieved.

'So I just stay on this road?' she asked.

'Yes, that's right,' he said.

He noticed the whites of Amanda's knuckles were showing and he reached out and touched her hand lightly.

'Relax, Lewis Hamilton.'

Amanda gave a nervous laugh. 'Yes, I'm a bit anxious,' she said, but she loosened her grip a little.

Simon looked at the sea as they passed. It was grey and still and the beaches were wide and empty.

'I wonder if it gets busy in the summer,' Amanda said with a glance at the sea.

'I don't think so. People tend to go down to Cornwall or Devon in the summer, or they go to Europe.'

'What a shame,' said Amanda. 'But better for us. I sometimes went to the Hamptons with my best friend Lainie. Her parents have a house there but it's kind of boring and very pretentious. I preferred Cape Elizabeth in Maine. Mom and I went there a few times. She would rent a room at this inn looking over the sea, and I would paint and draw and she would write and, I tell you, it was as near to perfect as anything else I have ever known. You know what I mean?'

Simon laughed. 'No, I don't actually. I don't think I've ever had such a visceral response to anything the way you just described. I feel like I'm missing out.'

'There's still time,' said Amanda.

'Are you always so positive?' he asked.

Amanda slowed down as they came towards the start of the village. 'Not always. I mean, as I said, my mom died not long ago. That was pretty awful,' she said, and he heard the pain in her voice.

'I'm sorry,' he said. 'That is awful.'

'Okay, where am I going?' she asked as the car crawled along the road.

'I think we need to find somewhere to park and then we can have a wander,' Simon said.

'Great idea,' said Amanda, her voice light again.

'There's one there.' Simon pointed ahead.

'Oh I can't park there,' said Amanda.

'Why not?' Simon said, turning to look at the empty parking space as they drove past.

'Because I can't parallel park when I'm on the right side of the road, let alone the left.'

Simon laughed as Amanda kept driving.

'Pull over,' he said, gesturing to the side of the road. 'I'll show you how to park.'

Amanda pulled over and turned the car off and turned to him.

'Sorry, I feel bad for making you come and do this, like I'm annoying you or something.'

Simon frowned. 'Do you think I'm annoyed?' he asked.

Amanda paused, and that was enough for him to know her answer.

'I can be brusque, not because I want to be rude, just because I don't have great people skills at the moment.'

'At the moment?' Amanda was smiling at him, seeming curious more than judgemental, he thought.

'Some things have happened that haven't made me love the human race lately.'

Amanda opened the door, got out of the car and walked around the back of the car to the passenger side, while Simon went around the front and slid into the driver's seat.

'Do you want to talk about it?' she asked as he clipped in his seat belt.

'Not really,' he answered.

'That's cool,' she said, and he turned on the indicator and drove onto the road and made a U-turn.

'Are you hungry?' he asked.

'I could eat,' Amanda said.

Simon was surprised at how well the car drove as he looked for a parking spot.

'Diana has really taken care of this little car. It's a corker,' he said.

'A corker?' Amanda asked.

'You know… like it's good, it goes well, a really solid little car.'

Amanda laughed. 'A corker, okay – a new phrase learned today.'

'Don't you know many English slang words?' he asked.

She shook her head. 'Mom didn't really say many of them. I mean, I used different terms for things like footpath over sidewalk and rubbish over trash because that's what I was taught, but not the slang words.'

'Then it will be a pleasure to teach you,' he said as he found a parking spot near the church and backed into it easily.

They stepped out of the car and Simon saw Amanda immediately move to the community noticeboard.

'Looking for piano lessons or a dog walker?' he joked, as he came to her side.

'Look,' she said, and she put her finger on the glass over one particular notice.

'The Foxfield gardening club,' he read. 'Meets every second Thursday at St Cuthbert's Church Hall. All welcome.'

'We should go and ask them for gardening advice,' she said, turning to him.

Simon made a face.

'What? Why the face?' she asked.

'It's the only face I have.' He chuckled to himself. He was surprised at his good mood. He had woken to another text from Charlie asking to talk and it had left him in a sour mood. When Amanda had asked him to help her drive the car, he was reluctant to agree as he wasn't fit to spend time with anyone, but Amanda was easy company really. She didn't pry, she laughed at his jokes and she was interesting.

'No, really, we don't know anything and we need help in the garden,' she said. She blew a curl out of her face. 'We could offer it to them to be a project or something.'

Simon looked at the notice and then at Amanda. 'And you think they would want to help us for free?'

Amanda shrugged. 'It's worth asking, isn't it? I mean, what have we got to lose?'

Simon couldn't argue with that and, besides, he had already lost everything and had nothing else left to weep over.

'Okay, you're the lady of the manor now.'

Amanda laughed and pushed him lightly. 'Don't say that. I hate it. It feels weird, as though I'm trying to be better than I am. I'm just lucky, that's all. Lucky my mom bought a ticket and lucky to have you to be my friend and help me.'

And she smiled a bright, true smile, one that Simon hadn't seen in a woman for so long. It made him wonder if Anika had ever really smiled at him with her whole heart – or was it always for Charlie from the start?

Diana – 1960s

Douglas was waiting for Diana when she came out of Moongate Manor, but he had a serious look on his face when she ran up to him and kissed his cheek.

'Hello,' she said, and pressed her body into his.

They had made love three times now and Diana wanted him again and again. All she could think about was Douglas naked and inside her. And as she'd told Helen, she thought she was getting better at sex with each time.

Helen had laughed and given her another condom but Diana had told her that Douglas knew how to pull out so she wouldn't become pregnant. Helen had laughed at her again and said that was a fool's way but Diana ignored her.

'Where are we going? Somewhere private?' she asked.

'Would your parents believe if you said you were staying at Helen's overnight?' he murmured in her ear.

'Probably not Helen, but maybe another school friend. I will ring them late and say the car broke down so I'm staying over. I'll be vague and deal with the drama tomorrow. Why?' She was intrigued.

'I have booked a hotel, in Middlesbrough. You will have to be Mrs Douglas McKay though,' he said and she pressed her mouth to his.

'I can't wait to be Mrs Douglas Mackay,' she said as she climbed onto the back of the bike and they took off.

A whole night in a hotel. Her mother would die but Diana didn't care anymore. This was her future now. Soon she would be Mrs Mackay in reality and there was nothing her parents could do about it.

It took an hour to ride to Middlesbrough and when they arrived it was late afternoon. Douglas parked the bike and they walked inside the hotel he had chosen. It was modern – to match her newfound persona, she decided – and as she waited while he booked them in she looked at the pamphlets for things to do in Middlesbrough, which wasn't much, she had to admit.

'Ready, Mrs Mackay?' Douglas asked and she turned and smiled at him.

'Ready, Mr Mackay,' she said.

Diana felt nervous when he opened the door with the key. A whole night with Douglas was something new, and she wondered what would happen. He was more experienced than her but she was a willing student.

The room was simple with a double bed, which she hadn't seen in person before. Her parents had single beds in sperate rooms, and Diana was still sleeping in her childhood bed.

It wasn't exactly Claridge's, she thought, but it would allow her to have a whole night with Douglas and she could ask him about their future.

Douglas took off his jacket and sat on the end of the bed. 'Diana, I have to tell you something.'

Diana sat next to him on the bed. This was it. This was the moment he told her how he felt and revealed all his ideas about their future.

'This is my last night here,' he said.

Diana felt her world spinning. 'What do you mean?' She felt her hands grasping at the eiderdown, as though hanging on to a lifeline.

'It's coming into autumn and it's getting colder,' he said as he smoothed away a strand of hair from her face. 'I don't want to do the ride through winter. It's too dangerous,' he said. 'And harder to get work.'

Diana couldn't breathe.

'But I'm going to come back,' Douglas said. He reached for her hand and though she could see him holding it she couldn't feel anything, except her future of adventure and partnership slipping away.

'I want to come back,' he said, looking at her closely, as though peering through a window. 'To you,' he said. 'And I want to meet your family, and I want you to stop hiding me from them.'

Diana blinked a few times, willing herself back into the room. 'You said you wanted a life of adventure,' she said slowly.

'I did and I do, but I want to do this first and then come

back here and create a life of adventure with you, Diana. I just want this one trip for me and then we can be together.'

'So you bought me to a hotel for one last night of passion and you're going to say whatever you need to so I lie there and let you do whatever you want while I dream of lace and orange blossom.' The words spat out of her mouth like nails.

'No, we don't have to do anything – I just want to be with you,' he said, his blue eyes imploring her.

Diana stood up. 'Take me home, please.'

'Diana,' he pleaded.

She stood against the wall. 'Now, or I will call the police and tell them you bought me here against my will.'

'Diana, please,' Douglas begged. 'Don't do this.'

'Do what?' She heard herself becoming shrill.

'Ruin this,' he said. 'I want to be with you. I'm going to come back, I promise you.'

Diana could feel the tears coming. She didn't want him to see her crying but it was too late.

Douglas slid off the bed and got onto one knee. 'Diana, marry me. Let's get engaged, and then you will know I'm serious.'

'And tell people you're now riding your motorbike around Europe? A proper engagement requires notices in the papers, a party, photos, planning. I haven't even met your family.'

Douglas shook his head. 'I don't have any. I was raised in Dean's Orphanage. I came here by chance and met some guys that night and went to the club with them. And then I met you.'

Diana was silent.

'And I stayed. I had one suit that I borrowed from one of

the guys I met and some money saved and that was it, but you were such a joy to be around. I've never met anyone like you, Diana. You make me laugh and made me want to protect you forever.'

'So why are you leaving me?' she asked, gulping for air as she cried.

'Because I want to do this one thing. Because I've always wanted to do it.'

Diana looked at the floor, noticing the red and blue fibres in the carpet.

'I want to be with you, Diana, I do,' he said, and she finally let herself look at him. 'But I want – I need – to take this trip first.' Douglas looked pale and worried as she spoke. 'I'll take you back now.' He got up from the floor, and Diana noticed the carpet marks on his trousers. 'It was a silly idea. I'm sorry.'

Diana stepped forward and said, 'Why did you bring me here only to tell me that you're going away tomorrow? It feels cruel.'

Douglas ran his hand through his hair and shook his head. 'I don't know. I wanted to be honest with you but I also wanted to be with you, spend a whole night with you, have memories of us while I am away.'

'Stay and make memories with me now,' she said, hearing her voice break.

They stood facing each other, each with their own agenda, and Diana knew she was beaten.

If he stayed, he would eventually resent her, and if he left now, she would feel she wasn't enough to stay for.

'Take me home,' she said, and she walked out of the hotel room.

14

Amanda

Amanda opened the door to the church hall with Simon standing behind her.

There was a group of six people sitting in a circle. Ranging in age from fifty to ancient, there were four women and two men.

'Hello,' she said, feeling nervous as the faces stared at her as though she was about to try and sell them life insurance. 'We're here for the gardening club.'

There was a murmur of voices and then the awful sound of chairs scraping across the floorboards as two women stood up and almost sprinted to her side.

'Are you sure?' asked a woman with pink, spiky hair and what looked to be a denim jacket with badges all over the front. Oh, she was a galah, the Australian bird, through and through.

'Yes. I'm sure. I'm Amanda Cox and this is my friend Simon. He's working on my new garden with me. We don't know much so we would like to learn,' said Amanda, whispering to Simon: 'Sorry, I don't know your last name.'

Amanda turned back to the woman. 'I really don't know

anything about gardening and I promised I would have it ready for people to visit in a year's time.'

The woman patted her arm. 'It'll be fine. Gardens find their gardeners, you know. They kind of call you until you can't ignore it anymore. I think it's a DNA connection to the land thing. I mean, all our ancestors had dirt under their nails, didn't they? Anyway, I'm Janet. Pleased to meet you both.'

Amanda liked Janet instantly. She definitely would have been friends with her mom and looking at the badges on her jacket she thought she would like to be friends with her also. Black Lives Matter, My Body My Choice, LGBTQI+, animal welfare, save the whales and some Amanda wasn't quite sure of.

'Come and meet everyone,' she insisted.

Amanda looked at Simon who had reverted to his sullen state.

'Try and be likeable,' she hissed.

'Simon the Likeable from *Get Smart* was a KAOS agent,' he whispered.

'I've never watched it,' she answered as Janet started introducing them to the rest of the club.

'This is Shelley and Frank. Shelley owns Shelley's Deli in the village. Shelley's from America.'

The woman gave Amanda a small wave.

'I can hear New York in your accent. Am I right?'

Amanda nodded. 'Yep, born and raised in Astoria.'

The woman elbowed Frank. 'Did you hear that? I grew up in the Bronx, but I had an aunt in Astoria. So close we could be cousins, so I basically know you.'

Frank gave a snort.

'It's true, in New York everyone knows everyone, even just by the borough, isn't that right?' Shelley asked Amanda.

'It's true.' Amanda smiled, already liking the group. Shelley and Frank reminded her of two noisy baboons but in a good way. Friendly and nosy and very opinionated.

'That's the thing about New Yorkers,' Shelley was saying to Frank. 'We're all survivors in a way. That city could be hard on you so, like the song said, you could make it anywhere if you survived New York's bitter winters, heartbreak, rental market and more.'

'This is Dennis, he's our reverend.' Janet was gesturing to a thin, older man who put out his hand to shake.

Amanda looked at Simon, who stepped forward.

Dennis shook both their hands. 'Pleased to see some younger people here,' he said. 'Foxfield doesn't have many young people.'

'Oh? That's a shame,' said Amanda. Dennis reminded her of a field mouse, unobtrusive and very timid.

'Perhaps you will have a baby and bring it up here,' said Shelley, and Simon coughed as though he was choking.

'Rude,' whispered Amanda.

'And this is my wife, Carole,' Janet was saying, as a woman with grey hair and cardigan and a pair of trousers stepped forward. 'She's also the local GP.'

Carole was a Persian cat, well groomed, graceful and with silver-laced hair and blue eyes.

'How lovely to have you join us. Please sit and let's hear all about your garden.'

Amanda and Simon sat on the chairs that Frank put down for them.

'Um, well, it's pretty overgrown, and we want to make it

nicer, of course,' said Amanda, wishing she had more words for describing the state of Moongate's garden.

'Lovely,' said Janet. 'So you've moved here recently?'

Amanda nodded. 'Just a few weeks ago,' she said.

'Nearby?' asked Shelley looking confused.

'Well not in the village, but further out. It's a house called Moongate Manor,' said Amanda.

The group leaned forward as one.

'Moongate? Where is Diana Graybrook-Moore?' asked Dennis the reverend.

'She's still there,' said Amanda. 'She lives in the gatehouse.'

'Are you family then?' asked Carole, her eyes wide.

'No?' Amanda shook her head, looking at Simon for help.

Simon crossed his legs. 'Amanda won Moongate Manor in a lottery. Her mother bought her a ticket and she won, so Diana has given her the house since there isn't any next of kin.'

'Well I'll be,' Frank mumbled.

'Are you serious?' Shelley asked.

'Totally serious. Why are you all freaking out?' Amanda asked.

'Because Diana Graybrook-Moore is basically a hermit. She never leaves that place, even though it's been going to wrack and ruin for the last ten years,' said Frank.

'A hermit? Really?' Amanda looked at Simon who shrugged and shook his head.

'We never see her,' said Janet.

'I've never met her,' said Shelley. 'And I've been in Foxfield for twenty years.'

There was a definite judgemental tone to her statement.

Dennis interjected. 'We don't always know why people do what they do but it's lovely she's bequeathed the home to you and you're very welcome to Foxfield and to our humble gardening club.'

Amanda smiled at him. 'Thank you,' she said.

'I've always wanted to see the garden at Moongate,' admitted Carole. 'I remember it was quite beautiful many years ago, when I was younger but it wasn't open to the public. Does Diana want you to open it again?'

Amanda nodded. 'She wants me to hold something called the Moongate Festival. I don't know what it is exactly but we can't hold anything there right now – besides a weeding festival.'

Shelley snorted. 'You know, you could ask us to help. I mean we're all able-bodied – though some of us somewhat slower than others.' She looked at Dennis. 'No offence, Dennis.'

'None taken but I am an excellent rose pruner and I do have an eye for a weed versus an annual.'

Amanda looked at the gardening club. 'You know, I didn't come to ask for help other than your knowledge, but if you want to come and have a look and give me your ideas, that would be amazing.'

She glanced at Simon who was looking less sullen. 'And Simon and I can do all the heavy stuff. I mean we're young and strong, we just don't have the knowledge you guys all have.'

Amanda noticed them sit up a little straighter and prouder and realised this was important to them.

'Do any of you know what the Moongate Festival is?'

Frank cleared his throat. 'I went to one as a child. I don't have much memory of it but my parents had photos,' he said. 'I can bring them over for you to look at.'

'That would be great,' said Amanda.

'And there would be some information in the Foxfield Historical Club. We could put that on the agenda to discuss,' Dennis added.

'Oh amazing – when do they meet?' Amanda asked.

'After the gardening club meeting,' said Dennis.

Janet looked at her watch. 'Which is now. Gardening club from six until half seven and then historical society from half seven till eight thirty.'

Amanda looked at the door. 'So should I wait here for them?' she asked.

Dennis looked sheepish. 'Actually we are the historical club as well as the gardening club but sometimes we skip the history part of the meeting, because there is nothing new to report.'

'Until now,' said Janet clapping her hands excitedly.

'What do you think, Simon?' asked Dennis.

Simon's head snapped up as though surprised to be included. 'About what?'

'About any of this.' Dennis gestured to the room.

Simon shrugged. 'I think Amanda having friends here and some help and knowledge about the garden is great. I'm not here for long so she will need to get up to speed quickly.'

Amanda spoke to the group. 'Simon is just here for the summer, helping out. Diana hired him.'

Shelley looked at Carole who looked at Janet.

'That's nice, isn't it?' said Shelley, not being shy about the intimation.

Amanda felt herself blush. 'We're just friends,' she said.

'Where are you off to after the summer?' Dennis asked.

'Don't know yet,' Simon said. 'See where the winds take me.'

Dennis nodded. 'It's nice to be free and easy when you're young.'

Janet stood up. 'Time for a cup of tea and some of Shelley's apple cake.' She looked at Amanda and Simon. 'She always brings the leftover cakes from her deli, and I tell you, they are delicious. Frank cooks them.'

Amanda looked at Frank who was nodding proudly.

'Okay, so tea and cake it is,' she said.

The gardening club members were in the small kitchen organising and chatting, and Amanda stretched. 'They're all so great – I love them,' she said to Simon. 'Do you love them?'

Simon laughed. 'I don't love them but they seem pleasant enough.' He paused for a moment. 'But only you could make me come to a random country gardening club on a Thursday night and only you could bewitch the club to come and help with the garden. You really are something else, Amanda Cox.'

And with that he stood up and went into the kitchen for cake, and Amanda wondered if his observation was good or bad – or did it even matter what he thought about her?

15

Diana

Diana was ready to walk Trotsky and when she opened the front door she found a woman with pink hair and a denim jacket standing in her front garden assessing her petunias.

'Excuse me, can I help you?' Diana asked.

The woman jumped back. 'Oh goodness, I'm sorry, I thought this was part of Moongate.'

'It is, it's the gatehouse,' said Diana with a sniff.

'You're Diana Graybrook-Moore,' said the woman putting her hand out. 'Janet Swan, president of the Foxfield Gardening Club and new friend of Amanda.'

Diana took the hand briefly and then clicked her tongue for Trotsky to come. 'Amanda is in the house,' Diana said as she leaned down and put on Trotsky's leash.

The pain in her hip was quite pronounced but she held it in while the woman was invading her space.

'Oh I know, Amanda just gave us a brief tour and then told us to have a wander around, get the lay of the land, so to speak.'

'Well the lay of the land doesn't include my home,' said Diana. 'If you can inform the others.'

Diana pulled on the lead for Trotsky to follow her as Janet scuttled from the garden and back towards the main house.

There was a reason Diana had avoided spending time with others and more so people from the village; they were all busybodies and more than likely liked to gossip about her and what they assumed would be her sad, lonely life.

As Diana walked along the driveway towards the road Amanda popped out from the moon gate.

'Diana, I was coming to see you,' she said, her smile brighter than ever.

Diana took in Amanda's apple-green sundress with work boots and a battered straw hat. Her skin was pale, with a light sprinkling of freckles.

'That hat looks familiar,' said Diana, peering at it closely.

Amanda put her hand up self-consciously to touch the hat. 'I found it in one of the bedrooms. Did you want it back?'

Diana laughed. 'No, dear, I don't need it. I am just trying to think where it came from. Perhaps it was Mother's.'

Amanda looked back at the house. 'Will you come and meet the Foxfield gardening club?' she asked. 'I invited them for a tour, and they said they will help me clear it.'

'I already met one – she was in my front garden. She had pink hair.'

Amanda looked pleased at this news. 'Oh that's Janet – she's great. If I had to choose an animal to for Janet, it would be one of those Australian birds – the galah, you know? The one with a pink and grey crest, slightly plump and short body?'

Diana laughed. 'I am sure she would be thrilled to hear

that.' But then she became serious. 'I am sure she's "great" as you state, but having her amongst my petunias wasn't what I was expecting when I came out for my walk.'

Amanda laughed. 'That's hilarious. I'm sure she meant no harm. She's super excited to see the garden properly; it's like the most exciting thing ever for this club.'

Without realising, Diana had been following Amanda up the path towards the house, and watched as the woman with pink hair came forward.

'Diana, I must apologise again for intruding,' she said and Diana nodded.

'No harm done,' she replied.

'I'm loving having the opportunity to have a stickybeak at this garden – it's wonderful,' she said.

'Stickybeak?' said Diana with a look at Amanda who stifled a giggle.

'Yes, a good look around,' said Janet. 'Those wild hollyhocks are incredible.' She pointed to the side of one of the garden beds. 'Look at those thick stalks. Legs like milkmaid's stools.'

Diana laughed in spite of herself. Janet did have the same infectious energy that Amanda had; no wonder she liked her galah-like friend.

'I so love these Granny's bonnets. We don't see them enough anymore. Everyone seems to like those succulents; they call it low-maintenance gardening. But that's not gardening in my opinion,' Janet said and Diana had to agree with her.

'The bees love this lavender, but it's a bit scraggly now. Look at the old rose. Diana, was that once a hedge?' Janet asked.

'Yes, it was, went all the way around the kitchen garden.'

She looked around. 'This was the kitchen garden. Not that we grew more than herbs and a few beans one year. I wasn't much into growing vegetables and fruit, but it's very popular now,' she mused as she looked at the rose and lavender, with the sparse and woody stems letting the morning light onto the path.

'Yes, well with the cost of living now, we need to grow what we can and be sensible,' said Janet.

Diana nodded but wondered why she hadn't grown food. Probably an unspoken rule of her mother's, she thought. Growing food was for farmers, not for young women whose role was to arrange the flowers that she grew.

A woman approached them, a little younger than Janet, Diana thought. She was more conservative with pearl stud earrings and a knitted jumper with a small brooch of a black cat with green jewelled eyes.

'Hello, I'm Carole Melton, Janet's wife. What a wonderful gift this is to Amanda and in turn us, by her asking us to come and see the garden.'

Diana liked Carole immediately.

'How long have you been in Foxfield?' Diana was surprised at her own curiosity about the women.

'Oh ten years – actually, closer to eleven, I think,' Janet said. 'Carole and I met in Manchester and then found a place to buy here. It's lovely and Carole's kids come and see us often. We're grannies now, as her eldest just had their first – a little girl called Molly.'

Diana tried to take in all the information about these women whom she had just met.

'Carole's the GP here,' said Janet as though Diana might know anything about her.

'Oh?' Diana looked at Carole. 'I see Dr Diamond in Newcastle.'

'He's a very good doctor. I see him at training and information sessions.'

Diana liked Carole even more for confirming her choice in health professional and not having her nose out of joint with Diana for seeing someone else.

'Have you met everyone else?' asked Janet, looking around.

Diana realised she had a choice. She could leave and continue her walk with Trotsky and then return home and make tea and sit with her book she was reading. Then she would have lunch, and perhaps assess her petunias and refill the bird feeder. Later she would doze in her chair and then wake in time to do a spot of tidying, or as much as her arthritis would let her, and then she would make a light dinner of cold meat and green salad. Perhaps a little BBC and more tea and then bed.

The schedule that lay ahead of her suddenly felt like a punishment. Once she had revelled in the simplicity, but now she looked around and saw Amanda's straw hat bobbing about some roses that needed a good prune, and she could hear her talking and laughing. This is what she came here for, Diana reminded herself.

She looked at Carole and Janet, who were waiting patiently, and made her decision.

'No, I haven't met anyone else,' she said. 'Yet.'

'Perfect, let me do the honours, and then we are planning on indulging in some cake from Shelley's Deli, while we sit and have a natter,' Janet said. 'I want to talk gardening, if that's not boring to you?'

Diana shook her head. 'I could talk gardening all day,' she said truthfully. She realised she still wanted to talk about gardening; she just didn't have anyone to talk about it with anymore. Until now.

She unclipped Trotsky's lead and let him wander off to explore at his own leisure and took Janet's arm when it was offered to her.

'Did Amanda show you where the koi pond used to be?'

Janet shook her head. 'No, how fascinating. How did you protect them from the birds?'

'Let me show you,' said Diana.

1960s

It had been two months since Douglas had left her at the gates of Moongate. Diana spent her days waiting for something but she wasn't sure what it was that she was hoping for. She knew Douglas wasn't coming back anytime soon, especially when she had walked away without a goodbye when he had taken her back to Moongate after the disastrous hotel trip. Douglas had said he would return to marry her but she didn't believe him. If he had wanted to marry her then he would have stayed.

She had tried to distract herself with shopping, books, going out to clubs with Helen, anything – but she couldn't focus. She missed Douglas; she missed his hands and mouth and laughter. She missed riding on his motorbike and, more than anything, she missed having a secret.

Diana had thought about Douglas every day since he left and the heartbreak hadn't left her. She was sick to the bone, tired, her body ached, her head ached, nothing working properly anymore, she noticed.

But the sickness came in waves. Sometimes when she woke in the morning, she would lie with her eyes closed and hope that if she kept them closed all day then the tears and nausea wouldn't come.

It was Helen who called it first.

'I can't be – I was careful,' Diana hissed over the phone.

'Not careful enough it seems,' said Helen.

Diana didn't speak; instead she sat on the Queen Anne chair in the hallway where the phone was kept in Moongate Manor.

'You can go to a doctor in Newcastle. There is a new lady doctor there; she has a clinic for women's issues,' Helen was saying but Diana couldn't think clearly.

A baby? She couldn't have a baby. Douglas had left her. She was supposed to be finding a husband and getting married and wearing a white moiré wedding dress by Victor Stiebel with a chapel-length veil and carrying a bouquet of white eucharis and lily of the valley.

A baby. No, she couldn't. Diana hung up the phone without saying anything more to Helen.

If she didn't talk about it, it wasn't happening, she told herself.

Her mother appeared in the hallway. 'Diana, why are you sitting there as though you don't have things to do?'

Diana stood up. 'What do I have to do, Mother? Tell me, please. I would love something to do. A job, studying at university, a task – anything would be a pleasure over sitting here waiting for my life to start.'

Her mother's mouth dropped open. 'Diana, you have never spoken to me like that before. What's happened to you?'

'Nothing's happened to me. That's the problem, Mother. I'm bored, I'm so bored I could die. I need an adventure. I need to see Europe, see the world, ride a motorbike.'

'Ride a motorbike? Diana, what's happened to you? Are you ill?' She called out: 'Edward, Diana is unwell.'

'I'm not unwell,' said Diana. 'I just hate it here.' And with that she turned and ran upstairs to her room.

She lay on her bed and closed her eyes, willing everything to go back to how it was before.

A few moments later her mother knocked at her door and opened it slowly, as though afraid that Diana would throw something at her.

'Diana, I have spoken to your father, and he suggested I take you to Europe for the summer next year. We can go before the Moongate Festival and be back in time for the exciting event. That's something to look forward to, isn't it?'

Diana rolled over and stared at the wall.

She didn't want to go to Europe with her mother. She wanted to be on the back of Douglas's motorbike, hands around his waist, her face resting on his back as they drove through the Black Forest.

Diana's mother closed the door again, leaving her alone.

Diana felt tears fall from her eyes. Deep inside her, she knew Helen was right; she just didn't want it to be real.

16

Amanda

Amanda watched Janet walk Diana around the garden, introducing her to the others in the club.

She walked over to Simon who was assessing a garden bed with scraggly plants fighting for survival.

'Are you watching this?' she asked Simon, nodding her head towards Diana.

'Yeah, it's nice,' said Simon.

'Can you hear that?' asked Amanda, straining to listen.

'What? No, I can't hear anything,' Simon said as he bent down and pulled a flower from one of the plants. 'Do you know what this is?' he asked.

Amanda shrugged. 'Don't ask me, I'm still working through the flower books and can't name anything other than a daisy, but I'm trying to learn.' Amanda put her hands on her hips and closed her eyes. 'I can still hear it. It's a phone ringing.' She leaned down and then quickly straightened. 'It's your pocket ringing.'

Simon reached in and took it out and Amanda leaned over and looked at the screen.

'Who's Charlie?' she asked.

'None of your business,' he snapped, but Amanda laughed at him.

'You don't get to hide your life from me if you're going to be my friend,' she said. 'Is Charlie your ex?'

Simon snorted. 'Not bloody likely.'

The phone rang again and Amanda grabbed it from his hand and answered. 'Hello, Simon's line. Can I assist you?'

She turned to see Simon's jaw agape.

'Charlie? I don't know of a Charlie – he has never mentioned you. Your last name please?' She paused, looking at Simon with her tongue out. 'B.R.I.N.D.L.E. Where is Simon now? He's with clients. I'm sorry, he can't speak now.'

Simon started to laugh and shake his head.

Amanda listened to the man on the line. 'I can't guarantee he will get back to you anytime soon. His days are filled for the next few weeks with some specific new things he's planting and shaping. A lot of digging deep, so he will have his hands dirty, I'm afraid.'

Simon was bent double trying to stifle his laughter.

'A message?'

Simon stopped laughing now and Amanda watched him.

'You're sorry, and so is Anika. Okay, anything else? Just to call him? Alright, I'll pass that on.'

Amanda looked at the phone and then at Simon and it all made sense. She ended the call.

'What an absolute fucking asshole,' she said.

Simon sighed. 'I suppose I should be mad at you for that, but part of me is glad that he's wondering why an American is answering my phone and what projects I have my hands in.' He put his hands in the pockets of his work pants. 'Anika left me the day of our wedding, for Charlie.'

Amanda gasped. 'Oh man, I should have told him to jump off a bridge.'

Simon shrugged. 'We were business partners and he also screwed me over and left me with nothing financially. Anika clearly chose the smarter one.'

Amanda pushed him gently with her hand. 'Never say that, okay? Never. It's their moral compass that's broken, it's not a sign that you're lacking in any way. Never, ever speak about yourself like that.'

Simon turned and looked out over the garden. 'I look back and I can see it all so clearly now, but I didn't then. The furtive phone calls. Anika at the office claiming to be waiting for me but supposedly forgetting that I had said I would be home. Me signing papers in a rush and not looking at the fine print. I was stupid.'

Amanda came to his side. 'You're not stupid – they were lying to you. It's easy to be hard on yourself now but seeing the best in people isn't a fault, and becoming cynical and suspicious of people is poisonous. I would rather believe people are good. I mean, look at all of this.' Amanda gestured to the garden.

Dennis and Frank were in deep discussion about a shrub, picking the leaves and inspecting them. Shelley was chatting to Carole as they set up a table and chairs outside on the cleared lawn that Simon had recently mowed, while Diana and Janet were standing next to the empty pond, Diana pointing at something with her walking stick.

'I was given a house, and these people are here to help with nothing in return for them but the opportunity to be a part of something. Diana gave you a job at face value and you showed up. You're always making a difference to Moongate and to me, because you're my friend and even though you can be a grump, you're a good person; I can just tell.'

Simon was staring at her, silent. A muscle in his jaw was twitching but he wasn't angry, he was just listening intently.

'Are you always so upbeat? Is it an American thing?' he finally asked.

'Usually. I mean, I try to be.' She laughed, embarrassed. 'I don't know if it's American as much as it is who I am as a person. Lainie, my best friend, said I'm too soft for New York, which is her way of saying I'm naïve and not tough, but I'm tough in my own way.'

Simon nodded. 'You're tough. I mean, who takes this on with no prior experience and assumes it's possible?'

'You don't think it's possible?' she asked.

Simon shook his head. 'No, I think you, Amanda Cox, can make anything happen. You have that sort of magic about you.'

Amanda knew she was blushing but also she knew it was true.

'Maybe we're good for each other,' he said.

Amanda pushed him gently with her shoulder. 'Then we really are friends,' she said and he leaned in to her momentarily.

'I guess we are. Now come on and tell me what I'm doing with this pond that Diana is always going on about.'

Simon and Amanda walked to Janet and Diana, who were deep in discussion.

'We would need a heater system installed for winter if Amanda were to replenish the pond,' Diana was saying.

'Absolutely, and a small stream or water flow would be helpful,' Janet replied.

'What am I replenishing?' Amanda asked with a smile.

Diana turned to her. 'I was explaining to Janet that I did have koi in here for many years but one harsh winter it iced over and the fish died and it was very sad.'

Amanda looked at the large and deep pond. 'What did it used to look like, this whole area?' she asked Diana.

'I have some old photos in the gatehouse that I can show you but I think the garden needs a renovation not a replication. We must always try and improve things if we can. Leave them better than they were before we came.'

Janet nodded. 'You know, Simon, you should come and see our pond set-up. While we only have goldfish, it is still very tranquil. There are ferns surrounding it, which would look lovely here,' Janet said.

Diana looked at the ground nearest to her at the pond's edge. 'There were ferns here, and papyrus, and creeping Jenny,' she said.

'Creeping Jenny – what a terrible name,' said Amanda. 'Imagine being the Jenny that the person named it after. "Jenny, you're such a stalker that I'm going to name a plant after you."'

Simon laughed and Amanda joined in but Diana and Janet looked at her as though she had lost her mind.

'Come on, that's a good joke, isn't it?' She looked at Simon for confirmation who nodded.

'It's funny,' he admitted and Amanda crossed her arms.

'Since Simon is the only appreciative audience member here, we're going to find cake and other people who think we're funny. You coming?' she asked Simon and when he nodded they walked towards the table where Shelley and Frank had set up morning tea.

'I think Diana and Janet are becoming friends,' she said to Simon as they walked away. 'We should encourage that.'

Absolutely,' Simon agreed.

Diana watched Simon and Amanda walk away and looked at Janet.

'I think there could be a spark there,' she said. 'We should encourage that.'

Janet nodded in agreement. 'Absolutely,' she said, turning to Diana. 'Shall we get some cake and observe?'

Diana looked at the woman beside her. She had to be twenty years younger than her, and presumably, by the badges on her jacket, they had nothing in common, but she could feel a stirring she hadn't felt in years.

Friendship.

'I couldn't think of anything I would like more,' she answered.

17

Simon

The stench of lavender was heavy in the air as Simon tugged on the last clump of roots from the shrubs that Frank had pulled out on the weekend.

Clearing the garden wasn't as easy as Simon had thought it would be and they had filled two skip bins with the rubbish and dead plants from Moongate.

The last two weekends had been filled with clearing with the gardening club and Amanda and Simon doing more of it during the week but, with this last push, it would finally be clear.

Carole and Janet had tip-pruned the roses and Shelley and Dennis tied back the climbing roses and the wisteria, but Carole said they were not to prune the wisteria until it had finished flowering, which would be in a week to ten days.

Simon was amazed at the collective knowledge of the club members, although they did disagree sometimes, mainly about the arrangement of the gardening beds; but Simon thought it was funny listening to them all bicker about plantings and if dahlias were worth all the glory they were given.

It was Diana that he learned the most about the garden and the planting from. She was almost Buddhist in her view that everything in the garden was connected, from the flower to the insect that needed it for food, that would then pollinate the fruits and vegetables in other nearby gardens. She wanted to feed the birds and give the wildlife a place to shelter. There were deer and shews and squirrels, and even stoats.

Simon realised how little he saw wildlife in London, other than the foxes rummaging through rubbish late at night.

The days were hard work but Simon enjoyed feeling the gentle heat of the mid-summer sunshine and the ache of his body as he grew stronger and fitter. He ate with Amanda more and more and found he was actually hungry for the first time in a long while.

But what he liked most was seeing the order and structure come back to the garden. Diana had told him the beds were orderly so the plants could be wild within them.

'The magic is in what you can't see,' Diana explained to him. 'The worms in the soil, aerating it, and the organic matter – the minerals, the gases and liquids that give us life. That's the magic, underneath it all. The rest is just tricks to get you to look,' she had said.

It was close to five in the afternoon now and the sun was still high in the sky, with plenty of warmth left in the air.

'Simon?' he heard Amanda call from the window overlooking the front garden and he walked up towards her.

'Do you like fish?' she called.

'I do, why?' he asked.

'I'm making fish and salads for dinner. I've invited Diana

as well, but she said she's not sure, as she is seeing Janet today and it might be too much to have two events in one day.'

Amanda had decided that they would eat together more often than not, as she said being alone at night was weird. She had never lived alone, she admitted to Simon, except for after her mother had died.

'What can I bring?' he called.

'Nothing,' she said.

'Then let me pay you for the dinner.'

Amanda frowned. 'Why would you do that?' she asked.

'Because you keep feeing me, and you don't have a job and I do – unless you have a fortune I don't know about.'

Amanda sighed. 'No fortune sadly. But you don't have to pay. You can make me dinner tomorrow night. How's that?'

Simon made a face at her.

'What? Don't you want to make me dinner?' She seemed insulted.

'No, I do but I don't think you would want to eat my dinners. They consist of beans and toast and maybe an egg if I'm feeling fancy.'

'No salad or vegetables?' she asked.

'No, I probably have scurvy.' He looked at the skin on his arms. 'No marks yet but soon to come, I expect.'

'I can't tell if you're joking or not,' Amanda said.

'I'm not sure I am,' admitted Simon. He hadn't been eating well since he had left London and food wasn't anything he had been interested in much before the disastrous wedding day. He knew he had lost weight and muscle tone, as the few clothes he had with him were looser than ever.

'I will see you at six, after I shower,' he said with a smile and he walked down to the gatehouse to see if Diana was back from Janet's.

As he came to the house, Janet's car arrived with Diana in the passenger seat.

He came around and opened the door and Trotsky jumped out first and then Diana's stick emerged and he assisted her from the car as she moved slowly and carefully.

'You must go to Janet's and see the pond, Simon. It's simply lovely and Janet has been potting up all sorts of lovely bits and bobs for the garden from her house.'

Janet came around the front of the car with a basket of things in her arm.

'Will I pop these inside, Di?'

'Thanks, Jan,' Diana replied holding out a house key.

Di and Jan? He couldn't wait to tell Amanda about this growing friendship between the women.

Diana held on to his arm as Janet went ahead and opened the door with the key that Diana had given her.

'Jan and Carole have given me a lovely basket of goodies from Shelley's Deli. So many lovely things for dinner or to have with a cup of tea. I'm quite spoiled,' she said as they walked through the small gate and into her front garden.

'Amanda was wondering if you were coming for dinner actually. She said she had invited you.'

'Can you please tell her not tonight? I want to sit with Trotsky and watch some BBC and have a nibble on something nice and then head off to bed. A very busy day for me. I'm not used to it now.' Diana laughed to herself.

'I will tell her, no problem,' Simon said as they came to the front door.

Janet came bustling forward and took over from him to ensure Diana's stability.

'I'm off to get ready for dinner then,' he said.

'He's having dinner with Amanda,' Diana said to Janet with a tone in her voice he couldn't understand.

'Oh how lovely,' said Janet very enthusiastically, as though Diana had just announced he was heading to dinner with a movie star.

'Okay,' said Simon, confused, and he left them and went to his place to get ready.

Soon he was ready and on his way to Moongate Manor. He didn't have many clothes with him but his jeans and a clean T-shirt would have to do. He was grateful that Amanda had let him use the old top-loader washing machine at the manor and had now organised internet at the house. Simon was thinking of buying a small laptop, and maybe he could start trading again with the little savings he had. Starting to rebuild everything he had lost wouldn't be easy, but at least he didn't have to worry about having an underhanded business partner this time; he only had to rely on himself.

He came through the kitchen door, where Amanda was sitting at the table, painting.

She looked up. 'You're early,' she said.

'I can sit outside and wait if you like,' he said, half joking.

'Don't be silly, come in and you can wash the lettuce while I finish this.' He came inside and looked over her shoulder.

It was a watercolour of Moongate Manor at night, with fairy lights around the house and lanterns and bunting hanging from the trees and the moon gate. The moon was full above the house, in a navy sky filled with stars. Simon wondered if he had ever seen anything quite as beautiful.

'My God, Amanda, that is incredible.'

Amanda looked up at him and smiled, and he noticed the tiny flecks of yellow and little shards of green in amongst the brown of her eyes.

'Hazel,' he said aloud.

'What?' She looked at the painting and then back to him.

'Your eyes,' he said. 'I thought they were brown but they're actually hazel.'

Amanda swallowed and nodded. 'It depends on the light,' she said. 'Or my mood.'

'Oh?' He was still looking down at her eyes.

'When I'm angry they go darker. I don't know why.'

'And now? What mood are you in now?'

She paused; their eyes locked. 'I'm happy,' she said.

'Good.' He pulled his gaze away and went to the kitchen.

'Is it bad if I ask you how to wash a lettuce? Just tell me and I'll do it,' he said.

'You haven't washed a lettuce before?' she asked.

'No, if I buy lettuce, its prebagged,' he said. 'From Tesco.'

'Oh this is from Frank and Shelley's garden,' she said, standing up, opening the old refrigerator and taking out a large lettuce. 'I'll give you a biology lesson on this lettuce.' She washed her hands and dried them on a tea towel.

'This is the core of the lettuce, which leads to the heart,' she explained and she took a small paring knife from the drawer and cut the core out. The heart pulled out with it and she put it in the compost bin.

'I can't believe you haven't washed a lettuce before.' Amanda laughed. 'Didn't you have salads growing up?'

Simon sighed. 'My mum wasn't much of a cook. We did a lot of takeaway. She's a historian, would prefer to be reading or at the university lecturing students about the Scandinavian world in the early Middle Ages, including Viking activity and the history of Scandinavian arts and crafts.'

'Wow, that's very specific,' said Amanda.

'Yes, she's quite knowledgeable if you would like to know the military tactics of Vikings and their hunting skills and habits, but not so great on the day-to-day stuff.'

'What a shame the Vikings didn't make salads, then you would know how to do this,' teased Amanda and he laughed.

'So, your mum was a good cook then?' he asked as Amanda washed the lettuce and he watched.

'She was not bad – a little experimental sometimes, and there was a whole season when she was obsessed with vegan food, which I didn't love but eventually she caved and we ended up getting Chinese food – including the sweet and sour chicken – and our vegan phase was over.'

Amanda washed the lettuce and then put it in the spinner she had pulled out from the cupboard.

'You can spin it,' she said and Simon did so, making sure the lid was on properly.

'So, what about as an adult? Didn't you learn to cook?'

Simon thought back to the last ten years. He ate in restaurants and ordered a lot of delivery. He thought about all money he had spent on not making his own food and he wished he had even a quarter of that money now. Anika used to order sushi for every lunch and then again for dinner. It was always her first choice.

'I remember cooking with my grandmother – scones and maybe icing a cake – but she died when I was nine and my mother wasn't a cook. So as an adult, I ate out a lot,' he said. 'Do you want me to at least cut up some tomatoes or something? I'm not completely useless, I promise.'

Soon they had the salad made and Amanda prepared the fish.

'Thank God Frank gave me all of the salad things, because I am going to need to get a job soon or I will be living in their veggie patch.'

'That bad huh?' asked Simon.

Amanda laughed. 'Yep. I'm a poor starving artist from New York who lucked out with this house, but it costs money to live here and I have student loans that probably cost the same amount as a new roof for this place, and if I don't pay them they draw interest and then it would cost more than this whole place is worth. I got some severance pay from my old work in New York but I don't want to spend it on that.'

'Are you going to sell it?' Simon was shocked.

'No,' Amanda cried. 'I'm just saying I have to get a job. I have to do the garden and it's a lot, but I guess it will work out. It usually does, doesn't it?'

Simon thought about her statement. 'Does it? Do you really think so? Even with your mum dying?'

'I can feel down, for sure, and if you had said to me a month ago that I would feel happy more often than I do sad, I wouldn't have believed you. But I'm feeling more hopeful now. I just need to get a job soon.'

She put a frypan on the stove and added some butter.

'Arnold, the guy I used to get coffee from back in New York, used to say that life could turn on a dime, and I think that's true. One day you're poor; one day you're rich.

One day you're being evicted; the next day you're the new owner of an English country home.' She shrugged. 'You can't assume anything is finished and done. There's always a chance things will turn around.'

Simon walked to the French doors and looked out at the back gardens.

Was there a second act to his and Anika's story? Was there a resolution for him and Charlie?

He didn't know the answer to those questions but, for the first time, he wondered if perhaps he should return to London to find out.

But what was there for him? Anika didn't want him and Charlie was a lying prick. His mother was exhausting and demanding and the thought of sitting in front of a screen day after day gave him a headache.

'You okay?' he heard Amanda ask and he turned.

'I'm fine, just musing over my life and where to go next,' he said with a sigh.

'Where do you think you will go? Where would you like to go?' she asked.

Simon thought for a moment. 'I don't know to be honest. It feels like wherever I go this feeling will come with me.'

Amanda nodded. 'Then stay here for as long as you need. Even after the summer is over. I'm sure there are other gardens and work that people might need a hand with around the area. The answer for your next journey will come when you're ready or have a decision to make. You don't know yet because you're not ready to leave, and that's my and Diana's win.' She flashed him a smile and went back to cooking.

Simon pondered her words. She was right. The answer

would come when he had a decision to make and the only decision he had to make right now was what to plant for the autumn.

Diana – 1960s

Diana pulled her coat tighter around herself as she and her mother crossed Bond Street.

The Christmas lights sparkled as shoppers rushed about like festive little ants in their coats and boots. There was a little snow, which looked lovely from afar but was already turning to slush from the cars and many feet that passed over it.

'Come along, Diana, I want to get you a diary from Smythson, so you can fill it with fun events for next year. When we go to Europe, you can make sightseeing itineraries and put the keepsakes in the pages. The snakeskin ones are too gaudy but the crocodile covers are lovely. But do get the silver lettering for the cover; the gold is far too gauche.'

Diana wasn't listening; instead she slowed as they passed a small shop with children's clothes in the window. A tiny romper in pink gingham with a matching pink bonnet was on display.

Diana's mother kept walking and then turned and walked back to Diana who hadn't moved from the window.

'Why are you looking at that? You're a long way from that. We can go to Harrods and look at going-away suits if you like.'

Diana still didn't move but the baby did. She could feel the flutters in her womb, like something soft stroking her from inside. It felt like the softest feather and she put her hand on her stomach.

'Diana?' Her mother was peering at her, and then she looked down at her daughter's hand.

'No,' she said, almost to herself. 'No,' she said again; this time she was firm.

Diana looked at her mother. She had a choice and it scared her more than anything she had ever faced in her young life. She could either tell the truth and deal with the consequences from her parents or she could run away and try and cope on her own. But how would she cope? She didn't have any skills or talents. She didn't have her own money or any independence. She was reliant on her parents, just as the child growing inside her was reliant on her. She took a deep breath and let the truth come out. 'Yes, I'm pregnant, Mother.'

Diana's mother gasped. 'You're not keeping it; we can see someone about that.'

Diana stepped away from the woman who had given birth to her, who had tried for so long to have Diana – the heartbreak after heartbreak that was the legacy Diana grew up hearing about. Diana was always told she was special because she had survived. Why couldn't her mother see that this baby was special too?

'I am keeping it, Mother. This is your grandchild.'

'No, no, no.' Diana's mother grabbed Diana by the arm. 'We're going back to the hotel and will return to Moongate tomorrow. Your father is going to be furious.'

But Diana didn't feel any concern at the news of her

father's impending wrath. She realised this was what she was looking for the whole time. Something to love and to love her. Douglas was merely the conduit to that love.

Her parents would have to learn to live with her decision and, above all, they would have to learn to love her baby.

This realisation lifted the cloud from Diana's soul and she knew that when she went back to Moongate and faced her father's anger and shaming it wouldn't matter. She was going to have a purpose now, and she would do everything in her power to make sure her child was safe, loved and encouraged.

Her father had other ideas.

'Where is the father? He needs to return home to marry you.'

'He's riding a motorbike around Europe, last I heard,' she had said calmly, her hands in her lap as she faced her father in his study.

'Write to him, tell him to return.'

'I can't, I don't know his address,' she said.

'Then I can get a private detective to look for him.'

Diana put her head to one side. 'And then what, Father? Ask him to return to fulfil his responsibilities? Force him at gunpoint like in the films?'

Her father snorted. 'I should.'

'If he wanted to be here, he would be here, Father. He's not.'

Her father knew he was outplayed on that one.

'If it's too late to have it seen to then you will have to go away and give it up for adoption.'

'No, I'm not doing that,' she answered.

'Which?' Her father was confused.

'Going away or giving the baby up,' she said.

'And what am I supposed to tell people?' He was standing now, pacing in front of the French windows to the outdoor patio.

Diana shrugged. 'I don't care what you tell them; I just know I'm having my baby, your grandchild, the next Moongate heir.'

She knew this would touch on her father's lineage worries. He'd nearly lost all hope of the Graybrook-Moore blood continuing before they had Diana, and now Diana was ensuring another generation after her.

'But a bastard heir,' said her father.

Diana stood up. 'Don't ever call my child a bastard or I will go and you won't have anyone to continue Moongate.'

Her father lifted his chin and squared his shoulders. 'Go to your room, Diana. We will talk about this later.'

Diana went to her room and lay on her bed. She was tired but she had told the truth about the situation. Her parents just had to get used to it, and then they would come up with some sort of lie that everyone would go along with. No one would believe it, of course, but they would be too polite to mention it.

Diana didn't mind being talked about; it was better than being dismissed or overlooked.

Let her parents deal with the details – she was having a baby.

18

Amanda

Amanda had arranged for Diana to come for lunch since she seemed to decline every dinner invitation that was sent her way.

'I don't want to walk in the dark.' A reasonable concern but Amanda had offered to walk with a powerful torch to light the way.

'I go to bed early.' An offer of an early supper didn't work for Diana, who said she liked to sit with Trotsky in the kitchen where they ate together.

'I don't want to get in the way of your growing friendship with Simon,' was the final excuse. Amanda had explained that she and Simon were friends already and weren't growing anything but the seeds they were sowing in the garden.

Amanda had the feeling that Diana was pushing her and Simon to be more than friends and had said so to Simon who had laughed.

'I think Janet is trying too. She asked me all about you the other day when I went to her house to see the pond and pick up the plants.'

'Meddling old matchmakers,' Amanda had said, slightly peeved at the audacity of the women.

No matter what Amanda tried, Diana had said no to any dinner invitation, claiming that she had a routine and she liked the way her life worked. 'It's been like this for half a century so I won't be changing it for anyone or anything.'

Eventually Amanda gave up on trying to get Diana to Moongate for dinner and had settled on lunch instead. She had made a Caesar salad and had some lemon mineral water, and dessert was one of Shelley's apple cakes with cream.

Diana arrived walking with her arm through Simon's for support.

'Hello, are you coming also?' Amanda panicked when she saw him. She didn't think she could stretch the meal to three servings.

'No, no, just delivering your guest. I've been raking the gravel on the driveway in preparation for some new gravel I ordered, and I should get back to finish up.'

'How did you pay for it?' asked Amanda. She certainly didn't have any money to pay for a truckload of gravel.

'I paid for it,' said Diana as she walked into the house.

'Diana, you shouldn't do that,' Amanda said. 'I'm supposed to pay for those things.'

'It wasn't a huge amount of money and I do like to hear the crunch of the car wheels on the fresh gravel,' she said.

Simon gave them a wave and headed down to the front of the garden as Amanda closed the door, while Diana went through to the sitting room and sat on the sofa.

Amanda walked in and sat down on an armchair.

Diana was silent for a moment, looking around at the room with its formal sofas and painting.

'I have always hated this room,' she said.

'Kitchen?' asked Amanda.

'Much better,' said Diana and they walked through to the kitchen. Diana's tension seemed to ease as she sat at the table.

'I never liked formality, despite my appearance,' Diana said, touching the brooch attached to her pale blue cotton jumper over a white shirt dress.

'My mom always said that caring about the way you look doesn't mean you care about what people think. I love to wear clothes that I know people think don't match but they make me happy and so I don't care.' Amanda looked down at her pink shorts and orange strapless top. 'I look like gelato... but happy gelato.' She laughed. 'I love clothes; they're a weakness of mine. I left a lot of them in New York. I had a bunch of vintage dresses from thrift shops and markets.'

Amanda poured them a mineral water each and sat down opposite Diana.

'There are so many old clothes in the attic. You're welcome to sort through them,' Diana said. 'Some were mine and some were my mother's. Maybe my grandmother's and before that also,' she said.

'Really? Wow, that would be amazing,' Amanda said. 'I've made us a Caesar salad, anchovies on the side in case you're not a fan.'

Diana looked up. 'I love anchovies. I'll take extra.'

'You're like my mom – she loves them.' Amanda paused. 'Loved, I should say.'

'You must miss her very much.'

'I do,' said Amanda, as she arranged the salads for them. 'But I started to miss her when she became sick. The illness, it took over everything, the best parts of her. I felt like I lost her before she died.'

Diana frowned. 'That's very sad. I'm sorry you and she didn't have more time together.'

Amanda poached two eggs and then put them carefully on the plates and brought then to the table.

'I got to have twenty-six years with her though. That's better than nothing. One of my friends from school, her mom died when she was twelve. I mean, that's unfair, isn't it?'

Diana nodded. 'It is unfair – very.' She looked down at her plate. 'This looks delicious.'

'Yes, but let's hope it tastes as good as it looks.'

They tucked into their lunch and chatted about the garden, and the progress Amanda, Simon and the gardening club had made in the clearing.

When it was time for the apple cake, Amanda took the plunge with Diana.

'I think I'm going to have to get a job,' she said. 'Because I have to pay my student loans and pay for my life here.'

'Of course, dear, you must work. I wished I had worked. I had wanted to but eventually I had to give that dream up. I just didn't have any real transferrable skills – well raised but useless other than being a wife and mother, of which I was neither in the end.'

Amanda gave a sigh of relief. 'I was worried you would be mad if I worked. I thought you wanted me here digging up weeds full-time.'

Diana gasped. 'What? Why on earth would I be mad, as you put it, that you worked? Of course you need your own money and to have something to do. Don't end up like me, knowing everything about roses but nothing else.'

Amanda shook her head. 'I don't think that's true. You probably know more than you think.'

Diana shrugged. 'Perhaps. Now, do you have any pictures of your mother and you as a child? I'd love to know more about your life in New York. It always seemed so fascinating to me.'

Amanda jumped from her chair. 'I would love to – let me get my laptop.'

She came back to the table, opened her computer, clicked on the photo album folder and it opened full screen on a picture of her mom pregnant with Amanda.

'Here's Mom – she had me that night. I was born just before midnight on a full moon. My dad took the photo.'

Amanda's finger touched her mother's face on the screen.

'Where is your dad now?' Diana asked, moving closer to the screen.

'He died when I was nine. He wasn't really around much after I was born. He was a musician apparently, never had any fame or anything, but played guitar. He died in a car accident.'

'I'm sorry for your loss.' Diana seemed genuinely sad for Amanda. She didn't want the poor woman to dwell on her sorry tale of her dead parents so she quickly moved on to the next image.

'This is me when I was one,' she said, showing a photo of her face covered in cake, her hair sprouting from her head like a Chia Pets toy.

Diana laughed. 'Look at you, cheeky monkey,' she said.

Amanda looked at her. 'That's what my mom used to call me. How funny.'

Diana smiled. 'You do look very cheeky though.'

'I was very cheeky – I still can be.' Amanda smiled at Diana fondly. She was starting to care for the older woman. Her generosity with the house was one thing but her kindness to Simon was another, and being open to the gardening club.

'I see you're becoming friends with Janet. She's great, isn't she?'

'She is a lovely woman, and so is Carole. They came together later in life, when Carole had a reckoning about who she really was. Very brave to be true to herself and her feelings. It's not easy when people can be so short-sighted.'

Amanda patted her hand. 'Good on you – you're an ally,' she said.

'An ally?' Diana asked.

'An ally is someone who supports a marginalised community. It could be a person of colour, or someone with a different sexual identity.'

'Oh lovely, I suppose I am an ally then,' Diana said, seemingly pleased with the title.

Amanda flicked through some more photos, showing Diana when she started school, Halloween costumes and her prom.

'You look lovely,' said Diana, peering at Amanda in the 1950s-style prom dress.

'It was vintage,' said Amanda. 'Mom helped me fix it as it was ripped at the bodice when I got it. She sewed it with the tiniest stiches, like a little mouse.'

Diana smiled. 'So your mother was creative?'

'Very,' Amanda said. 'She said New York helped her be creative. It was the city of possibilities, although it was less like that for me.'

'Why was that?' Diana asked.

Amanda sighed, trying to think how to explain how New York made her feel.

'Mom always wanted to live in New York she told me, ever since she was a child. She loved the hustle but I never relaxed. My favourite times were when we went to the beach at the cape and just hung out. That's when I would draw and think and paint.'

'How does it feel being here?' asked Diana, gesturing to everything around her. 'I don't want it to be a source of stress for you.'

'I feel nothing but joy here,' she said. Her hand instinctively reached out and held the older woman's hand. 'This is the first time I have thought about painting since Mom got sick. I have even started sketching some pictures for a book that she wrote. We were going to do something with it and then the diagnosis happened and everything stopped.'

'Your mother wrote a book?' Diana seemed surprised.

'She worked as a court stenographer but her life outside of her job was filled with ideas and decorating and cooking and dancing and singing and more. She was always learning something new.'

Diana was listening intently.

'I wonder sometimes,' Amanda said, 'if she tried to do everything because she knew her time was limited.'

Diana smiled gently. 'Sometimes we tell ourselves what we need to hear, just so we can get through to the next day.'

Amanda nodded, suddenly feeling tears well up. She

hadn't looked at photos of her mom like this in a while. Remembering hurt, yet it was a pain tempered with such deep love it made her throat clench as the tears sprang.

'I'm sorry, I just miss her,' she said to Diana who in turn patted her hand.

'I understand, more than you know.'

And Amanda thought perhaps Diana did know and wondered what had happened to her in her past.

19

Simon

Amanda's cheekiness answering his phone to Charlie had set off a chain of events back in London that Simon found amusing. Charlie had always been the charismatic one in the friendship, ever since university. That's why Simon was surprised when Anika had first shown interest in him instead.

Simon wasn't as handsome as Charlie but he was tall and he was cleverer with numbers. The business idea had been his but Charlie had the connections with the cool crowd in society circles. The boys who wanted to get richer faster.

When Simon had left university early to focus on the business with Charlie, his mother was horrified. But when he started to bring home more money than she had ever seen as a university professor, she had to admit his idea had worked. Then Anika came into his life at twenty-five and he bought an apartment upon her advice along the Riverwalk in London. It was Charlie who suggested that he buy it through the business, something about it being a tax write-off, and Simon did it because he wanted to be with Anika and because it meant he didn't have to live with his mother anymore.

Anika had finally called him recently but he didn't take the call. What would he say? And he didn't want to hear any excuses about her cheating. Anika had always had an excuse for her poor behaviour, even when she was clearly in the wrong.

She's Charlie's problem now, he thought as he lay on his bed scrolling through the photos on his phone. Photos of his former life, but what was the life he was living now?

Trying to learn how to garden, earning a minimal wage and living in what was ostensibly a shed that had been done up to accommodate a person living there short-term.

It wasn't an ideal situation so why did he wake up happy to start the day? He went to bed thinking about the garden and woke up wondering what had happened overnight. Were the seeds sprouting? Would the wisteria survive Frank's pruning? What was Amanda planning for the day?

As the sun rose, Simon was in the garden with a cup of tea in the old tin mug from the cupboard under the sink.

A year ago he would have been on his way to the office. He laughed to himself, thinking about how important he thought he was back then. Whenever anyone asked him how he was, he would answer that he was busy.

Busy isn't a state of mind, he thought, it's a trap.

His phone rang and he saw it was his mother. She would never usually ring this early unless it was about something urgent, so he answered.

'Finally you've decided to speak to you mother,' she said.

'What's happened? Why are you calling so early?' He put his tea down on a low wall.

'Nothing's happened but I thought I would try you

earlier in the day since you avoid me at every other time of the day.'

'I'm not avoiding you, Mother,' he said. He remained still as he watched a roe deer with a new fawn stagger across the grass at the fence line near Diana's house. The baby tottered behind its mother, who was warily making her way to the forest behind them.

'You are – you're avoiding everything and Charlie said you have an American assistant? What are you doing?'

Simon rolled his eyes at the phone. 'She's not my assistant, she's my friend – and why are you talking to Charlie, Mother. Do you have no loyalty?'

His mother snorted. 'Of course I have loyalty. I can't stand Charlie; always thought he was a little pretend aristocrat with his airs and graces. He was so desperate to be in *Tatler* or marry someone with a title it was ridiculous.'

'So why were you speaking with him?' asked Simon. 'You know you're a gossip, Mum.'

'I'm not,' she stated.

'You study history, Mum – much of which is hearsay and gossip.'

'No, it's facts, and we can deduce the stories from the facts. And the fact in this case is that Charlie rang me to ask about the American, as he was concerned and wondered where you were working.'

'I bet he was,' Simon muttered. 'I'm fine, Mum. I'm working and I'm enjoying myself. It's nice to have a break for a while.'

'That's good. I'm glad you're feeling better.' She paused. 'Anika also called me,' she added.

'Christ, Mum, why didn't you just have them over for dinner?'

Sometimes his mother was so frustrating it made him want to scream. Did she not understand that her decision to speak to the people who broke his heart was disloyal?

'She and Charlie broke up.'

Simon sat down on the wall next to his mug of tea. 'What?'

'Yes, apparently she made a mistake,' his mother said.

'Which part? Cheating or lying or the choice of the bloke?'

'Don't be bitter, darling, you're not a grapefruit,' his mother scolded.

'Mum, I don't know why Anika is calling you or Charlie, but I really don't want you talking to them anymore. And the reason I don't take your calls is because I know you still talk to people and news will get around about me.'

'Simon,' his mother protested.

'If you can't put your own son ahead of the people who fucked me over, then you and I can't speak,' he said. 'So you decide if you want to be a part of my life or theirs. Until then, I have work to do.'

Simon ended the call and turned off his phone. He stared down the garden to the view of the sea.

'Morning!' he heard, and turned to see Amanda walking towards him. She was wearing a pale turquoise kimono with a dress or a nightgown underneath, and had a mug in hand.

He was extremely pleased to see her after such an awful phone call.

'Hello,' he said and he looked in her mug. 'Coffee?'

'Absolutely,' she said. 'How long have you been up?'

'Not long but my mother rang.' He sighed.

'Oh, is that not good?'

Amanda sat next to him on the wall.

'She finds it hard to put loyalty above her own self-importance,' he said. 'She isn't deliberately mean but she's just a bit… I don't know.' He struggled to find the word.

'Thoughtless?' Amanda asked and he nodded.

'Yes, that's it.'

'I'm sorry, that's a shitty way to start a morning as beautiful as this.'

'Thank you,' he said.

Amanda crossed her legs.

He glanced down and then back to the view. Amanda was the sort of girl he used to go out with at school and at university. Pretty, sensible, dependable and kind. Why did he get so swept up with Anika? Besides her beauty there was nothing else he admired about her and he realised, sitting next to Amanda in comfortable silence, that he had been kidding himself.

'I've realised I don't like myself very much,' he said.

He was surprised he'd said it aloud but on a morning as still and as beautiful as this, he felt it would be impossible to lie. There are times when the surroundings ask you to tell the truth about yourself; your fears and your dreams. Like when you're sitting by a campfire at night or watching a particularly stunning sunrise.

'Why?' Amanda asked.

He liked that she didn't try and dissuade him from his opinion on himself. No false compliments or pandering accolades. Just a simple question: why?

'Because I think I went out with my fiancée because I liked that people looked at me and her together. She was a model and beautiful... externally,' he added.

'Ouch, that's a terrible thing to realise,' Amanda said. 'Wow, you really admitted that about yourself. You went there.'

Simon laughed. 'I know it's a terrible thing to admit but I admitted it.'

'So why did she go out with you?' Amanda asked.

Simon looked at her, pretending to be insulted.

'Are you saying I'm not handsome enough to be a model?' He shook his head.

'No, you're not.' Amanda laughed. 'But neither am I, so we're even.'

Simon was quiet for a moment. 'She went out with me because I had money.'

Amanda pretended to look around him and behind him. 'And where is this fortune now?' she teased. 'Why are you working in this garden for next to nothing?'

Simon sipped his tea. 'Because my ex business partner, Charlie, stole it all. Signed my side of the business to himself and claimed I knew. I didn't but once Anika had left me for him, I didn't care anymore. I just wanted to be away from them both.'

Amanda put her hand on his arm. 'I'm really sorry, Simon. That's awful and such a deep betrayal.'

He let out a huge sigh, one which felt as though he had been hanging on to it for the past few months.

'Thank you, and thank you for listening. I think having you as a friend has saved me. Diana, too.'

Amanda leaned against his arm briefly.

'We're going to be okay,' she said, and Simon looked out towards the sea. With the sun starting to warm him, while sitting next to a new friend, he actually believed it was true.

We're going to be okay, he repeated her words to himself.

20

Amanda

The car putted into Newcastle with Amanda behind the wheel and she looked for a car park she could drive into and not one she had to parallel park. She still found it disconcerting to do from the opposite side and wasn't confident enough to do it when she had to be at an appointment.

Amanda found a parking spot and then checked her lipstick in her phone camera.

She had dressed for the job as a receptionist at the day spa, with her hair pulled back and smothered in hairspray to keep the curls down flat, simple silver studs in her ears and a pretty pink lipstick. A white shirt and some nice linen pants finished the look with some sensible flats, the ones she had worn for her mother's funeral. Amanda thought she looked boring but Diana told her she looked smart and offered her a brooch from her extensive collection.

Amanda had declined but had enjoyed looking at Diana's jewellery and hearing her stories about them.

'There was a beautiful double strand of pearls but I can't find them anymore. Mother probably misplaced them,' Diana had said as they looked at the collection.

Now Amanda wished she had added something fun to her outfit. She looked boring, she thought, as she stepped out of the car and walked in the direction of the spa.

The outside of the day spa looked lovely, very chic and minimalist, and suddenly Amanda was thankful she was dressed the way she was, despite her earlier misgivings.

She pushed open the door and the scent of fragrant citrus oils greeted her, along with some melodic music over rainforest sounds. It made Amanda want to lie on the sofa in the waiting area and have a nap.

A woman a little older than Amanda came through a door. She wore a white uniform with her hair slicked back. She had a poise that Amanda doubted she would achieve in this lifetime. The woman's makeup was artfully applied and her nails were an elegant length with a soft pink polish. Amanda put her hands behind her back, aware that while they were clean, there was a chance there was the odd spot of soil under the nails.

'You're Amanda? Hello, I'm Maggie,' said the woman. 'Come through and we can have a chat.'

Her smile was reassuring and Amanda followed her through to a small office that was as simple and elegant as the rest of the establishment.

'Have a seat,' said the woman and Amanda did as she was asked.

'So you're from New York?' Maggie asked. 'I've always wanted to go. Why on earth would you want to come to…' She paused and looked at Amanda's CV on the desk. 'Foxfield? Most people want to escape a village as small as that.' She laughed but not meanly. 'My mother-in-law was born there – hated it,' she said.

Amanda smiled. 'I like it, but I don't really live in Foxfield. It's further out, near the sea,' she said. 'It's an old house called Moongate Manor.'

'Oh really? That's amazing. My mother-in-law used to be friends with the woman who lived in that house but apparently she became a bit of a hermit, stopped speaking to everyone.' Maggie leaned over the desk. 'My mother-in-law's father was the gardener there. Said it was a very unhappy house, especially when she lost the baby.'

Amanda was confused. 'A baby?'

'Yes, the woman who lived there fell pregnant and stopped speaking to my mother-in-law. Other than an odd birthday card and sending a baby gift when my husband and his brothers were born, she drifted away over the years. My mother-in-law still talks about her though. I think they were very good friends before it all fell apart. It's always sad when a friendship ends.'

Amanda nodded, trying to process what this stranger had told her about Diana.

'How did you come to live there, if you don't mind me asking? I know the house; I've driven past it. It's a bit overgrown and wild now but wasn't when I was younger.'

Amanda swallowed before she spoke. Telling people about the way she came to live at Moongate Manor always felt like she was telling a huge lie, but sometimes the most fanciful-sounding things in the world were actually true.

'I won it in a lottery. My mum bought the ticket,' she said and waited for Maggie's response of surprise and shock.

Maggie gasped and Amanda nodded. 'Yes, it sounds crazy.'

'It does. But also very exciting.'

'The owner is hoping I will return the garden to its former glory but that takes money, which I don't really have.'

'That's true – so you need a job,' Maggie said. 'You know, you should come and meet my mother-in-law, Helen. She could tell you all about the house and the woman who used to live there.'

Amanda nodded. 'Sure.' She paused. 'You said she lost a baby? What did you mean? Do you know what happened to it?'

Maggie shrugged. 'No idea, to be honest. I just remember Helen saying there was a pregnancy and then the baby wasn't with the woman when she returned to the house. And my mother-in-law stopped seeing her. All very sad.'

'Yes, very,' Amanda said but her mind was elsewhere.

Diana had a baby? She said she didn't have children. She needed to think this over.

'Do you like going to spas?' asked Maggie.

Amanda paused. 'You know, I've never really been to one. It's not something I have thought about doing.'

Maggie nodded and looked down.

Amanda was silent, thinking for a moment.

'I don't think I'm right for this job,' she said and she pulled her hair out of the bun. Her curls sprung from her head. 'I'm sure you will find someone great but I think I would prefer something outside, in nature.'

Maggie smiled. 'Of course. Maybe you weren't here for the job but to hear about Moongate Manor. Life has a funny way of directing us onto the right path if we stay open.'

Amanda smiled. Maggie's philosophy made sense.

'I like that idea,' Amanda said.

'Do you want my mother-in-law's number? She would love to chat to you, I'm sure. She can talk the leg off a chair,' Maggie joked.

'I would love that,' she said. 'Thank you.'

Maggie opened her phone, wrote the number on a piece of notepaper and handed it to Amanda.

'Here you go,' she said, and then she opened a cupboard next to her and took out some small bottles and tubes and put them into a gift bag.

'Have some samples – hand creams and sunscreen. Look after your skin if you're going to be outside so much.'

Amanda took the bag. 'This is so nice of you, especially since I've wasted your time.'

Maggie laughed. 'You didn't – it's fine. I've had lots of girls apply anyway. I was interested to meet you when I found out you were American.'

Amanda liked Maggie more and more with each moment.

'You know there's a garden centre that's looking for someone. My friend owns it. Perhaps that would be a better fit for you?'

'Oh wow, that would be amazing.'

'Let me call them and then I'll let you know what they say. Does that work?'

Amanda could have cried. Working at a garden centre would mean she could learn and maybe even have a discount on plants.

'I feel like it's serendipity that I came here today.' Amanda could have hugged this woman.

'It was meant to be, wasn't it?' Maggie beamed at her and Amanda nodded.

'It absolutely was,' Amanda said, though she suddenly felt a gnawing sense that something wasn't right with Diana's story and she was almost afraid to find out the truth.

Diana – 1960s

Diana was allowed out of Moongate until she was six months pregnant but then her mother found many reasons for her not to go to Newcastle or even the village of Foxfield.

So Diana decided to do the unthinkable and went to Newcastle with Helen when her mother was at bridge and her father was in Manchester, in order to sit for her driving test. She had practised on Helen's dad's car without anyone knowing – apart from Helen – while he was at Moongate working in the garden. They had driven on the road a few times and hadn't killed themselves or anyone else, so Diana thought she was ready to sit for her licence.

It wasn't so hard and even though she messed up the parking a little, she had put her hand on her belly and looked sadly at the man testing her and said, 'How will my baby and I get around?'

The man had taken pity on her when she explained her husband was at sea and was hoping she would pass the test.

The next stop was a pawn shop in the Grainger Market, where Diana took her small Omega dress watch and a pair of sapphire earrings that were a present from her godparents in India.

She slipped off the gold ring she had borrowed from her mother's jewellery box for the driving test. She would return it when she went home but now she needed the man in the pawn shop to feel her plight.

She opened up her coat and went into the shop and put the items on the glass counter.

'Yeah?' asked the young man who had a jeweller's loop around his neck and hair down to his collar. He was wearing very fashionable clothing, as though he had come from London, and he smelled of exotic cigarettes that Diana had once smelled at a party held by students from Northumbria University.

'Hello, how much could I get for these?'

The man looked at the watch, turning it over in his hands. Then he looked at the earrings through the loop. 'Fifty quid,' he said.

Diana scoffed the way her father would if he had been here.

'Thanks anyway, but that's not going to help me at this stage.' She touched her stomach and he looked at her and then the earrings again.

'Seventy.'

'I could get three hundred alone for those earrings in Hatton Garden.'

'Then you better head off to Hatton Garden, love,' he said.

She held her nerve.

He kept picking up the earrings and putting them down. She knew he liked them more than he would tell her.

'One hundred,' he said.

'One fifty,' she countered.

He paused and then nodded and pulled out the receipt book and started writing.

Half an hour later, she was in a car yard in Tyne and Wear, with Helen looking worried.

'This looks like a place where stray dogs live,' Helen whispered.

'Maybe they do, but when I get my car, we can drive away quick sticks,' Diana said a with a smile.

This was the smartest thing she had ever done, she thought, as a man came towards her with the keys to the blue Hillman Imp.

'All yours, darling, drive safe,' said the man.

The car was one hundred pounds and the fifty paid for petrol, registration and insurance. Diana was now free to come and go from the house as she pleased.

'Your dad is going to be mad,' said Helen.

'He's already mad – he can add it to the tally,' Diana said as they got into the car.

'You're like a different person now,' said Helen as she touched the dashboard and the seats inside.

'I am. I'm going to be a mother,' said Diana proudly. She started the car and slowly backed out of the car yard and drove them back to Moongate.

21

Amanda

When Amanda woke that morning, her first thought didn't go to her mother's death. It was becoming less of a place her mind went to since moving to Moongate Manor, as there was always something else to think about. At that moment, she was focused on her aching muscles from working in the garden. Her hands hurt from using the secateurs so much and her hamstrings complained as she moved her legs. And she had another day of the demands from the garden, asking for her toil and trouble, ahead of her.

She gingerly walked to the bathroom and cleaned her teeth, then took a shower to try and loosen her muscles.

Who knew gardening was such hard work? No wonder Diana was in such great shape.

After breakfast, she headed down to the pond to work.

By ten in the morning, the sun was beating down. Even the shade of the fernery wasn't a relief.

'It's so hot,' Amanda complained to Simon as they dug out around the pond. 'I didn't think England got as hot as this.'

'You can thank climate change for that,' he said. 'We were in a drought last year.'

Simon had resealed the pond, thanks to a video online that he had watched with Diana, and they planned to put in the small ferns and cuttings from Janet's garden around it.

'We shouldn't plant these when it's so hot,' he said. 'Maybe later today, before the sun goes down or first thing in the morning.'

Amanda wiped her face with her hand and a smear of dirt went across her forehead. 'Do you want to call it a day and go for a swim?'

'Where?' He looked around.

'In the sea, you idiot,' she teased.

'Do you know how cold that water is? It's the North Sea,' he said.

'Come on, it can't be that bad. I didn't see any penguins. You can at least put your feet in.' Amanda had already pulled off her gardening gloves and thrown the vines and weeds into the wheelbarrow.

'I don't think I have any swimmers,' he said.

'Are swimmers British for swimsuit?' she asked.

'Yes.' He laughed.

'Then swim in your underwear. I don't care, let's just go and cool down.'

'You're crazy. Swim? In my underwear?' he said.

'Yes, Captain Prude, in your underwear. I won't tell and no one else will notice, I promise.'

She stuck her garden fork in the ground. 'I'll meet you at the moon gate in ten minutes.'

Exactly to the minute, Amanda was ready and waiting

for Simon at the gate. A bathroom towel would suffice, she thought, along with a cooler bag with some beers and a fresh breadstick from Shelley's, along with cheese, salami and dips. It was a perfect afternoon and the water across from the house sparkled in the sunshine.

'Here he comes,' she called out as Simon walked towards her wearing a T-shirt and shorts.

'Where did you get those from?' she asked.

'They're my trousers. I just cut them off into shorts,' he admitted and Amanda burst out laughing.

'Are you serious?'

'Absolutely,' he said. 'I can get new trousers and it's probably better to be gardening in shorts in this weather.'

They crossed the road and walked down the path towards the beach.

There were people on the sand further up towards the village but Amanda and Simon had their area to themselves.

Amanda put her towel on the sand and the cooler next to it and slipped off her sundress.

'Last one in's a rotten egg,' she cried and ran down towards the water.

As her feet hit the water she turned and danced, facing the beach. 'It's freezing,' she called out.

'I told you,' Simon said, turning around and looking at her.

'Come in.' She waved at him.

Amanda waded out further into the water as her body became used to the temperature. Soon she was waist-deep and then up to her shoulders.

She looked back to shore and saw Simon sitting on the sand.

'The water is fine,' she yelled but Simon didn't seem to hear her.

Amanda swam a little further out and then realised she couldn't stand anymore and turned to swim back, when suddenly she felt her body being dragged out further to sea. No matter how hard she tried to swim the other way, she was pulled further out. It felt like a magnet under the sea was pulling her, dragging her under.

The water also felt faster than where she had been swimming only moments before.

Simon was becoming smaller the further she was pulled out and Amanda started to panic.

She tried to put her hand up but she was pulled down and she swallowed water, then came up gasping up for air.

'Simon,' she called weakly but he wasn't in view anymore. 'Simon!' she cried, but her legs felt like lead and her head went under the water again.

Fight, fight, she told herself but she couldn't. Her ears hurt and her lungs felt as though they were about to explode. They burned and she closed her eyes, terror enveloping her body, when she suddenly felt arms around her waist. She was being pulled towards someone.

Her arms instinctively wrapped around the person's neck and she gasped for air.

'You're okay. We're in a rip. Lie back with me and let's just float, okay?'

Amanda couldn't see. Her eyes burned from the salt and she felt herself being turned onto her back, lying on someone's chest, and she floated.

'Slow your breathing,' she heard the person say. 'No,

like this. Feel your breath with mine,' they said. Their hand was on her diaphragm, soothing as she felt her breath slow down and her mind stopped panicking.

'We're going to float and this will take us to a sandbank I can see, so just lie back. I have you, you're safe.'

Amanda did, but the tears came, and she cried as they floated until it felt as though they were not moving anymore. Then she realised she could feel sand below her feet.

'We're okay, we're safe now. We're safe together,' she heard and she reluctantly pulled away and stood up, hip-deep in water. She turned and there was Simon.

'Thank you,' she cried and fell into his arms, sobbing onto his shoulder. 'You saved my life,' she said.

His arms wrapped around her again and her held her tight.

'That was a nasty rip,' he said. 'I got up to warn you, as I could see it from the shore where I was sitting, but then you just went under, as though pulled down.'

Amanda nodded into his neck. 'It felt like a magnet,' she said.

'You're safe now but we need to take you to a doctor and get you checked.'

'Why?' she asked, pulling away.

'Because of secondary drowning,' he said. 'You've swallowed a lot of water. Come on, we can walk in to shore and go back to the house to get the car. I'll get our things later. There's nothing of any value there so I'm not concerned.'

They walked through the water, Amanda holding on to Simon's arm, her chest hurting. She coughed as she made it to the sand on the shore.

'I'm going to walk you to the house and you can get dressed and then we are going to see Carole.'

She held on to Simon every step back to the house and he waited outside the room while she changed into a dress. She was so tired and so she sat on the bed for a moment and then lay down.

Simon's knock on the door was insistent.

'Just a moment,' she said.

Simon opened the door and saw her on the bed. 'You can't go to sleep,' he said, his voice thin and tight.

'I just need to rest.'

'You need to get checked by a doctor,' he said and came to the bed and sat down.

Amanda put her hand out for him to take and he held it. His hand felt warm and cold at the same time. A perfect temperature.

She shivered in the bed and Simon stood up and put a quilt over her.

'Come on, I'm taking you to Janet's,' he said. His voice sounded firm now.

She looked at him and saw he was still in his wet shorts and no top or shoes.

'Go and get changed,' she said.

'No, it doesn't matter,' he said brusquely.

'You can't go and see Carole and Janet with no top on – it will be the talk of Foxfield.' She smiled at him and he laughed.

'I don't care.'

And with that he picked her up, quilt and all, and carried her down the stairs and out to the car.

She leaned against him, knowing she had no energy to do

anything more, and he managed to open the car door and propped it wide with his foot and helped her into the car.

'God, I'm so tired,' she said.

Simon bent down and put her seatbelt on. 'Sit there quietly and breathe slowly. Don't stress your lungs out.'

Amanda grabbed his arm. 'Simon?'

His face was inches from hers. 'Yes, Amanda?' he asked.

'Thank you,' she said, feeling her eyes hurting from tears this time, not just the salt water.

He seemed as though he was about to speak but instead, he nodded. 'You're safe now. I promise.'

And as he closed the door and moved to the driver's side of the car, she remembered his words in the sea.

'We're okay, we're safe now. We're safe together.'

The words rang in her ears all the way to the village.

22

Simon

Simon had called ahead so Carole was already at the front of the house when they arrived, and she ushered Amanda into the front sitting room while Simon went to the back garden with Janet.

'You need a drink,' Janet said. 'Sit down and I'll make a gin.'

He sat down on the wicker chair under the back patio and breathed a sigh of relief.

The minute he had called Janet from the gardening shed, she had suggested sending an ambulance and meeting them at Moongate. But Simon knew it would be faster to get to their house and at least there they would be in the hands of a doctor if they needed more assistance.

'What happened?' Janet came holding a tall glass of gin and tonic for each of them and placed them on the table.

'A rip. It was fast and brutal. She wouldn't have had a chance if she was swimming alone.'

'God,' said Janet. 'That's terrifying. So lucky you were there.'

Simon thought he was going to be ill at the idea of what could have happened.

Carole came outside. 'She's okay – she's just very tired. I couldn't hear anything on her lungs but they've had a workout, that's for sure. She's resting now.'

Carole sat down. 'And what about you, Simon? Do you need me to check you?'

'No, I'm fine, I promise.'

'How did you know how to do that?' asked Carole. 'Not many people can identify a rip or rescue someone who is near to drowning.'

'I spent a year in Australia actually, and I did the lifesaving course because it was given on Bondi Beach and I thought it would be fun. I've never used what I learned until today.'

'Lucky for everyone then,' said Carole and they sat in silence, each of them processing what could have happened.

'It's a privilege being alive,' Carole stated, but it was almost to herself, Simon thought.

'It is,' he agreed.

'We cannot waste a moment of it being bitter or angry or resentful. All we have is the now.'

Simon wasn't sure if it was meant for him or if it was her thinking aloud but her words ran through him like cold water.

The sudden need to calm the chaos in his mind was overwhelming and he put his drink down and rested his head in his hands.

He was tired of being angry and he was tired of being filled with shame.

'Simon, are you okay?' He heard Janet's voice and then she was next to him now, her hand on his shoulder.

'I just… I'm just thinking about everything that brought me to Foxfield and Moongate and how Amanda is so integral to that. I mean, she's like sunshine, you know?' He looked at the women who nodded.

'Yes, she is.'

'And we nearly lost her.'

'But we didn't,' Carole reminded him.

'But I nearly did,' he said again.

'But you didn't,' Janet said. 'You saved her.'

He swallowed, unsure if he should cry or scream out loud. 'I just...' He tried to find the words but the feeling was unfamiliar. He couldn't think of how to express what he felt. Fear, trauma, worry, stress.

'You're having a response to the incident,' said Carole, taking the drink away from in front of him. 'You need something sugary and some sleep. Come on,' she said and she took his hand.

'You can lie down in our room; Amanda is in the spare room. I'll bring you a tea.'

Simon followed dutifully and went into a lovely bedroom of soft furnishings and shutters that dimmed the room enough to nap.

He sat on the bed as Carole turned on the fan in the corner, and a cool breeze blew over him.

Janet arrived with a tea in a mug that read, *Honk once if you're a goose*, and he smiled as he took it.

'You two women are amazing,' he said, feeling his eyes prick with tears. He hadn't cried when Anika had betrayed him or Charlie had ripped him off, but now he was ready to weep in the arms of these lovely women who knew exactly what to do to make him and Amanda feel safe.

He sipped the tea, feeling the warm liquid soothe his nerves.

'We'll leave you to rest,' said Janet.

'Wake me if Amanda needs me,' he said.

'We will. Don't fret, pet,' said Janet as she closed the door.

Simon put down the mug on the bedside table and looked at a photo of Janet and Carole together, smiling at the camera.

The love was so present between them and he wondered if photos of him and Anika together had ever made people wish they had a love like theirs.

He highly doubted it.

Simon turned onto his back and closed his eyes.

He could feel Amanda in his arms still, hanging on to him, her face so close to his in the car.

Everything that happened before today didn't matter anymore. None of it. There was only now.

And then he slept.

Diana – 1960s

The car gave Diana a sense of independence that not even her mother was able to enjoy.

Her mother had never learned to drive. She was driven everywhere and, despite her general disapproval, she had asked Diana how hard the test was and had even gone out for a drive a few times with Diana, including to Diana's doctor's appointment in Newcastle.

'The baby is breech,' the doctor had told her. 'It might turn but if it doesn't, you will have to have a caesarean.'

Diana had frowned at this news but her mother had patted her hand.

'You were the same, my dear. You and this baby seemed to want to enter the world standing on your own two feet.'

It was the first time her mother had said anything about the baby in a sentimental way, even a positive way, and Diana was touched.

She was eight months pregnant now and her mother had taken a few things of Diana's down from the attic. A Moses basket with linen that she had the staff wash, and some small items of clothing, but it wasn't enough for a new baby.

Diana had asked her father for some money and though he said he would do something to help her, nothing had materialized yet.

She knew she was having the baby in hospital, as she'd arranged it herself, but nothing else had been organised beyond that.

'Is Father going to help me at all?' she asked her mother one day when they were arranging Easter flowers for the church at St Cuthbert's. This was her mother's contribution to the community every year and the flowers were always lovely – and the only thing Diana enjoyed about attending the service.

'Help with what, Diana?' Her mother was looking at the display while holding a single jonquil and deciding where it belonged.

'With the baby. I don't have anything for it besides what you gave me from upstairs.'

Her mother sighed. 'I have spoken to him and I will again. Don't worry about it – babies don't need much when you bring them home. My great-grandmother slept in a dresser drawer.'

Diana had worried that *she* was going to have to sleep in a dresser drawer soon if her father kept ignoring her, but for some reason she had faith in her mother.

'Shall I help you take these up to the church before the service?' she asked her mother who had finally found a home for the jonquil.

'Father thinks it best you don't come to church, dear,' she said. 'It will be too tiring. You need to rest.'

Diana narrowed her eyes at her mother. 'Is it because I'm pregnant and he doesn't want me to shame the family name in the village?'

'No, dear,' said her mother, but Diana knew it was a lie. Diana had been respectful of her father's wishes to remain out of sight for the most part. Aside from her trips to Newcastle to the doctor's and the occasional lunch with Helen, she hadn't seen anyone she knew since her belly started showing.

But this upset her.

'Does he plan on hiding the baby when I bring it home?' she challenged.

'No, dear, I think he's just concerned you're doing too much.'

Diana snorted in an unladylike way. 'That's a lie and you know it, Mother.'

The next morning, Diana heard her father's car start and she looked out of her window. She saw some of the staff carefully laying down the flowers in the back seat of the Jaguar, while her mother, dressed in her Easter finery, and her father in a suit got into the car and headed to the church.

Diana dressed in her best pregnancy dress, a pale-yellow smock with pretty lace cuffs and collar and wore the only shoes that fit her swollen feet – a pair of white sandals with a slight kitten heel. She pulled her blonde hair back into a ponytail and tied a yellow ribbon in it and put on a slick of pink lipstick that Helen had given her for her birthday.

Diana went downstairs and to her car. She got inside it and adjusted the seat back to accommodate her baby bump. For years Diana had tried to avoid Easter Sunday service and her parents would never let her, and now she wasn't allowed to go, there was nowhere else she wanted to be. She knew why they wanted her to stay home and she wasn't having it. She would go to church and show everyone her belly, then there would be no more hiding or excuses from her parents. The moment she revealed her baby was real, then her father could stop living in a world that he thought he controlled.

She opened her bag to take out her keys but they were not inside. She emptied her purse on the seat to check but came up empty-handed.

She got out of the car and went up to her room again to check. Her feet were already hurting in the sandals and she wished she could wear her slip-on shoes that Mother said were too low class to leave the house in.

Diana hunted through her room, even getting on all fours to look under the bed, which took some effort to do and to get up from.

She was sure she had put them back into her handbag the day before when she had taken a little drive along the cliffs for something to do. She'd returned before dinner and had left her handbag on the hallstand, which her mother told her off for, and told her she had put it in her bedroom.

Had her mother taken the keys?

Diana sat on her bed in defeat and for the first time since she had told her parents she was pregnant, she felt fearful of what was to come.

23

Amanda

Amanda clomped up the stairs to the attic of the house. Carole had prescribed no gardening or being out in the heat for a week, which was frustrating, but Carole was more than intimidating when she was in doctor mode.

The last two days had been spent sleeping, doing some drawing and having lunch at Diana's house. Amanda didn't tell her what had happened and asked Simon, Janet and Carole to keep it to themselves also. Diana was old and she didn't need to worry about Amanda.

But today she was grumpy in her boredom until she remembered that Diana had said the attic was filled with old clothes that she could have.

Lainie had insisted she send photos of anything cool when she had told her about it, so Amanda went upstairs with her phone to document the items.

The attic was at the very top of the house, up a tiny staircase that was just larger than a ladder.

Thankfully the light worked when Amanda turned it on and she looked at the mess of suitcases, wooden tea chests, boxes, and old furniture.

It was bigger and more chaotic than Amanda had imagined and it was also filled with very musty old air that she was sure she could have chewed through.

She pushed through the mess to a window, opened the latch and pushed but it was stuck. She banged on the frame with her hand and heard the window loosen and then it slid up with some noisy protestation.

'Thank God,' Amanda said to herself as she surveyed the scene.

She could handle mess – her mother was messy – but to organise it, that was a bigger process.

The side of some of the tea chests had the word *books* written on them. Other ones read *china*. Another read *misc* and many were unlabelled.

Amanda lifted an old leather suitcase on top of one of the chests and opened the clasps.

Lifting the lid, she found a men's dinner suit, with several shirts and ties. There were some dress shoes – worn but well looked after – and a number of pairs of braces.

She closed the case back up and put it to the side.

Amanda decided she would organise into four piles.

- Keep.
- Go through with Diana.
- Charity shop.
- Throw out.

The next case was larger and was filled with dresses from the 1960s or maybe earlier. Many were from brands Amanda didn't know, but they were lovely and still in tissue paper. It was obvious they had been carefully put away by someone.

Amanda looked at each one, fascinated by the detail and stitching. They were so beautiful, she thought and she held up a peach georgette one, with a bow on one shoulder.

It was gorgeous and she laid it on the case and took a photo of it and the label, then sent it to Lainie.

Divine. Cocktail dress. You could get a lot of money for it online.

Amanda kept sending pictures of the dresses and Lainie sent back similar ones online for more money than Amanda had imagined they would be worth. Lainie texted back:

You're sitting on a month's rent in New York, baby

Amanda put the suitcase to the side to go through with Diana. Despite Diana's insistence that all of it was hers now, she would never dream of selling or getting rid of anything without Diana's approval, and it would be nice to talk to Diana about them and where she wore them. The memories that came with the dresses would no doubt make them even more beautiful and fascinating.

There were more dresses in cases, some older, perhaps from Diana's mother, more matronly but always excellent quality.

There was a trunk of hats, which Amanda adored. The silk shone when she turned the hat, and the brim was stiff and proud. She texted Simon a photo of a black top hat in perfect condition on her head at a rakish angle.

My new gardening hat?

You look fantastic. You should wear it all the time, not just in the garden.

Amanda giggled as she kept exploring.

There were coats, so many coats, she thought as she put them to one side.

A few broken shoes – she wasn't sure why they were being kept – and sadly, a box of knits that some moths had feasted on. A pile of newspapers, which she thought were a fire hazard and so made a note to ask Simon to come and get rid of them for her.

The various piles were growing, and she wondered if she should take a break when she spotted a cream suitcase, smaller than the others and more feminine. Probably Diana's, she thought with a smile as she put it up on the chest to open it.

She clicked the latches and opened it up.

Inside she found a number of dresses, nightgowns and slippers.

There was a bag of toiletries and then smaller dresses and some pants and shirts and cardigans. The suitcase was crammed full of items that Amanda carefully unpacked. And then at the bottom of the case was a baby dress with smocking across the front. It was very old-fashioned but lovely, in a light, pale pink cotton. There was a crocheted shawl that was so soft and begging to be washed. Thankfully the moths had not found their way into this case, she thought.

Next there was a little white romper for a baby, with tiny little yellow flowers embroidered on the front with a matching white cardigan. They were beautiful baby clothes but why were they in this case? It didn't make any sense, Amanda thought, as she took everything out and started to refold the items.

There was a tiny rip in the lining of the case and when Amanda touched it she felt something like the shape of a ring.

She put her fingers in and pulled out a small ruby dress ring, but she could feel more.

Gently pulling back the lining, Amanda found a more rings with different stones and a string of pearls.

She counted the pearls. There were one hundred and forty of them framing a blue stone in a gold pendant. They were incredible, and she took a photo and sent it to Simon.

I just found these in the attic.

They will look great with the top hat. But seriously, what the hell? Why are they in the attic?

No idea, but I'm going to show Diana.

Amanda put everything back into the case except the jewellery and carefully made her way downstairs.

She needed to think about what she had just seen before she spoke to Diana about the jewellery and the case. Nothing made sense.

Amanda went to the kitchen and laid the pearls out on the table. They were in beautiful condition considering they had been shut in a suitcase for decades.

She remembered her mother saying that pearls needed to be worn – something about the pearls absorbing the natural oils of the skin and rehydrating – so she put them around her neck, feeling them against her skin, cool but not cold, weighty but not heavy.

She went to the living room, where a mirror was hung on one wall and looked at them.

They were beautiful, she thought, looking up at the picture of Diana, who was wearing the pearls in her portrait, and the painting of Diana's mother, who was also wearing them in hers. She glanced at herself again in the mirror and for a moment she looked like one of the women in the paintings or perhaps she was wishing she was one of them. She touched the pearls and then shook her head. She shouldn't be wearing them. She took them off and put them on the small table. It wasn't any of her business but something wasn't sitting right with Amanda.

Diana was entitled to keep what happened to her private but there seemed to be so many unanswered questions that Amanda couldn't help but be curious. No, it was more than curiosity, she thought. It was intrigue, and Amanda couldn't help thinking that Diana was deliberately hiding something from her. The more she pondered on what she found, the more questions she had for Diana.

24

Amanda

Diana was out with Janet when Amanda went to the gatehouse but the door was open, which wasn't surprising since Simon had said he would care for Trotsky and would return him later. There was no chance of anyone coming to the gatehouse without being seen by Simon, so Diana had happily it unlocked.

Amanda walked inside and looked around for a safe place to leave the pearls.

Diana's house was lovely, she thought, more modern than Moongate with a fully renovated kitchen and a wall unit air conditioner.

Amanda went into the living area and placed the pearls on the coffee table with the rings.

There was a small secretaire with a notepad, and Amanda wrote a quick note.

Found these in the attic, along with some rings. I think they're the pearls you mentioned. Let me know when you're free to chat.

Amanda left the note next to the jewellery and walked outside, closing the door firmly behind her.

She walked through the garden and found Simon eating a sandwich, sitting by the cool of the pond, which he had filled with water.

'Hey,' she said.

'Hey yourself,' he answered as she sat by him.

'No top hat and pearls?' he teased.

'No,' she answered.

'You okay?' Simon asked, looking at her and frowning.

'I don't know.'

'Do you need to see Carole?'

'No, it's not that – I'm not feeling unwell,' she said, stretching her legs out in front of her. 'Just something feels off.'

'Okay? Talk me through it,' he said, putting his sandwich down.

Amanda squinted as she thought, trying to piece it all together. 'I think Diana is not telling me the truth.'

'About what?' he asked.

'About everything,' she said. 'But if I ask her outright and I'm wrong then I look like an ungrateful bitch.'

'Give me an example.' Simon had turned to look at her and she twisted to face him and blew a curl out of her eyes.

'So, I asked Diana if she had any children and she said no, but then I met this woman whose mother-in-law used to be friends with Diana, and she said Diana had a baby but no one knew what happened to it. I think it might have died.'

'That's sad,' said Simon with a frown. 'But she doesn't

have to tell you about that; that's her story and she can keep it private.'

'I agree but I found a suitcase in the attic that was clearly meant for someone who was going to a hospital to have a baby. It was filled with maternity wear and toiletries and a few baby clothes, but they were really old-fashioned, the baby clothes I mean. Like, for a baby in the 1940s. And in the case was the pearls that Diana and her mother are wearing in their formal portraits, along with some other jewellery that had been hidden in the lining.'

'All right, Nancy Drew, you might be overimagining things a little. She probably hid it up there so she never had to think about it again, especially if the baby didn't survive.'

But Amanda shook her head. 'Something doesn't feel right; it never has. I get Mom bought a ticket but Diana is evasive when I try to ask her questions about the competition to win the house, and sometimes, there's just a funny feeling that she's not telling me the truth about things. Not that I feel she's doing anything untoward, but it feels as though she's deliberately editing her life for my benefit.' Amanda paused. 'And... Okay, this is crazy, so hear me out.'

Simon listened intently.

'I think I look a bit like Diana and her mom in the portraits of them in the living room. I can't explain it but they're wearing the pearls in those paintings and when I put the pearls on – to try, you know?'

Simon nodded.

'I looked at myself in the mirror and then at the paintings and I could see it. The skin tone, the nose shape, the eyebrow definition. They only difference is I'm a redhead, and my mom was a redhead.'

Simon sighed. 'Okay, I hear you but it's all based on assumptions. You need more evidence than that and you won't get anywhere with accusations.'

'I know. It seems so far-fetched but something isn't sitting properly with me.'

'What about your mother? Who were her family?'

Amanda scratched her head, thinking. 'Mom was adopted, but she didn't like her adoptive family. Super strict and religious, according to her. They were also abusive. She left for New York and never went back.'

'That's sad for her,' said Simon. 'She must have felt very unwanted.'

'That's why she called me Amanda, she said. It means "worthy of love" in Latin.'

Simon laughed. 'Do you know what Simon means?'

Amanda smiled at his laughter. 'No. What does it mean?'

'"Reputation", which is shite, by all accounts.'

Amanda laughed. 'Don't be so mean about yourself. It's Anika's and Charlie's reputations that are shite, as you say – also, great word. I'm going to steal it and use it.'

'That's a gift to you from us Brits,' he said.

'Thanks, you're so kind to me.' She laughed again.

'So what are you going to do?' he asked.

'I'm going to wait for Diana to see the jewellery. I left it at her place with a note. I'll see if she wants to talk about it. The ball's in her court now.'

'You know, you could research your mum and her adoption. I'm sure you can get the papers now she's passed and you're next of kin.'

Amanda slapped her own leg. 'Great idea, I will. God, why didn't I think of that?'

'Because you're not as brilliant as me?' he teased.

'Clearly! You should be wearing the top hat – it would look great with your gardening shorts.'

'Why thank you, ma'am,' Simon said, and pretended to tip his pretend top hat.

Are we flirting? wondered Amanda for a moment but then pushed it from her mind. Simon was just being funny. It was clear he was still pining after Anika.

'Okay, I'm off to be Detective Amanda Cox, the dual-passport-holding, brilliantly talented and intuitive mystery solver.'

'What's your catchphrase? They always have a catchphrase.'

'Hmmm.' Amanda thought for a moment. 'How about: I know what's up.'

'What's up where?' Simon looked confused.

'The news, the clues, the mystery,' she said. 'Okay, that one doesn't translate so well.'

She thought again. 'Mysteries, I solve them.'

'Wow, straight to the point.' Simon laughed.

'Or I attempt to.' She laughed with him and stood up. 'Thanks for the chat,' she said.

'Anytime. I'm going to keep planting out the pool.'

Amanda's phone rang and she pulled it out of her pocket and looked at the number.

'I don't know who this is,' she said.

'Answer it – you might have won another house.' Simon wiggled his eyebrows at her.

'Very funny,' she said as she answered the phone.

'Hello, Amanda speaking.'

Amanda listened to the voice on the end of the line and looked at Simon.

'I can, absolutely. Can you text the address to me on this number? Amazing, thank you – I'll see you tomorrow.'

Amanda put the phone back in her pocket. 'I have a job interview tomorrow, at a garden centre – the one the girl at the spa told me about.'

She jumped up and down and Simon jumped to his feet and grabbed her hands.

'That's amazing, how great,' he cried and she jumped into his arms, hugging him close.

'I know! I can learn stuff and get a discount on the plants.'

Amanda hugged him tightly and she felt his stubble on his cheek where it was pressed against hers. She breathed in the scent of the soil and his perspiration and felt his arm encircling her and she nestled into his neck.

His mouth was so close, she thought, just a slight move and they would kiss and then she would...

Amanda pulled herself away.

Do not do this, Amanda, she told herself. *Do not embarrass yourself by doing this. He's not interested and you're just lonely.*

She smiled at him as she stepped back.

'It's three days a week, which is great. I can still help in the garden and we can make this spectacular.' Amanda did a spin. 'Seriously, life here is so perfect, isn't it?'

Before Simon could answer, she ran towards Moongate Manor. 'I have to find something to wear,' she called.

'You can borrow my gardening shorts and top hat,' he called out and Amanda laughed all the way to the house.

25

Diana

Diana returned from Janet's with an armful of dahlias ready for a vase and the deep satisfaction of a day well spent. Janet had taken her to the cinema to see a lovely French film about a girl who worked in an art gallery who fell in love with a man in a painting. It was charming and the cinematography was beautiful.

Janet had taken out a container of strawberries from her bag and they ate them along with the two chocolate-covered ice creams they'd bought.

It had been so long since Diana had done anything with a friend; she could have watched two flies walking up a wall with Janet and been as happy as she was now.

When Janet dropped her home Trotsky wagged his tail upon her return.

A dog will always be happy to see you come through the door, she thought, as she put down her bag and went into the kitchen to place the dahlias in a beautiful Émile Gallé cameo vase that had been her great-grandmother's. The pinks and burgundies of the flowers looked spectacular in the vase, she decided, as she carefully carried it into the sitting room to place on the sideboard.

Diana stood back to admire them and then sat in her armchair to see how they looked from that vantage point.

As she looked around the room, she saw the gleam of something unusual on the table. She stood, walked to the table and leaned down.

'Oh my,' she said, picking up the pearls and feeling their weight in her hand. She read the note from Amanda then she sat back down and held the necklace, closing her eyes.

It was so long ago, and she was so depressed after returning from the hospital without the baby, she had forgotten where they were. She was so sad for so long that perhaps she had blocked it from her memory.

Whatever the reason, the pain and anguish came rushing back and Diana was suddenly eighteen again, the memories bubbling up and spilling over, demanding she remember them.

1960s

Diana and her father had barely spoken for the past six months and when she asked him about the keys he denied it, as did her mother, but then her keys were found on the driveway by Helen's father, Peter, who swore he hadn't seen them there the day before when he raked the gravel.

Diana had taken the keys and hid them in her room so this would never happen again, and she had gone downstairs to speak to her mother when she heard her parents talking in her father's study, the door slightly ajar.

'I have told the village the Moongate Festival is cancelled this year. I told them there is an illness in the family,' her father was saying.

'It's the first time in one hundred years we aren't having one, Edward. Are you sure you don't want it? We can send Diana to London.'

Diana felt tears welling as she heard them speak of her ruining things. Her hand stroked her stomach and her child kicked in response.

'No, we will just get it over with and then next year we can pretend it never happened and start again.'

'If you're sure, Edward,' her mother was saying but she sounded uncertain.

Diana crept back to her room. They were planning something, she was sure. This was why her father hadn't helped buy anything for the baby and why he had hidden her car keys.

Diana found a suitcase in the box room and took it to her bedroom. She laid it on the bed. She packed as much as she could and then she went to her mother's room and opened the jewellery box. The Moongate pearls lay on blue velvet and Diana held them for a moment before slipping them into her pocket along with some smaller dress rings and earrings. They would have to be sold to pay for things for the baby. Diana would head to London and try and find a job and care for her child alone. It wasn't going to be easy but it could be done. She had read about other women who did it alone.

Diana stepped out of her mother's room and went to her bedroom where she took her car keys from the hiding place and put them in her handbag. Diana unpicked the lining of the suitcase and put the jewellery into a silk bag and then a sock and laid it flat, and then she sewed the lining up again. It was terrible handiwork but it would do, she thought, as she did up the suitcase and looked around her room.

She would leave tomorrow, she decided, first thing in the morning, and she slipped the suitcase under her bed. This would be the last night she ever slept in this house, she told herself, but she didn't feel a moment of guilt. She needed to keep her baby safe and she was sure that wouldn't happen while she lived here.

26

Amanda

Amanda pulled up at the garden centre, adjusted her pink striped shirt and brushed invisible lint from her jeans.

This felt much more like her, she thought as she looked in the rear-view mirror and moved her curls back from her face.

She stepped out of the car and went to the front entrance of the gardening centre with the sign across the top. NEWCASTLE UPON TYNE GARDEN CENTRE. Not the most creative of names, she thought, but it said what it was and there was no mistake about what they sold.

Inside there was a large display of indoor plants – real ones, not plastic, she noted, remembering the ones in her and her mom's apartment.

There were pots and knick-knacks for sale and beautiful prints of different local artists on the walls. Shells in baskets and notebooks with beautiful covers on a spinning stand greeted her, and pretty scarves and shawls hung from a large bamboo ladder.

It was so lovely Amanda thought she might like to live there forever.

'Amanda?' She turned to see a man in a T-shirt and shorts, and a large-brimmed straw hat and sunglasses.

'Yes, hi,' she said, as he took off his sunglasses.

'I'm David. We spoke on the phone,' he said, and he shook her hand. 'Nice to meet you. Fancy a tour?'

'I would love one. The gift shop is gorgeous. I would like my house to look like that.' She laughed.

'That's my wife Tilly's work. It's all her – she has great taste.'

David walked her through the garden centre, pointing out the plants and the different areas. He showed her the bags of potting mix and compost and soil and the large stakes and more. It was a lot, but Amanda soaked it in.

'How much do you know about gardening and plants?' David asked her as they walked into the office.

On the wall was a mess of children's drawings and photos of two small children with David and a smiling woman.

'That's the art wall from my little family.' He smiled proudly.

'Your children are so cute,' she said, peering at the photos of the happy faces. David was definitely giving off Labrador energy; a golden one, all tail wagging and happy with their lot in life.

'Yes, and a lot of work! Tilly, who also works here, is pregnant with our third, so we need help. I know it's not full-time but there might be a little overtime here and there.' He looked at her hopefully as they sat down.

'To be honest, I would love three days. You asked me if I knew much about gardening and plants. I do and I don't. I'm learning. I have a large garden at the house I've just moved into. It was apparently an amazing garden, but it's since gone to ruin and I've been charged with returning it to its former glory.' She laughed. 'So, as you can imagine, I'm on a huge learning curve.'

'Really?' asked David. 'Where is the garden? We sponsor the open gardens here every summer.'

'It's called Moongate Manor,' she said. 'Down by the sea on North Road.'

'Moongate? Oh wow, I've heard that was incredible in its day.'

'Yes, I've seen photos and drawings, but it needs a lot of work to get it back where it was. A huge amount of work.'

'Do you have help?' asked David.

'I have a friend, Simon, working there, and the Foxfield gardening club, who have a lot of knowledge, but it comes with a fair amount of arguing about where to put the seeds and they take a lot of breaks for tea.'

David burst out laughing. 'That's fantastic – I love that.'

'They have been amazing, and so generous with their time and help, but I need to do as much as I can myself. I promised the woman whose house it was.'

David sat back in his chair. 'You know, I could come and take a look, give you some of my horticultural smarts. I've designed some major gardens in the area, and I can set you up with some things to do over the rest of the summer to get you set up with the planning for autumn.'

'Really?' Amanda couldn't believe her ears.

'Absolutely, but the bigger question is, when can you start?'

Amanda gasped. 'Now?'

'We're okay today but how about tomorrow? Eight a.m. start, finish at three.'

'Seriously, you don't know how much this means to me. I'll work so hard and learn all the plants – I'll be a plantopaedia.'

David laughed. 'I think I'm going to like you, Amanda.'

Amanda stood up and put her hand out to him. 'I will see you tomorrow. And thank you.'

Amanda felt like her car was flying home as she drove back to Moongate Manor. And the person she couldn't wait to tell was Simon.

Diana – 1960s

It was two in the morning when Diana woke thinking she had wet the bed. As she stepped out onto the floor, more water rushed down and then a contraction came, taking her breath away.

The baby was coming.

Terrible timing, she thought, and she stood waiting for another contraction, counting in her head.

Five minutes apart, she thought. Was that enough time to drive herself to the hospital?

She could pull over when they came, she thought, and pulled her suitcase from under the bed as another contraction started. She buried her face into the bedclothes to muffle her moan and breathed through the pain until it passed.

She had no time to even dress. She took her handbag,

suitcase and a coat, and carefully and quietly left her room and headed down the stairs and towards the front door.

It was all going to plan but then a contraction came unexpectedly quickly and she cried out in pain and dropped her case.

Bending over, she panted, trying to will the pain to subside.

'Diana?' It was her father at the top of the stairs.

She looked up at him. 'I'm going to the hospital,' she said as she opened the door.

'Don't be ridiculous, I will drive you. Let me get your mother.'

Diana almost screamed her protestations. 'No, I'll take myself.' She picked up the case and walked to her car.

Please don't let another one come for a while, she silently prayed as she put the case in the boot and closed it firmly. She had managed to get into the car and was closing the door when another one hit her. She threw her head back and made a sound she didn't know she was capable of making.

'Out.' Her father had opened the car door and was holding her hand. 'I'm taking you now,' he said.

She noticed he was in his pyjamas, robe and slippers, as her mother came running out of the front door in a more respectable dress and shoes. She waved a bag at Diana. 'I have some things,' she said and Diana's hope rose. So her mother had packed a little bag for the baby; perhaps she had been imagining all of their refusal to discuss the baby's arrival and their plans to send her away.

Her father helped Diana over to the Jaguar and put her on the back seat.

'I will ruin the leather,' she said.

'It's only a car,' said her father with uncharacteristic nonchalance.

Soon they were on the road and her father was driving just above the speed limit, all the way to the Princess Mary Maternity Hospital, a choice which her father was not happy about.

'That's a hospital for poor women,' he said accusingly.

'No, it's a hospital for all women,' Diana said through gritted teeth.

'You could have gone private,' said Edward. 'She should have gone private,' he added to his wife.

'I didn't want to. My doctor can deliver the baby there,' she said as another contraction came, this time closer than the last.

'When did you make these arrangements?' he demanded to know.

'When I found out I was pregnant,' she said as another contraction arrived, stronger than the last.

Relief came as she saw the lights of the hospital, and when her father came around and opened the door, a porter arrived with a wheelchair.

'Straight in,' the porter said and he started to wheel Diana away.

She turned to her mother. 'Can I have the bag of things you brought?'

Her mother looked confused. 'What bag?'

'You said you had a bag of things when you were leaving the house.'

Her mother shook her head at Diana. 'No, dear, that was

for your father. He can't be expected to wear his nightclothes while in public. He can change in the bathrooms inside.'

The porter wheeled Diana away as she felt another contraction hit and she cried out in both pain and anger at her parents.

27

Amanda

Amanda drove up the driveway and saw Diana standing by the gatehouse. She waved but Diana turned and walked inside, as though she hadn't seen her, but Amanda knew she had. She was avoiding her.

Amanda drove up to the house and parked the car.

She wasn't ready to speak to Diana yet. She didn't want to ruin the good news about her job; instead she went searching for Simon in the garden.

He wasn't around, so she walked down to his place, but his motorbike wasn't there.

Amanda sighed and turned to walk back, her mood lowered with Diana's snub and Simon's absence.

She wandered back to the house, went inside and looked around. She was tired of the old interiors and the fading wallpaper and paint. She thought about how lovely the gift shop at the garden centre was and how she would like the inside of the house to be as lovely as the garden was supposed to be but that would cost even more than she could imagine.

She lay on the sofa in the living room and looked at the portrait of Diana. She was wearing the peach georgette dress with the bow on the shoulder in the portrait, she realised – the one Amanda had found in the attic. She had been so taken by the pearls she hadn't seen the dress, or the glint in Diana's eyes.

Amanda closed her own eyes and wished she could speak to her mother.

She would tell her all the right things to soothe her racing mind, help her understand her feelings for Simon that seemed to be growing and how to handle Diana while gently teasing out her secrets.

There was so much to do, Amanda thought, as she felt her eyes become heavier. She was supposed to cook dinner tonight for her and Simon. She was supposed to be researching her mom's adoption, while trying to salvage the garden and work. And then there were the clothes to go through with Diana and see if she could sell some things, because that money could help the garden. It was an endless list of tasks and each one created the next.

It was nearly too much, she thought, as she drifted off to sleep. Just a short nap, that's all she needed, and then she would get on with the list.

28

Amanda

A week later, the sun was up and so was Amanda, as she waited outside the house for David – her new boss – to come and see the garden.

Simon came walking towards her, his tin mug in hand, his hair still slightly sleep-worn.

'Morning.' She smiled at him.

'You look fresher than I feel. What time did you get up?' he asked her.

'About twenty minutes ago but I'm a morning person,' she said. 'I love coming out here and looking at everything in the garden. There are ladybugs on the roses.'

'Ladybirds,' Simon said.

'They're ladybugs where I come from.' She poked her tongue out at him.

'That's the North American lineage. Here they are ladybirds because they're not bugs, they're beetles.'

'You're a beetle,' Amanda said and Simon laughed.

'I'm a tired beetle.'

'Poor you,' said Amanda as a car drove up the driveway and stopped.

'David,' she called and waved as her new boss jumped from the car.

'Good morning,' he said.

'David, this is Simon, my friend who has been working in the garden.'

David and Simon shook hands and then David looked around.

'This is incredible,' he said.

'It could be,' Amanda said. 'But we need some guidance, I think. Simon and I are doing our best but it's so much work.'

David nodded to them both. 'But it doesn't need to be done all at once. A garden is always evolving and changing. I think this time next year you would both be surprised at the changes in the spaces.'

Amanda looked at Simon who was staring straight ahead.

Simon had only agreed to be here for the summer and hadn't said he had plans to stay any longer, but the mere thought of him leaving hurt her heart and head.

'Want to give me a tour?'

As they walked around the garden, Amanda listened to the way Simon spoke about the ground, the plants, the nurturing tone he used when handling the flowers and explaining the process of rebuilding the pond and planting out the shade-loving plants in the surrounding area.

'You will eventually build your own little microclimate here,' said David, looking around.

'That's really cool,' Amanda said to Simon.

'Right? We might get frogs here.'

Amanda liked the way he said 'we', but she wasn't ready

to ask him if he would stay because why would she assume he would stay for her?

Her last boyfriend hadn't even offered for her to move in when she was nearly homeless. Why would a man who was running away from his life want to stay here digging in the dirt for a living?

'Amanda?' Simon's voice interrupted her thoughts.

'Yes? Sorry, was thinking about the pond,' she said.

'David wants to know if we have had the soil tested.'

'For what?' she asked.

David smiled. 'To see the quality of it, if it's acidic or loam, or loam clay, or sandy, or all sorts of things. The more you know about the soil the better your plant growth will be. It's choosing the right plants for the right environment. Some things just aren't suited to some environments yet thrive in others.'

Amanda nodded as David spoke, thinking of herself in New York. She had never thrived in the city, no matter how much her mom loved living there, yet the moment she moved to Foxfield and Moongate, she was in her element.

'I think you should get the soil tested first. I assume the wind from the sea brings salt with it?'

Simon shook his head. 'Surprisingly no, the winds rarely blow onshore because that's a little bay down there and it's protected. The garden is actually in a little valley so the wind hits the roof before it hits the garden.'

'How do you know that?' Amanda asked.

'Diana told me. She did some surveying of the land back in the day.'

Simon looked at David. 'Diana is the previous owner. She

was an avid gardener but is getting on in years now. She let the garden go due to her health issues.'

'She would know the soil type then?' Amanda asked.

'She might but it's still worth doing new testing anyway, as things can change so much, and since the garden has been dormant for a long time it will have changed quite a lot since she was last planting it.'

Amanda nodded. 'It's all quite scientific, isn't it?'

'It is,' said David. 'I can give you a number for someone to come and check the soil and so on and then we can chat about it afterwards.'

'You should show David the seed box and maps and the watercolours you did,' Simon encouraged Amanda.

'Oh sure,' she said. 'I mean, he doesn't need to see my paintings.' She looked at David. 'I'm a visual person, so I needed to see how it would look from a picture.'

'I would love to see them,' David said.

29

Amanda

Amanda led David to the house and took him through the back door to the kitchen.

'Coffee? Tea?' she asked.

'Coffee would be great.'

'Finally an English person who isn't obsessed with tea,' she said as she turned the kettle on.

'I love tea but I like coffee first thing,' David said as he sat at the kitchen table.

'Simon, can you get the seed drawer and stuff? It's in the living room,' she said.

Soon Simon was back and he placed the items on the table in front of David.

'This is the book about Moongate's garden and the maps Diana drew for each of the seasons,' Simon explained to an entranced David. Amanda made the coffee and a fresh tea for Simon. She buttered some fruit loaf for them and placed it on a plate and then put it all on the table as they talked.

David looked up from the watercolours of Amanda's vision of the garden. 'You did these?' he asked.

She nodded.

'You're incredibly talented. What else have you done? Can I see?'

Amanda knew she was blushing and hated how easily she was pleased by praise for her artwork.

'It's silly,' she said, brushing him aside.

'No, it's not silly,' Simon said. 'Show him your work. Actually, show me also – I've hardly seen anything.'

Amanda groaned and went into the front sitting room and found her latest sketchbook of her animals. She went back and put it in front of them and looked away as they opened the book.

'My God,' said Simon. 'These are fantastic.'

Amanda gave him a small smile.

David was poring over them. 'These animals are gorgeous.'

Amanda nodded. 'Thank you, they're my favourite thing to draw but sadly no one wants to buy them.'

'Are you serious? These would sell out if I put them in the gallery. Do you have any completed? Ready for framing and hanging?'

Amanda laughed. 'I have a whole exhibition actually but it was never held because I couldn't afford the framing in New York.'

David banged his hand on the table. 'You know, my brother-in-law is a framer and he can do them for a discount. You could pay him once the pieces are sold at the garden centre.'

Amanda sat in shock. 'Do you really think they would sell? That people would want to buy a drawing of a pair of frogs on a tandem bicycle on the French Riviera?' She laughed as she said it aloud, aware of how ridiculous it sounded.

'Are you kidding? These will go instantly. They're perfect for country homes and whimsical decoration. I know my clientele and they will snap these up in a moment.'

He turned a page and saw a baby hedgehog in a cradle. 'God, my wife would love that for the baby's room.' He glanced at Simon. 'She's pregnant with our third, a boy this time after two girls.'

'Congratulations,' said Simon.

'I'm nervous about having a boy. I know what I'm doing with girls.' He laughed and then looked at Amanda. 'So, will you do an exhibition at the garden centre? It would be great for us and for you.'

Amanda looked at Simon in shock. 'What do you think?' she asked him.

Simon reached over and took her hand. 'I think you should do it. This is everything you wanted, isn't it?'

Amanda felt tears at the back of her throat but held them down. 'Yes, you're right.' She paused. 'Okay, let's do it,' she said.

David ate some fruit loaf and flicked through the Moongate book.

'You know, you should write a story about this garden and send it out to publishers. I think this would be a beautiful children's book.'

Amanda shook her head. 'Slow down, cowboy, one thing at a time, okay?'

David drained his coffee and stood up. 'Bring the art in when you can and we can go and see my brother-in-law together.' He looked at Simon. 'So good to meet you also. I'll think about the garden some more and send you a few ideas once you get the soil tested.'

Simon shook his hand and Amanda noticed how happy he seemed.

When David had left, she went back to the kitchen and looked at the sketchbook again as Simon came in behind her and looked over her shoulder.

'You are very talented, Amanda, really. Don't hide it from the world. I know you think your style isn't modern enough or cool enough, but it's gorgeous and you just have to find people who love it. They're out there – David being one of them.'

Amanda nodded and sighed. 'How is everything so different here from New York? I mean, it's like this whole country has made me feel so welcome, helped, cared for, wanted and supported.' She felt the tears come. 'I've never felt that for a day in New York, yet here I am, living in this crazy house, with a job and an art exhibition and so many friends, albeit they're almost all over fifty but still, I've been treated with so much kindness.' She let her tears fall as she looked at Simon.

'And you, you're my best friend here, and I look forward to every day with you in the garden.'

Simon swallowed. 'I know, I love it too.' he said. 'I love it here and I love seeing you every day, making our plans, having dinner, laughing.'

They held each other's gaze and Amanda wondered if he would say any more, and if she had anything else to say. But what did she want to say to him?

It was as though she wouldn't allow herself to have the feelings that were growing inside. He wanted Anika; he was pining for her. He was only here for the summer, she reminded herself.

And until he told her otherwise, that was all there was to it.

She looked down at her sketchbook and picked it up, wiping her tears with her free hand.

'Okay, well, I better get on with finding the drawings for David,' she said. 'See you for lunch?'

Simon looked as though he was about to speak and then closed his mouth. After a pause he said, 'I'm off to see Janet about some iris rhizomes.'

'That's a fancy word,' she teased.

'I'm a fancy man, didn't you know?' he said as he walked towards the back door.

'You can borrow my top hat,' she called out to him as he left, and she could hear him chuckling as he walked past the window, down the side of the house and towards the garden.

Amanda sat at the table and clutched the sketchbook, wishing she knew what he was thinking about her and Moongate. It was the middle of July now and summer would end before they knew it. If Simon didn't show any feelings by then, she would know the idea of them together was just a dream. But what an amazing dream it was…

Diana – 1960s

Diana woke from the anaesthetic. Her mouth was dry and her eyes hurt but she remembered what had just happened. She turned her head to see a nurse standing on the side of the bed.

'Where is my baby?' she asked, trying to lift her head from the bed to see if the baby was in a crib nearby.

The nurse looked at her watch and then at Diana. 'Stay here,' she said as though Diana was planning on making a run for it.

Diana dropped her head onto the pillow and let out a deep breath, which hurt.

She had been cut so the baby could come out. She could feel it, across her belly.

The door to her room opened and a different nurse, younger with a jolly face, smiled at her.

'New mum, are you? You've got the little beauty, the red-headed princess, don't you?'

'It's a girl?' Diana was thrilled at the news. She hadn't minded either way but the news pleased her more than she thought it would.

'Yes, and with a crop of red hair like I never did see. Everyone is talking about it in the nursery – she's quite a beauty,' said the nurse. 'I was going to bring her around for you to try nursing her. Have they sat you up yet?'

Diana shook her head and the nurse came to the end of the bed and kicked something and then started winding.

'It will hurt but you will get used to it and we can get you something for the pain,' she said.

Diana would have borne nails in her feet for the chance to finally meet her daughter, and she gripped the bedsheets as she came to a reclined sitting position.

'Righto, let me get the little beauty and bring her to you.'

The nurse bustled out of the room while Diana smoothed her hair down. Although she knew it was silly, she was nervous to meet her daughter.

She sat waiting, looking at the clock in the room, watching the minutes go by. Ten minutes passed and then twenty minutes and then half an hour. Diana wished she could drink something and tried to reach for the call button but couldn't find it along the side of the bed.

Finally the door opened and she smiled expectantly to greet her child.

Instead her parents stood in the doorway. Her mother looked as though she had been crying and her father looked stern.

'Diana,' he said, and he almost pushed her mother into the room and closed the door behind them.

'Where is my child?' Diana asked, feeling panic rising inside her.

'Diana, we need to talk to you,' he said from where he stood at the end of the bed.

'Where is she?' Diana wanted to scream but her throat was too dry.

'Diana, your father did what he thought was best,' her mother said, but her father put up his hand to silence her.

'Diana, we have given the child to a couple who cannot have any children. They are adopting her.'

Diana heard herself scream now. 'No, no, bring me my child,' she sobbed. 'You can't do that,' she said. 'It's not legal.'

'It's legal. You were under anaesthetic and we made the choice for the baby and for you to have the best life you can.'

Diana tasted blood in her mouth as the first nurse from earlier came rushing in.

'Be quiet – you're upsetting all the mothers,' she said before leaving the room again.

Diana's head was spinning and she pulled at the bedclothes, trying to get out, but her body was too weak.

'She's been taken home, Diana, to the home where she belongs,' her father said. 'Now you can get married and have your own family and raise them at Moongate one day.'

Diana had never felt hate before but now she knew it tasted like blood. She looked at her weak, pathetic mother, her overbearing, cruel father and she laughed at them.

'I will never have a family of my own. I will never marry and I will never have another child. That was my child and you stole her from me,' Diana said. 'The Moongate legacy finishes with me and you only have yourselves to blame.'

30

Amanda

The doorbell rang, and Amanda jumped in surprise.

She hadn't heard the bell ring before and she had been in deep concentration when it reverberated through the house.

Amanda stood up from the dining table, which she had turned into temporary art studio, and went to the front door and opened it to see Diana.

'Diana, you don't need to ring the bell. Just come in,' she said.

Diana was clutching a small silk bag, but it was still bigger than her thin hands. She was wearing a pair of linen pants and a pink-and-white-striped cotton top. It was unlike anything Amanda had seen her wear before.

'I love your outfit,' she said. 'You look so fresh. Come in.' She opened the door wider.

'I went shopping with Carole, and she chose this for me. I thought it far too young but apparently there are no rules on what you should wear at any age now.'

Amanda laughed. 'Good job, Carole. Are you coming in?'

Diana shook her head. 'No, I can't. I'm off to lunch with

Shelley and Frank and then to a gallery in Alnwick.' She handed Amanda the silk bag.

'What's this?' she asked, pulling the drawstring open.

'They're the pearls. They're a part of the house. They belong to you,' said Diana.

Amanda looked into the bag in shock. 'I can't take these,' she said, but Diana shook her head.

'They belong to you. They came with the house,' she repeated sternly.

Before Amanda could say anything else, she saw Frank's car pull up to the gatehouse. When she turned back to Diana the older woman stared her down.

'Don't argue with me about this or I will put them in the rubbish – you know I will,' she said firmly but with a smile. 'Have a lovely day.'

She turned and then was off down the driveway to her waiting ride to her lunch.

Amanda closed the door and went back to her artwork, putting the pearls on the table.

They were worth tens of thousands of pounds and Diana was handing them out as though they were a mere trinket.

Something wasn't right about this and Diana, for all her secrecy, was not playing it as subtly as she thought she was.

Amanda took her laptop from the table and typed into the search bar: *finding your biological family as an adoptee.*

Amanda walked outside and pulled a weed from a bed by the front garden. She pulled another, and another, feeling pleasure when they came out whole, the roots hanging down, and throwing them into a small mound. She used her hands to scrape through the dirt, pulling and raking, not bothering with gloves or even a gardening form. She just needed to do something physical that would produce immediate results.

While she worked, she thought about Diana. Everything was clouded in misty half-truths and yet Amanda felt she couldn't have asked Diana for the whole truth because what if she became angry and told her to leave? The uncertainty of her place at Moongate was always there. It still didn't feel like hers, even though the deed was now in her name.

The weeds came out easily enough and soon the small garden bed was cleared. Amanda stood back and looked at her work.

'It's easy to lose yourself in the weeding, isn't it?' she heard Simon say from behind her.

Amanda wiped her hands on her jeans. 'It is,' she said, and wondered if that's why Diana had become so obsessed with gardening. Here her only obstacles were caterpillars and weeds. Beyond the gates was the real world.

'Let me put these weeds in the wheelbarrow and I'll take them to the bin.' Amanda went to the pile but Simon shooed her away.

'I'm going there anyway,' he said, scooping them up with the rake and putting them in the barrow.

He looked down at her hands. 'You okay?' he asked. 'You seemed to be gardening with some sort of murderous intent towards those weeds.'

Amanda sighed. 'I'm just tired and everything is annoying me today.'

'I get that feeling most days.' He half laughed.

'Have you heard from Anika or Charlie lately?' Amanda asked.

Simon scoffed. 'No and I don't want to. There's nothing they can say to change what happened. They're living their lives and I'm living mine, here.'

Amanda was silent. Did that mean he was staying? she wondered. He sounded as though his choice to be here was punishing them in some way.

'Okay, I'm off to dump this in the bin and then I'm posting the soil test.' He picked up the barrow and went on his way.

Amanda knew what was troubling her but she couldn't quite voice her worry.

Amanda went inside the house and washed her hands and scrubbed her fingernails with the nail brush that Janet had given her, and then she realised she knew what to do and who she needed to speak to.

Her mother used to say there was meaning in everything and there were no coincidences in life, and as Amanda dried her hands on the dish towel she realised she had been given the thread to follow through the mess of half-truths and vague facts from the beginning. She found her phone and dialled.

'Hello? Can I speak to Maggie please?' she asked.

31

Amanda

The woman who opened the door for Amanda looked older than Diana and she spoke with a rounded Northern accent, but she was smiling as Amanda came through the door.

'When Maggie told me you wanted to meet me, I felt as though I was a celebrity.' She laughed as she led Amanda down the narrow hallway of the small house in Newcastle. 'Not many people from America want to come and visit me. Come sit and I'll make a brew,' she said, moving slowly about the kitchen.

Amanda sat down at the wooden table, looking at the initials carved into the corner and her fingers ran over the worn wood.

'That's my boys that done that,' said Helen. 'Always making their mark wherever they went.' She laughed. 'And you're at Moongate now? Maggie told you I was friends with Diana back in the day. My dad was the gardener there for nigh on forty years, even worked his way up to head gardener, but in the end it was just him and Diana, so the title didn't mean much – not to him anyway. Diana's still there?' she asked.

'Yes, Diana's still there, but in the gatehouse now,' she said.

'She all right?' asked Helen, and Amanda could see the genuine concern on the old woman's face.

'She is. A little frail, but okay,' said Amanda.

'And you wanted to know about the house? She would know more than me,' Helen said as she swirled hot water around in the teapot.

Amanda paused. 'Actually I want to know about Diana.'

She saw Helen's shoulders straighten.

'Oh and why's that?' she asked, turning to Amanda. 'I don't really talk out of school about people.'

Amanda nodded. 'I know but I think there is something Diana isn't telling me about why I'm here and I need to figure it out. I know I sound nosy but it's more than that. I feel like this has something to do with me but I can't quite say how. Nothing is making sense.'

Helen came to the table and sat down on a chair with a number of cushions on the seat. It was well worn, as though she had sat there for fifty years or more.

'You can ask me questions and I will try to answer as best I can but I'm not sharing in any gossip.'

Amanda liked this old friend of Diana's. She was loyal, just like she knew Lainie would be if faced with someone asking about her own life.

'Was Diana ever married?'

Helen shook her head. 'Not that I know of. She thought she was going to marry Douglas but then he never came back from his trip to Europe.'

'Douglas?'

Helen nodded. 'Yes, Douglas. Let me think what his

last name was… Kay? No, McKay, I think. Oh he was handsome, but then Diana was beautiful too, so they were well matched. They had a whirlwind romance but then he left for Europe. He told her he'd be back but she didn't believe him and she was right because she never heard hide nor hair of him again. Diana was in shock after his departure; so was I, but I thought he would see reason and return soon enough. Diana was a catch.'

The kettle on the stove started to whistle and Helen started to stand to turn it off, but Amanda jumped up. 'Let me,' she said, and Helen didn't protest at her offer.

Amanda poured out the old hot water, put three spoonfuls of tea into the infuser and refilled the pot. Then she put the lid on and came and sat back down.

'Why did he go to Europe?' asked Amanda. She was curious about this Douglas now. Where was he? Why didn't he come back?

'He wanted to ride his motorbike through Europe – I think the Black Forest in Germany was his dream – and he said he would be back before the winter. That was all he told her. I remember she was heartbroken when he left. She sobbed and sobbed at my place. Men say all sorts of things to women to have their way, don't they?'

Amanda thought about a young Diana's heart being broken and she thought about her old boyfriend Mike, who never made any promises to her but also never made any effort either. She wasn't sure which was worse.

'Maggie said Diana had a baby,' she said.

Helen stared at Amanda for a long time. 'Why do you want to know about that?'

Amanda wasn't sure why she wanted to know but she knew she needed to know.

'I think...' she said slowly, 'I think there is something more to me being at Moongate than Diana is saying but I can't prove anything. My mother was born here but then she was adopted. She never came back to the UK but then, after she dies, suddenly I win a house here, while the owner of said house is still alive? And I can't find any evidence of a lottery at all, even though Diana is adamant there was one. She said my mother bought a ticket but I think she's covering up something.'

Helen leaned forward. 'Do you think you're Diana's granddaughter?'

'I can't answer that and I don't think Diana will tell me the truth. Short of paperwork and a DNA test, I'm in the dark, trying to put it all together.'

Helen sighed. 'Pour the tea and I'll tell you what I know.'

With a mug in hand, Amanda listened to Helen tell the story from what she had seen and what she had heard from her father.

'And then she came home without the baby. I tried to go and see her so many times but she wouldn't speak to anyone, not even me. She stopped eating, talking, leaving her room. It was so bad her father was going to put her in the psychiatric hospital except her mother put her foot down, my dad said. He said there was a hell of a row that day and Mrs Graybrook-Moore said she would never put her daughter in there and right she was – they did all sorts of terrible things up at that hospital.'

She paused as Amanda refilled her mug with tea.

'I never spoke to her again after that. She became a hermit of sorts. I think her family kept people away. I mean, I did try and see her, but when I called they said she was asleep or couldn't speak at the time. It was my dad who would let her know how I was doing. When I got married and had my first – Darren – I didn't think she would want to see me, with a baby and all. I didn't want to upset her.'

'So no one knew what happened to the baby? If it lived or died?'

Helen shook her head. 'No, but I do know that Diana never spoke to her father again until the day he died.'

'What did she say to him then?' Amanda was intrigued.

'I don't know exactly but I know that's when she started to garden with my dad. She spent all day in that place, became almost obsessive, Dad said. But perhaps, and I think about this sometimes, perhaps it saved her from whatever happened. So much loss for her. She stopped living when she came back from the hospital, never saw anyone, did anything, just gardened until it became too much.'

'Why didn't she hire someone else after your dad?' asked Amanda.

'There wasn't that sort of money, I don't think. She was left some by her parents and she used to open the gardens throughout the year and make some money that way. I don't think she was rich but I don't think she was poor either.'

Amanda listened, thinking of Diana, and knowing if she had fallen pregnant at a young age, like Diana, her mother would have helped her, whatever decision she made.

'Do you know when she had the baby?' she asked Helen.

Helen frowned. 'She was eighteen, and I was a year older than her. In 1963, it must have been.'

Amanda held her breath.

'Yes, the May of 1963. I can't remember the day though. When was your mum born?' Helen asked.

Amanda heard her words but couldn't believe her ears.

'May 20th, 1963,' she said aloud.

Helen looked as shocked as Amanda felt. 'Well then, I think you might be on to something.'

Amanda was silent, her mind flying with ideas, conversations to have with Diana. It felt chaotic yet it all made sense.

'Why wouldn't she just tell me? Why did she do all this elaborate cover-up?' Amanda asked.

Helen shrugged. 'You don't know what the truth is yet – it's all guessing right now. But you need proof before you go accusing her of anything. And remember, Diana was very broken after what happened. I don't think she's ever recovered. You can't assume you know what it was like for her.'

Amanda listened and nodded in agreement.

'Whatever happened after she had that baby broke her. So be careful in whatever you do next.'

'You're a good friend, Helen,' Amanda said, missing Lainie more than ever at that moment.

'I know, and she was to me also. Just because we don't see each other now doesn't mean I don't care about her anymore. She was my best friend. That never stops, not even after death.'

Amanda thought about her mom as Helen spoke.

'Some people just understand you more than others. It can be a friend, a husband, a sister or a brother, but once you have that, it never goes away. Diana and I were that for each other.' She smiled at Amanda. 'Like your mum. I reckon she's with you every moment.'

'I hope so,' Amanda said.

'A big adventure like this that you're having? Of course she is,' Helen stated.

'A big adventure. I like that,' Amanda said.

'That's all it is, love, and when you think of it like that then life is much easier. Trust me, I've been around long enough to know.'

32

Simon

'So there was a baby?' Simon asked as Amanda opened a bottle of wine he had brought with him.

'Yes, born the same month and year as my mom, so I really need to get the adoption papers. But I chickened out when I went to submit the application,' Amanda admitted as she poured them each a glass .

Simon reached out for his wine and Amanda winced.

'Wow, that's a terrible scratch,' she said, turning his arm over and looking at the length of the wound.

'From a nasty vine. Can't remember the name but it got me well and good,' he said. 'But it's just a surface scratch.'

Amanda looked closely, her fingertips on his skin. 'Did you wash it?'

'Of course I did. I'm not a complete idiot.'

'I'm going to put something on it anyway,' Amanda said, opening the cupboard above the fridge and taking out a small first aid box.

'Is that from Diana's day? I doubt it's usable now.'

Amanda rolled her eyes. 'No, Frank gave it to me in case I needed it for a reason exactly like this.'

She took out a tube of antibiotic cream and some cotton wool and came back to sit at the table.

'Put your arm out,' she said as she dabbed the cream onto the cotton wool ball.

She gently applied the cream to the top of the wound as Simon took a sharp breath.

'Relax, breathe slowly,' she said. 'You will get used to it faster if you breathe slowly.'

Making sure she covered the wound from the elbow to the wrist, Amanda worked slowly and methodically.

Simon watched her every move. 'I'm almost certain you're using a painting technique to apply that cream.'

'Maybe I am, maybe I'm not,' she said, looking up at him.

His face was brown from all the time spent under the summer sun and his skin clear. He'd put on weight – maybe muscle? – and his curly hair was longer than when he'd arrived.

'What?' he asked.

'What, what?' she asked, putting the lid back on the tube of cream.

'What were you thinking when you looked at me just now? Your face changed.'

Amanda blushed. 'I was just thinking you looked well, compared to when I first met you.'

Simon laughed. 'Wouldn't be hard. I was a walking ghost when Diana found me at the front of the house.'

'Nothing like a bit of outdoor work, wine and pasta with me to solve your worries,' she said as she put the first aid box away.

'You're not wrong,' he said. 'I love coming for dinner here.' He paused. 'I'll miss it.'

Amanda stood still at the stove, watching the water in the pot boil.

'Why will you miss it?' she finally asked. 'You going somewhere?'

This was it, the conversation that she had been avoiding having with him.

'At the end of summer. Diana only hired me for the summer,' he reminded her.

Amanda leaned against the cupboards for support. 'That's a while away yet,' she said. 'We have lots to do before then.' She tried to keep her voice casual as she spoke but it came out a little squeaky.

'We do,' said Simon, twisting the wine glass in his hand. 'So tell me about this man Diana was seeing. Dougal?'

'Douglas,' corrected Amanda, putting the pasta into the water. 'He went riding away on his motorbike and though he said he would come back for Diana, he was never heard from again.'

'Have you done a search for him online?' asked Simon.

'Not yet,' she said. 'Use my laptop and you start looking while I do this.'

Simon took her laptop from the bench and opened it.

'And what's his surname?'

'McKay.'

Simon typed the name and watched the results roll in. 'We're searching for a needle in a haystack. Do you know how many Douglas McKays there are in the UK?'

'I knew it wouldn't be easy,' said Amanda, blowing air out of her cheeks.

Simon thought for a moment. 'You know, Helen said he went overseas; maybe he ended up living there?'

'Or maybe something else happened,' Amanda said slowly as she sat down next to Simon. 'Helen said she was surprised he didn't come back. She thought he was serious about Diana, that Diana was a catch. I mean, what if something happened to him in Europe?'

'God, you're making it harder now,' Simon said.

'No, Helen said he was in the Black Forest, which is in Germany. Is there any way we can see newspapers from that time? Maybe there's something in there?'

'Amanda, you keep making it harder,' Simon said. 'Do you speak German?' he asked.

'No? Why?'

'Because all the articles will be in German,' he said.

'That's what the translation button is for,' she said, waving his concerns away.

Simon typed and then scrolled.

'So what year was this? Did you say 1963?'

'Yes,' Amanda said.

'Black Forest?'

'*Ja*,' she said.

'So you do speak German,' he teased.

'*Ein bisschen*.' She made a face at him and went back to check the pasta.

Simon searched as Amanda finished making their dinner, mixing some fresh pesto from Shelley through the pasta.

'Cheese?' she asked.

'Always,' he answered, staring at the screen.

Amanda bought the bowls to the table and placed them down. 'Leave it and eat,' she said.

'No, I can't. I need to keep looking. It's annoying me now. I want to know what happened to him.'

They ate while Simon scoured the internet.

'So many accidents reported. I guess the roads and cars weren't very safe,' he said as he ate his pasta.

'He was on a motorbike,' Amanda reminded him.

'Yes, I would imagine that wouldn't have been the safest either, especially if the roads were icy.'

'Even if something did happen, there's no guarantee it was reported on.' Amanda sighed. 'If anything happened at all, that is. Maybe he just took his trip, lived his life and never thought about Diana again.'

'Wait,' said Simon, looking closer at the screen. 'Wait, wait, wait.'

'I'm waiting.' Amanda laughed at Simon's sudden seriousness.

'That's it, that's it. He's here!'

'What?' Amanda forgot about the pasta and moved over next to Simon.

'Here.' Simon clicked through to an article and made it larger.

'The side panel translates the article. This appeared in a newspaper called the *Weiner Zeitung* around that time.' He started to read: 'A man has died on the Black Forest High Road, after losing control of his motorbike. No next of kin has been found but the man had his passport on him and a gold ring inscribed: *For Diana*. If anyone knows anything please contact the police at Baden-Baden.'

Amanda gasped. 'That's him!'

'No way,' said Simon.

'Oh my God,' she said. 'This is insane. How the hell did we find that? I can't even call myself a detective anymore – it's like I'm being guided to the clues.' She looked up at the ceiling. 'Mom? Is it you? Knock once if it's you. Douglas, knock twice if it's you.'

Simon burst out laughing. 'You can't be serious?'

'No, but also, why not?' Amanda said, taking a large gulp of wine. 'Nothing has been normal since I came here, so you have to wonder if sometimes there aren't special things happening that you can't see.'

Simon was looking at her with an amused expression on his face. 'You really are remarkable. I don't know anyone like you,' he said.

Amanda smiled. 'Is that a good thing or a bad thing?'

'It's a good thing,' he said. 'Being with you is like being on a big adventure.'

Amanda shook her head. 'See? It's crazy. That's what Helen said to me today. Life is a big adventure and when you treat it like that then it's easy to get through.'

'I think life would be very easy to do with you in it.'

Amanda swallowed. 'Then you shouldn't leave at the end of summer.'

Simon leaned back in his chair. 'Amanda,' he said, but she put her hand up.

'Don't. I don't want to be rejected. I had that in New York. I don't want it here.' She moved back to her seat and stabbed at her pasta.

'I'm not rejecting you,' said Simon. 'I just need to settle a few things with Anika and Charlie first.'

Amanda waved her fork at him. 'It is settled. She's with your ex best friend – not sure how much more finished it can be.'

As she spoke, she was shocked at her own bitterness. Why was Simon wasting time with Anika?

'Don't you think we have something more than friendship here? Or we might have?' she asked.

Simon paused and Amanda felt her face redden.

'Oh you don't think that way? God, how embarrassing.'

Simon closed the laptop. 'It's not that, Amanda. It's complicated.'

'What is? Your feelings towards Anika, or me?'

'No, it's just that I have things to sort out, and I have nothing to bring to us right now. I'm hiding from the world. I need to face up to what happened and try and find a path to what's happening next.'

'But not with me,' she said.

'I didn't say that,' he insisted

'But you also didn't say you could see something between us.'

'Stop twisting things, Amanda. I think I'm going to go,' he said.

'Yes, you probably should,' she said, putting her fork down, her appetite suddenly gone.

Simon stood up and went to the door. 'I don't understand what just happened,' he said.

Amanda looked at him. 'And I don't understand why you want to go back to your ex and why you don't want to stay here. So I guess we're even.'

Simon opened his mouth as though to say something, but then turned and left, closing the door behind him. Amanda sat at the table, wishing she could undo what had just been done.

33

Simon

Diana walked through the garden towards the pond, hanging on to Simon's arm. Trotsky was running ahead, enjoying the sniffs on offer in the freshly dug garden beds.

'How have you been?' she asked him.

'Good. Busy,' he answered.

'And how are things with Amanda?' Diana asked.

'Fine,' Simon said. 'She's busy also.'

Except it wasn't fine. They hadn't spoken since her outburst, not that he hadn't tried, but because she was working or she said she was too busy painting for the exhibition or she was seeing Shelley or Janet.

She was avoiding him and he knew why.

'Here we are,' he said as they came to the pond.

He had planted it out with the ferns and the papyrus and daylilies from Janet and in the pond were water iris, duckweed and some water lilies. It wasn't yet flowering, but Janet said it would next year.

'Oh it's lovely, Simon, really lovely,' Diana said. He saw her wipe a tear and he put his arm around her shoulder. 'You've done so well.'

'That's not the surprise,' he said. 'Look down.'

Diana peered into the pond and then she clapped her hands. 'Koi!' she cried.

'Yes, baby koi, so they can grow into the pond. There are nine, as it's supposed to be good luck to have that number,' he said.

'I remember,' said Diana.

'And I've put the black netting that you told Janet about over it, so the birds can't get them.'

'Clever man,' said Diana. She sat on the edge of the pond, taking care with her movement, and looked into the water. 'Sit,' she instructed him. 'Let's watch them swim.'

They sat in comfortable silence for a while.

'When I was younger, I loved the koi. I would come see them every day, and then when I was eighteen my life changed, and I stopped visiting them.'

Simon was silent, listening carefully.

'Shortly after they died, one by one, over nine months,' she said. 'I was so used to loss by then, I never replaced them. It felt futile...'

Simon could hear the bees not too far away. The water was calm, but the pump was making it ripple gently, and there was a scent of jasmine in the air.

'What did you lose?' he asked softly.

'Not what, who.' She said. 'Two loves I wrongly believed would last forever.' She gave a sad smile and then shook her head, as though buoying herself back into the present and positivity. 'But enough about that sadness. Why are you wasting your time with Amanda and not telling her how you feel?'

Simon laughed. 'And how do I feel about her? Perhaps you need to tell me. She's a great friend.'

Diana rolled her eyes, which was so funny to see from a woman in her late seventies.

'You are better for being around her.'

'Perhaps I'm better for being here, at Moongate,' he said.

'You can quibble, Simon, but I am aware you have feelings towards her and also that you are avoiding them because you don't want to recover from the hurt you experienced before coming here. Anika betrayed you and so did you friend Charlie. It is a deeply painful thing to go through.'

Simon was silent.

'Do you think about Anika and Charlie and what happened when you're with Amanda?' Diana asked.

'Not really,' he said. 'But she's always talking and coming up with ideas about things. There's not always a lot of quiet time.'

Diana laughed. 'She is a dynamo, yes. But let me ask you, do you look forward to seeing her?'

Simon nodded. 'I do, she's a great friend.'

'Oh shush, I don't believe in that. You like her; she adores you. Why haven't you done something about it?'

Simon looked at Diana. 'I don't want to have this conversation, Diana. I'm sorry but I already have a meddling mother; I don't need a meddling grandmother.' He stood up. 'Should I help you back to the gatehouse?'

'Sit down now,' she said and he did. It almost felt like his body didn't have a choice. 'Do not waste a moment when you find the right one. Write your own story, Simon. You are happy here; you love what you do. You could be with Amanda and make a go of it. The whole of Moongate is for you and her if you want it to be.'

He looked down at the fish, floating in their little watery

world. 'I don't know if Amanda feels that way,' he said finally. 'It's one thing to assume there is an attraction and another to say, "hey, can I live with you for the rest of my days?"'

'If you don't ask then you won't know,' Diana said. She took another look at the fish. 'Okay, I'm ready to go home now. Is Amanda working?'

He nodded.

'Don't forget it's her birthday party at Janet's tomorrow night.'

'I haven't,' he said.

'You can take us both in the car.'

'Yes, no problem,' he answered.

'I know it won't be a problem because I just told you,' she said with a frown and Simon tried to hide a smile as they walked back to the gatehouse together.

'You don't often take no for an answer, do you?' he teased as they came to the gate, Trotsky heading in first as he was wont to do.

Diana walked through the gate and turned to Simon, leaning on her stick.

'I have never taken no for answer but once a decision was made for me that I had no control over, and I swore I would never feel like that again. But in doing that, I have kept myself isolated and lonely for too many years.' She paused. 'Don't be like me, Simon. Don't let the anger eat you into a shell of a person. It's a sad place to live.'

And with that she turned and walked into the house, leaving him to wonder how he had managed to be ambushed by a septuagenarian who saw him better than he saw himself.

*

1980s

Diana spent the next two decades living at Moongate Manor, watching her mother fade away into dementia as the years passed, asking her where the pearls were, and when was the baby coming. Diana couldn't remember where the pearls were and couldn't answer about the baby without wanting to tear her own hair out.

Diana was gentle with her mother though. She had married a brute and had suffered for it deeply.

Her father had called for her when he was on his death bed, and she went to his room and simply looked at him in silence, waiting for whatever he wanted to say before he died of cancer.

'Diana,' he said.

She stared at him. She was thirty-eight now. Her father nearly eighty-eight. She hadn't married, she hadn't had another child and she hadn't ever heard from Douglas again.

Instead she stayed every day in her parents' home, reminding them it all stopped with her.

They took away her future so she took away their legacy.

Her father was pale, gaunt, his eyes briefly open and his head lying on the pillow in a way that looked uncomfortable, a nurse by his side.

'I want to tell you,' he said, his voice thin with age and sickness.

She had waited for his apology for twenty years, but now

that it was close she felt nothing anymore. She was tired of everything; she was tired of punishing him and herself.

She turned to leave the room and she heard him say: 'In the safe. Her birthday.'

She paused, her back towards him.

'I'm sorry,' he said, and finally she turned to him.

'Father, whatever you're feeling at the end of your life, whatever forgiveness you're looking for, you won't get it from me. You could have had it all: the loving daughter, the loving granddaughter, maybe I would have married again, had more children, but you will never know. You took away my life and now everything you built – your legacy – is in my hands. I will sell off this house – every piece of furniture, every painting. I will salt the earth, and then I will leave the house open to be taken over by animals and tourists and anyone else who wants to partake in the misery of these walls and the pain of this family.'

Her father was unmoving in the bed. The nurse was looking at her hands, probably wishing she wasn't there, thought Diana, but she didn't care.

She saw a single tear fall down his weathered face.

'Goodbye, Father, go well.'

Her father slipped into unconsciousness and died four days later. Diana spent most of that time outside. She walked around the garden, picking off rosehips, pulling off the deadheads of the daisies. She could see Helen's father in the distance, now in his sixties, trimming the whips of the wisteria from the walls of the garden.

She walked over to him. 'Pete,' she said. 'How are you?'

'All right,' he said. 'Helen had another boy,' he said.

'Oh wonderful, I will send her a little present,' Diana said.

Helen had married a mechanic from Newcastle and had three boys and now she'd had her fourth. She was busy but happy. Diana had gone into herself when her baby was taken and had stopped going out. Idle gossip with Helen about boys and parties wasn't something Diana could partake in anymore. And how could Diana watch Helen raise a family when she had lost everything she had ever wanted? She didn't begrudge Helen's happiness but she also knew her own personal limit to what she could bear.

'Do you like gardening, Pete? I mean, I know you do it through the week here, but do you like it?'

Pete looked at her for what felt like a long time. His face was lined and brown from the sun, his bucket hat sitting on top of grey curls that needed a cut.

'I can't rightly think of anything else I'd rather do. There's something special about growing things. These plants are like my children. You have to water them, feed them, prune them when they're being too wild, and you can get generations from a single plant if you know what you're doing.'

Diana was silent. The symbolism of his words wasn't lost on her.

'I would like to learn to garden,' she said. 'If you would teach me?'

Pete smiled. 'Gardening can't be taught; it has to be a trust between the gardener and the garden. Plants will grow if they trust you.'

She looked closely at him and realised he knew everything. Of course he would know. He would have seen her coming and going as the baby grew.

'You knew? Why didn't you say something?' she asked.

'Not my business,' he said.

'Did you notice me or did Helen tell you?' she asked.

Pete looked down at his feet, his boots kicking some dirt away.

'Both,' he said. 'But don't be angry with Helen – she was so distressed when you told her what happened to your daughter. She wanted to try and find her, asked me to help, but what could I do? I'm so sorry, Diana.'

Diana crossed her arms and walked a few steps towards the pond where a white water lily with a yellow centre was blooming.

'I was going to name her Selene,' she said. 'The Greek goddess of the moon, since I am named for Diana, the Roman goddess of the moon.'

'That's a lovely name,' said Pete, reaching into the pool and picking up a bee that was struggling in the water. He placed it carefully on the side of the pond.

Diana smiled as the bee began to move slowly, shaking its wings to dry off.

'Thank you.' Diana turned and sat on the edge of the pond. 'My father told me there is something in the safe – something about my daughter. I haven't opened it yet,' she said.

Pete looked at her and then gave her a pat on the shoulder.

'You'll know when it's the right time to open it.'

Diana nodded; he was right.

'Can I come and watch you work tomorrow? Pick up a few tips?' she asked.

'I start at seven,' he said. 'I'm working on the roses tomorrow.'

'I'll be there,' she said.

Diana walked back to the house and looked at the door to her father's study.

She reminded herself of Pete's words and went to the kitchen to make tea.

She would know when the right time was.

34

Amanda

Amanda walked downstairs in the peach georgette dress that she had found in the attic and some pretty ballerina slippers she had found at a boutique in Newcastle on her lunch break.

Diana had helped her handwash the dress and showed her how to steam it so the draping fell the right way.

'I can't believe you found it,' Diana had said when Amanda went through the clothes with her.

'Sell anything you want. I won't need it and you might as well make some money,' Diana insisted.

But with every dress of Diana's she had a story to go with the garment. Even the top hat had a story.

'That was my great-grandfather's silk hat. He told my father that top hats were never seen between Saturday and Sunday because they weren't suited to church. Only the new moneyed wore them to church, which was considered very déclassé.'

Amanda had laughed. 'I've been wearing it around the house. I call it my thinking cap.'

Diana laughed. 'Oh that's marvellous – a thumb at the nose of snobbery and tradition. I love it.'

But Amanda hadn't asked her about the baby clothes in the suitcase. It felt rude and prying and she had done enough for now. She was waiting on her mother's adoption papers and then she would know the truth. But it could take weeks even months, the website had stated.

Now Amanda walked down the stairs to where Simon was standing, wearing a suit.

'A suit? What is happening?' She laughed.

Things were still awkward between them but Amanda was prepared to forget it ever happened, especially since it was her birthday… the first without her mother. It felt wrong to celebrate it without her.

'Janet said the dress code is cocktail, so this is cocktail,' he said, doing a spin.

'You look great,' she said, meaning it. He looked handsome – almost too handsome, she thought, as she saw the curls touching his collar. She wished she could run her fingers through them.

'Not as good as you look. That dress is incredible and you make it even more so,' he said. Amanda was reached the bottom step of the stairs, making them nearly the same height.

'It's Diana's. She wore it on her eighteenth birthday. It just fits but I won't be having too much cake,' she said, patting her stomach.

They were at eye level, and Amanda could smell his soapy, lovely scent and she wished she could kiss him. Instead she stepped down and walked past him. 'Okay – off to get Mrs Graybrook-Moore.'

Simon followed her outside and she got into the back seat as he was driving.

'I think Diana is a front-seat person,' she said with a laugh.

'Agreed,' said Simon. He drove the short distance down to Diana's house and went inside to escort her to the car.

Diana emerged in a black chiffon dress that was an older style but so beautifully made. It had a cape with tiny little stars embroidered on it and she had a different walking cane, black with the silver top of a crescent moon.

'Diana, you look incredible,' Amanda called from the window.

'I know but don't call from the window, dear – it's very unexpected.'

Amanda burst out laughing as Simon helped Diana into the car and closed the door.

Diana turned slightly to Amanda.

'The georgette looks lovely, dear,' she said.

Simon started the car and off they went to Janet's house.

'Are you having a lovely time?' Frank asked Amanda as she watched Shelley dancing around with Diana who was on a chair on the dance floor in Janet and Carole's living room.

Amanda looked around at the balloons and the streamers and the handmade sign saying *Happy birthday Amanda* and she nodded to Frank.

'It's great, yes,' she said.

Frank gave a shrug. 'It's hard being without your parents for the first birthday, or the first Christmas, the first anything really. But you're a good egg for putting on a show for Janet and Carole and Shelley.'

Dennis came by with a bottle of champagne. 'Top-up?' he asked, and Amanda held out her glass.

'I never thought I would see a man of God on bartending duty,' she said to Dennis.

'I do it every Sunday when I hand out the holy wine,' he said, and Amanda laughed.

'Touché,' she said, and Dennis gave a little bow.

She turned to Frank. 'It's hard, and I feel like having a cry, but everyone has made such an effort,' she said.

'Go outside and get some fresh air and I'll cover for you,' he said.

'Thanks, Frank, you're the best.' She handed him her champagne glass and snuck out into the back garden.

She walked down to the pond at the end of the garden and there was Simon.

'Oh gosh, sorry,' she said, and turned to go back up the path.

'Don't go,' he said, grabbing her wrist and gently pulling her towards him.

Without thinking, or perhaps it was the champagne, Amanda's arms were around his neck and they started to sway to the music that was drifting into the garden from inside.

'Happy birthday,' he said.

'Thank you,' she said, laying her head on his shoulder.

His arms were around her and she felt him pull her a little closer.

She put her head up as he leaned down and their lips met for the first time.

It was a tentative kiss, soft, gentle, sweet. She smiled at

him in the darkness. She could just see him in the light from the house.

Then he kissed her again, and this time it was hungry, passionate and wanting. She felt her body respond and as she leaned into him, his hands moved down her back and she felt how much he needed her. 'Amanda,' he whispered, but she pulled away.

'What happened?' he asked.

Amanda felt the bow on her shoulder drop and she pulled it up and smoothed out her dress.

'We've drunk champagne, and it's a party. It's not real,' she said.

Simon frowned. 'I thought you wanted this – me.'

But Amanda shook her head. 'No, not like this. I don't want just sex. I don't want to be a rebound for you, someone for you to get over Anika.'

Simon's mouth dropped open. 'Do you think that's what this is?'

She put her hands on her hips. 'Isn't it? You were the one who told me you have unfinished business with her.'

Simon was silent. 'I'm sorry, I was inappropriate just now,' he said, stepping backwards, but before Amanda could say anything, Simon had fallen in the small pond, his legs up in the air.

Amanda wasn't sure if it was the timing, the image or the absurdity of the moment but she bent over in laughter. She laughed harder than she had in years, with tears streaking down her face, which bought the rest of the guests to the garden.

'My fish!' cried Janet.

'Never mind the fish, what about my suit?' said Simon, putting his hand out to Dennis and Frank to pull him out.

'It's a wet suit now,' said Shelley, and Amanda screamed in laughter again.

Then everyone began to join in as Simon looked at them all laughing at him.

Even Diana was laughing. Amanda saw him notice and realise he had a choice. He could become sullen and angry and act like a spoiled idiot or he could see how funny this moment was and join in.

He patted his jacket pockets.

'No fish in there,' he said. 'But thanks for the party, Janet, it went swimmingly.'

The laughter erupted again and he looked at Amanda who was still laughing and now hanging on to Shelley.

She smiled at him. 'That was the best present you could have got me, Simon. I have needed that laugh since my mom became sick. I actually never thought I would laugh like that again, so thank you from the very muddy bottom of my pond.'

He nodded. 'My pleasure – it's my gift to you.'

Later, he walked Diana to the gatehouse while Amanda waited in the car, then drove the short distance to the main house and parked the car.

Amanda was quiet for a moment. 'Do you want to come in?' she asked.

Simon stared ahead. 'I probably shouldn't.'

Amanda felt her heart crack a little but she would never demand anything from someone who wasn't one hundred per cent interested.

'Okay, well… goodnight,' she said. She opened the car door and walked towards the house.

'Goodnight, Amanda,' she heard him say, but she didn't turn back.

There was no point. He simply didn't want her.

35

Amanda

Amanda woke with a dry mouth and a headache that felt like she had slammed her head into a wall at some point in the night but she knew she hadn't. It was the champagne.

She dragged herself from bed and managed to go downstairs for water and pain relief, and she looked at her phone.

A missed call from Simon and a voice message.

He could wait, she thought.

And then she remembered the kiss. God, she had never been kissed like that before. So passionate and filled with desire.

It was intimate and beautiful and she hadn't wanted it to stop but it had. Because he was still in love with the idea of someone else.

Amanda looked at the coffee pot and decided to stick to water just to be safe.

She opened her laptop and looked at her email, seeing one from Lainie that was filled with photos and news. She decided to save it for the next day, when she was feeling more human.

She scrolled down and saw another from the Adoption Contact Register and clicked on it.

Dear Ms Cox,

Please find the details of your mother's adoption in 1963.

If you have any queries, please contact us at this email and refer to your case number which is listed in the subject of this email.

Amanda paused, her finger quivering over the attachment to the email. This would tell her everything or it would tell her nothing.

Finally she clicked on it, and waited for the document to load.

She scrolled down and there it was.

Baby Girl born to Diana Graybrook-Moore, aged 18

Amanda didn't know whether to cry and rage. All of this secrecy and drama from Diana instead of being honest.

She scrolled down.

Father – Unknown.

Well that wasn't true, Amanda thought, and she came to the signature.

Sir Edward Graybrook-Moore

Diana hadn't signed the birth certificate. Why not?

She pored over the document and came up with no more answers, only questions.

She texted Simon.

Are you in the garden? Come to the house, I need to show you something.

The message was delivered but no answer came.

Amanda pulled on sneakers and a cardigan over her pyjamas and went into the garden.

Simon wasn't anywhere that she could see, so she walked over to his house, wishing she had worn sunglasses.

As she came to the house, she saw his motorbike was gone.

Where was he? She peered through the window and tried the door. It opened and she stepped inside.

The house was empty of anything belonging to Simon. He was gone.

She called his phone again but this time it didn't ring through. He was really gone.

Amanda sat on the bed and looked at the empty room.

Last night's kiss clearly meant nothing to him, and now he had left her with a garden to manage and a huge house and a lying grandmother in the gatehouse.

You couldn't even write something as outrageous as this, Amanda thought, and the more she thought about it, the angrier she became.

How dare he leave? How dare he not say goodbye to her?

And Diana had lied all this time. She couldn't trust anyone.

Amanda didn't often allow anger to consume her; in fact,

she had never felt as enraged as she did at this moment. Her hangover was gone and replaced by the sort of spitting fury that was both foreign and thrilling.

If Simon had gone without a word, then she would confront Diana about all the rubbish and subterfuge and then she would pack up and head back to New York.

That was it – she'd had it. She would rather struggle in New York than stay here and deal with all the drama. She could stay with Lainie until she got on her feet and she would never speak to Diana or Simon again.

She pushed open the gate and walked up to Diana's door. Just about to knock, she saw it was already ajar. Trotsky came around to the front of the garden and pushed past her to go inside.

'Trotsky, why are you outside?' Amanda asked the dog as he walked inside and then she saw Diana on the floor, still in her nightgown.

'Shit, God, oh God!' she said and ran to Diana's side.

She was unconscious but breathing as Amanda called 999 for an ambulance and texted Carole while she was on the phone.

Diana is unconscious, have called an ambulance.

Within moments a text came back.

On my way.

Amanda listened to the operator talk her through the process of putting Diana into the recovery position while she waited.

Amanda stroked Diana's thick, grey hair. 'It's okay, it's okay, someone's coming,' she said over and over, like a mantra.

It felt like hours before Carole arrived but Amanda knew it had only been a few minutes and Carole had likely broken the speed limit by quite a bit to get there in the time she did.

Carole dropped to her knees, checking Diana's pulse and then listening to her heart through her stethoscope.

She lifted an eyelid and shone a small torch into it and then the other.

'What's happened to her?' Amanda asked.

'I don't know, love, could be a stroke. How far away is the ambulance?'

'I rang them when I texted you but they have to come from Newcastle, don't they?'

Carole nodded. 'She needs a blanket. Can you get one from her bedroom? We need to keep her warm.'

Amanda went to the bedroom, took a comforter off the end of the bed and came back and draped it over Diana.

'Have you told Simon?' Carole asked.

Amanda shook her head. 'Don't ask.'

Amanda heard the ambulance in the distance and went outside to meet them.

'Put Trotsky out the back,' Carole called and Amanda went and did as she said, feeling sick from worry now. And to think she was going to confront Diana and tell her she was leaving Moongate because she hadn't told her the whole truth. She felt terrible as she watched Diana being bundled into the back of the ambulance.

After Carole had spoken to one of the paramedics in

depth, she came to Amanda's side. 'We think it's a stroke. She needs urgent attention.' Carole reached out and held Amanda's hand. 'We have to be prepared for the worst but hope for the best,' she said.

Amanda started to cry. 'Oh it's so terrible, it's awful.'

Carole pulled her into a hug. 'It is, it's awful. Now go and get dressed and grab the dog – you're coming to ours,' she said. 'And then we'll go to the hospital.'

Amanda had packed a bag and took her computer and charger, but ran back into the house and grabbed the pearls in their silk bag. They were too precious to be left unattended.

She was soon in Carole's car and they were on their way to Carole and Janet's house, with Trotsky sitting in the back seat with all of his canine accoutrements next to him, including his bed.

'I haven't even showered,' said Amanda.

'You can shower at ours and then we can head to hospital. They won't let us in until they have done an assessment and have answers anyway.'

Amanda clenched and unclenched her hands.

'So, where was Simon?' Carole asked in a calm voice.

'He's left.'

'Left?' Carole glanced at Amanda.

'Yes, he's packed up and gone.' Amanda looked out the window.

'Did he send you a message at least? Say when he would be back?'

Amanda felt the tears starting again. 'God, I keep crying

– it's so annoying,' she said, shaking her head as though trying to get rid of a fly that was annoying her.

'Of course you're crying. You're stressed and you've had a traumatic experience,' Carole said. 'Cry all the stress out.'

Amanda closed her eyes.

'Did you and Simon have a fight?' Carole asked.

'No,' Amanda said. 'Maybe, I don't know.' She sighed. 'I don't care now – I only care about Diana. Simon is collateral damage.'

'Ouch,' said Carole.

Amanda shrugged. 'Simon had to choose between me and Anika. He chose Anika.'

Carole pulled up to her and Janet's house. 'I'm sorry, Amanda,' she said. 'I really am.'

'Don't be,' Amanda said as she opened the car door.

Inside, Janet was waiting for them both, immediately taking Trotsky's lead from Carole.

'Amanda needs a shower and then we're going to head up to the hospital,' Carole informed her wife.

'What can I get you?' Janet asked Amanda.

Amanda thought for a moment. 'I can't believe I'm saying this, but can I get a tea? I need something warm but don't want coffee.'

'We'll make an Englishwoman of you yet,' said Janet.

Amanda showered quickly and came out to the kitchen where her tea was waiting for her with a croissant.

'Eat something,' Carole instructed.

Amanda tore a piece of the pastry off and ate it while she sipped her tea. 'Okay, are we going now?' she asked Carole.

'Finish those both,' said Carole firmly. 'And sit down when you eat.'

Amanda gave a little laugh and sat at the table and looked around. She had only been at the house after Simon had rescued her and for her party when it was dark, so she had never really paid much attention to the surrounds.

The inside of the cottage was a mix of country softness and modern living with some sensible IKEA pieces between the overstuffed armchairs and comfortable, modern sofa. It was entirely Janet and Carole – practical and cosy.

Amanda put down the rest of the croissant, and the sick feeling returned.

'I have to tell you both something,' she said. 'Before we go.'

'Okay,' Janet said, her face serious and concerned.

'Diana is my grandmother. I only found out today, I went to confront her and she was on the floor.'

Carole gasped. 'Oh you poor thing. Three shocks in one morning – it's too much.'

'Three?' asked Janet.

'Simon's flown the coop, and not a word as to why.'

Janet sighed. 'I'm not surprised about you and Diana being related; none of her lottery story made sense.'

Amanda put her head in her hands. 'I was so desperate to get out of New York I didn't really look into it. I mean, it was real – the house and everything – and life seemed better there than it had been in New York. Maybe I was kidding myself.'

Janet stepped forward and put her hands on Amanda's shoulders.

'This is not the Amanda we know; you are usually always so positive and optimistic. I know Diana went to some crazy lengths to hide the truth from you but she must have a reason. She's a principled person.'

Amanda looked at Janet and shrugged. 'I'm just hurt she didn't tell me. I felt so alone after my mom died. To know I had family would have helped me a lot.'

'I know you're hurt but I also think you're sad about Simon, and rightly so. But let's tackle on problem at a time, okay? First we'll go to the hospital and see how Diana is.'

Amanda nodded, grateful to be in the care of these wonderful women.

'Let's go,' she said, and she hugged them both. 'You're both the best, and my mom would have adored you.'

Carole and Janet smiled, clearly pleased at the compliment. 'Then we adore her in return. Now let's go.'

36

Simon

Simon rode away from Moongate knowing he was doing the right thing but also knowing it would be terrible for Amanda and he was letting Diana down. He had promised to stay the summer but he couldn't be around Amanda anymore. It was too much.

He couldn't stop thinking about her mouth on his, the curve of her waist, the way she pressed against him.

'Concentrate, mate,' he said aloud as he swerved to miss a station wagon backing out of a driveway.

'Idiot,' he called as he went past the car. 'Have a fucking look.'

But he also knew he was projecting his anger because he was angry with himself, and angry with Anika and Charlie.

It would be five hours before he hit London, give or take the traffic. He had five hours to plan what he would do when he saw Anika. He felt his stomach turn in knots at the thought of confronting her.

No more, he thought. It was time to stand up for himself.

⋆

Simon arrived at his mother's house, let himself in and poured himself a wine.

'Simon? Is that you?' His mother came out of her study, her glasses shoved onto her head, a book in hand.

'Hello, Mother.' He sipped his wine.

'Is that all I get? I haven't seen you in months and months. You've been hiding from me, from the world, like you committed a crime. And now you come back in and pour a glass of my cooking wine and act like nothing's happened?'

Simon looked into the glass. 'I was going to ask how you got the cat to balance on the bottle. Terrible taste.' He took another sip.

'Why are you here and why do you have a tone?' His mother put the book down on the kitchen bench.

'I'm here to get back what's mine,' he said, leaning forward and kissing his mother on the cheek. 'It's good to see you.'

His mother reached up and held his chin, turning his head from side to side. 'You have colour – you've been outdoors.'

'I have,' he answered.

She took his hands and inspected them and looked at the fading wound on his forearm that Amanda had dressed.

'You have dirt under your nails, and healed scratches... and your forearms have more definition.' She paused. 'Have you been in the wilderness?'

Moongate was wild but it wasn't the wilderness.

'Not quite.' He looked at his mother. 'I've been gardening,' he said.

'Gardening? How interesting.' She sat on one of the kitchen stools. 'Where were you?'

Simon took a stool on the other side of the kitchen bench.

'In Northumbria, outside of Newcastle,' he said.

His mother's mouth opened. 'Viking land,' she said.

'Apparently so, but I didn't see any,' he said.

'And whose garden was it?'

How could he explain anything to his mother in the short time he had before he faced his past so he could rebuild his future?

'You know, Mother, I will tell you everything; but first, I have to go and sort a few things out. Dinner tonight?'

'Yes, I'll cook,' she said.

Simon reached for her hand and held it. 'Promise me one thing, Mother?'

'Anything, Simon.'

'Don't cook anything that requires that wine – it's truly horrendous.'

'Noted, dear.'

37

Amanda

'A stroke,' said the doctor to Amanda as they stood in the hallway outside the emergency department. 'We have administered a drug to try and ease the pain and she's going to CT now so we can assess the damage and see if we have to perform surgery.'

Amanda held Carole and Janet's hands. 'Can I see her?' she asked.

'It's family only,' the doctor said.

'I'm her granddaughter,' Amanda said, and felt both women squeeze her hands. 'And these are my aunts,' she added.

The doctor shrugged, clearly occupied with other things that required his attention. 'Okay but she's in and out of awareness. Don't tire her.' He beckoned to a nurse. 'Can you take them to the woman with the stroke?'

The nurse smiled at them all. 'Come this way,' she said, and she used her pass to open the doors and lead them to the bay.

She moved back the curtain slightly to reveal Diana in a hospital bed. 'She's sleeping, but feel free to just sit with her and hold her hand, let her know you're here.'

Amanda stepped forward to Diana's side and picked up one of her thin hands. 'Diana, it's Amanda. I'm here, and so are Janet and Carole,' she said quietly.

The sound of the machines and the familiar hospital smells reminded her of when her mother was dying, and she wiped a tear that fell.

Diana's closed eyes flicked and she opened her mouth and then closed it again.

'It's okay, I'm here,' Amanda whispered. 'I know everything and it's okay. I don't understand but I will, so please stay and make sure I understand one day. You're the only family I have now.'

Diana opened her mouth again. 'Father?' she said but her words were slurred.

'No, it's Amanda,' she said.

'Don't take her,' Diana mumbled. 'No, leave her. She's mine.'

Diana's eyes opened but she was staring ahead, not seeing anything in the room it seemed.

'What's happened?' Amanda asked Carole.

'Her brain is injured. Old memories are coming back from long ago. Her synapses are making new pathways. It's common but not pleasant for her. I'll get the nurse.'

Carole left to find the nurse and Janet stepped away and left Amanda alone with Diana who was trying to say something.

'No, no,' she cried and Amanda held her hand.

'Diana, it's okay. Your baby is safe. She's here; she's with you. I'm here,' she repeated until Diana became quiet.

The curtain was pulled back and the nurse came in.

'She seems calm now,' she said to Carole.

Amanda leaned down and kissed Diana on the forehead. 'Sleep and I will see you tomorrow. I promise. I'm not going anywhere.'

'You have the knack,' said the nurse to Amanda. 'Getting her to settle.'

Amanda looked back at Diana. 'Sometimes you just need someone who can soothe your fears, you know?'

The nurse nodded. 'You're a good granddaughter. She's lucky to have you.'

'We're lucky to have each other.'

Diana – 1980s

A month after her father's death, Diana was ready to open the safe.

She had spent every day in the garden since her father had died and found it as healing and as meditative as Pete had said it would be. She turned things over in her mind as she turned the soil and ran over the past with every weed she pulled.

She was feeling strong and suntanned but her heart still ached.

Those years after they had taken her child away were some of the most painful Diana had ever known. Now she understood that she had needed help. She'd had a breakdown. Her milk coming in days after she was home from the hospital, the pain of the surgery, the few small things her mother had given her of Diana's as a baby were all reminders of the lack of life she had now.

She had been her father's prisoner and her mother was complicit.

Diana sat on her father's chair now and looked at the safe under the desk. His study was the embodiment of who he had been as a man. Wooden, stiff, and without any adornment beyond the leather-bound books. Not even a photo of his wife and daughter.

She thought back to his words. 'Her birthday', he had said.

She turned the dial six times to spell out her mother's birthday, but the safe didn't click to open.

Diana tried again with the same result. She frowned and then tried her own birthday as the combination, but nothing happened.

She sat back in the seat and tried to think. Who was 'her'?

His mother? *God help me*, Diana thought, *I have no idea when his mother was born*. She was dead a long time before Diana entered the world.

Diana looked at the safe again and then she put in the numbers of the day when her world was torn from inside her.

The safe clicked.

Diana gasped and she opened the steel door.

Inside lay a pile of papers and letters tied with a blue ribbon. She carefully lifted them onto the desk and pulled the bow on the satin ribbon so it fell away.

On top of the pile was a piece of paper folded into thirds, with her name on the top in her father's writing.

Diana paused. She wasn't sure she wanted to read the letter. She didn't need his disappointment from the grave as well.

Slowly she opened it and smoothed it out on the desk.

Dear Diana,

I don't think there are words for the pain and heartbreak I have caused you over these past twenty years.

I am ashamed and deeply sorry for the decision I made that I know was the wrong one.

I wanted you to know that just weeks after your daughter, my granddaughter, went to the adoptive parents' home, I went to retrieve her. I told them it was a mistake and you needed your baby back.

They refused to return her, and said it was a legal adoption. I told them I would get a solicitor on the case and they would be going to court and I would win because I knew many judges.

It was the wrong thing to say because when I went back to see them again, they were gone. I had private detectives try and find them over the years. I offered rewards to anyone who had seen them, but they simply vanished, with your child.

I know this doesn't make amends for the profound grief I have caused you but I wanted you to know I tried to fix it but, perhaps, I made it worse.

All I can do now is leave you the adoption papers, the correspondence with the family and the only photo I have of them with your child at six months old.

She was a dear little thing, with the bluest eyes and

copper hair and a pretty rosebud mouth like yours.

Perhaps you can find her, not for Moongate but for you. I don't care about Moongate now. I only ever wished you would speak to me again, but I know I am not worthy of that.

With deepest regret,
Your father

Diana put the letter down and sifted through the papers to find the photograph.

She looked at it closely, feeling silent tears fall down her face.

Her little baby was holding her hands in a fist and was squinting at the camera. It was black and white but Diana could make out the white knitted dress with smocking and wool stockings. The couple looked hard, the woman tired and the man thin, reedy and disappointed.

But her daughter was in good condition by the look of the photo and was clean and in nice clothes.

She turned the photo over and read the pencil writing on the back.

Clive, Peggy and Wendy, December 1963.

38

Amanda

Amanda hadn't been home to Moongate for seven weeks. Janet had gone there for her to get the rest of her clothes while Amanda was at the hospital with Diana, who was slowly improving and had moved to the rehabilitation centre.

Instead Amanda was living at Janet and Carole's house with Trotsky because it was easier to get to the hospital and because she didn't want to be in the house without Simon or Diana nearby.

She had told David she couldn't work at the nursery centre while Diana was in hospital and he was very understanding and told her the exhibition was always on offer when she was ready, but Amanda couldn't imagine doing that either with the current state of things.

She had one surviving family member left and she was going to do whatever it took to help her recover, but still hadn't told Diana she knew the truth. The doctors said Diana couldn't cope with any sudden shocks while her brain was recovering so Amanda had to wait, which was fine, she told them, as the last thing she wanted was to stress her out when she was just coming out of the worst of it.

And every day of those seven weeks she had checked to see if Simon had messaged her.

He hadn't.

She refused to text him but she had seen that Anika had changed her relationship on Facebook to 'It's Complicated' and she and Charlie had unfollowed each other on Instagram, not that Amanda was stalking or anything, she told herself.

Eventually Amanda stopped checking. She had more important things to think about now.

When she looked back at her life in New York and compared it to the one in England, she could hardly believe she was the same person. The fearful, anxious girl, afraid of herself and the world was no longer. At Moongate she was empowered by the house, Diana, by the friends she had made in the village and by the gentleness of her surroundings.

She wished her mother had seen her in the house, that her mom had even experienced it for a moment, but she couldn't think about that too much. *A life of regrets is one that is wasted*, she told herself.

And while living in New York might have seemed glamorous and exciting, the reality was quite different. Life at Moongate Manor was smaller yet gave her a bigger, richer experience and she was a better person for having experienced all of it. But she couldn't do it alone. She needed Diana and wanted her to stay around for as long as she could.

Amanda arrived at the rehab ward of the hospital as Diana was taking steps down the hallway with a frame.

'Look at this hideous thing,' she said. 'I want my stick, not this contraption.'

The physiotherapist rolled his eyes at Amanda.

'And don't roll your eyes, Isaac. I know you are. I can feel it.'

Amanda laughed.

'Amanda?' She turned to see the rehabilitation nurse standing outside her office. 'Can I have a word?'

'I'll be right back,' she said to Diana and followed the nurse into the office and sat down.

'We had a meeting about Diana today and we think she's ready to go home.'

'That's great news!' said Amanda.

'But she can't live alone. Not anymore. She either has to have someone with her or she will have to go to an assisted living facility.'

Amanda shook her head. 'No, she won't be going there. Diana can live with me.'

The nurse frowned. 'Are you sure? It's a big responsibility, caring for an ageing person.'

Amanda shook her head. 'I nursed my mother to the end when she had terminal brain cancer. I know what I'm doing.' She thought about Moongate Manor. 'And the house is big enough for the two of us. I will just need to make some adjustments. When were you thinking she'd be able to leave?'

The nurse looked at her notes. 'Next month. We just have to do some more work on her daily living skills.'

A month – that was doable.

'No problem,' she said.

The nurse looked at her. 'When you tell her that you know, she will be very emotional. Not just because of the news but also because a stroke can heighten emotional responses. Just be prepared for that and if there is an issue, you need to bring her right back to the hospital.'

'Okay,' said Amanda. 'I'm so grateful for everything you've done for her and for me. Truly.'

'That's my job,' said the nurse. 'But thank you. We have enjoyed Diana's company, even if she is very vocal about the quality of the food, the interiors, the lack of garden and the nurses' sneakers.'

Amanda laughed. 'Yes, she's a lot sometimes.'

Back at Janet and Carole's house, they made a plan.

'I can move her into the downstairs living room. It's huge and she can have her own little space in there, with her bed and her lounge suite from the gatehouse.'

'Is there a bathroom downstairs?' asked Carole.

'Only a toilet.' Amanda sighed.

'You could turn the butler's pantry into a bathroom, as the door opens into that room, doesn't it?' Janet asked as she looked at the sketches of the downstairs that Amanda had done.

'With what money?' Amanda laughed. 'I'm so poor I'm living off your food and am behind in my student loans and probably all the utilities have been disconnected at the house.' She looked down at the sketch. 'I mean, I could sell something.' And she looked up at them. 'Actually, I do have something I could sell.'

'We could help,' said Janet, and Carole nodded.

But Amanda shook her head. 'No, I have to do this for Diana and myself.' She got up and went to the guest room and came back and put the silk bag on the table in front of them.

'Do you know where I could sell these?' she asked.

Carole opened the bag and pulled the pearls out. 'My God, these are for royalty,' she said.

Janet gave a long slow whistle.

'Do you know what they would be worth?' she asked them.

'No idea, but I know someone who would know,' Janet said. 'She's a valuer from one of the fancy auction houses. I could ask her if you trust me to show her?'

Amanda threw her hands up. 'All yours, just tell her I need enough to fund a bathroom, and maybe a new kitchen.' She laughed.

'Are you sure?' Carole asked, looking at the clasp and holding the pearls up to her neck.

'It's either sell them or put Diana in a care home and I can't do that. It's not even an option.'

Janet took the pearls from Carole's hands. 'And no, we can't afford them,' she said to Carole who smiled.

'I know, but they're so very beautiful.' Carole sighed.

Janet put them back into the silk purse. 'Leave it with me. Are they insured?'

Amanda shrugged. 'No idea,' she said.

'We'll get insurance on them and then I can take them to our friend to get them valued.'

'Thank you,' said Amanda.

She looked out onto Janet and Carole's garden. It was filled with flowers bordering a central green lawn, and the flowers went from low to high so there was a kind of natural step for the eye. The back of the flower bed was filled with large dahlias in beautiful jewel-like colours.

'I can't imagine how bad the Moongate garden is.' She sighed. 'Seven weeks is a long time. It's going to be worse than before. Simon might as well not have ever been there. What a waste of time.'

Janet and Carole exchanged glances, like they did whenever Simon's name was mentioned, but Amanda ignored them.

'It might not be so bad,' Carole said.

But Amanda knew it would be a mess. She looked at Janet. 'Can you come up tomorrow with me to see what we have to do in the house? I can't face it alone,' she admitted.

'Of course, my love,' said Janet. 'And you never know, it might not be as bad as you think.'

Amanda scoffed. 'It will be, trust me. In the words of my dear departed mother, it's going to be an absolute shit show.'

39

Janet

Janet was up first thing in the morning, before Amanda was awake.

She drove into Newcastle with the pearls in her handbag and went to the hotel and up to room 302, as she had been instructed.

The door opened and she nodded and handed over the bag with the pearls. She was handed an envelope of cash in exchange.

She went to open it.

'It's all there.'

'I know, just force of habit.'

'Speak later.'

'Bye,' she said, and turned and went back to the elevator.

She opened the envelope when the doors closed and checked. Yes, it was all there.

Janet drove back to Foxfield where Carole was waiting in the front garden with Trotsky.

'Do you have to wee on my alyssums?' Janet scolded the dog who ignored her.

'Done?' Carole asked, looking around nervously.

'Done.' Janet patted her bag.

'Is she up?'

'In the shower,' Carole said.

Janet went inside and made tea and put the envelope on the counter and waited. It was a risk but she knew it was one she had to take.

Amanda wandered out with wet hair and in her jeans and T-shirt. 'We should go to Shelley's and get some coffee and pastries on the way to Moongate,' she said. 'I'm going to need something stronger than tea with what I'm about to face.'

Janet pushed the envelope towards Amanda. 'This is for you,' she said.

'What is it?' Amanda asked.

'Look inside.'

Amanda picked it up and opened it, and then dropped it. 'What the hell?'

'It's for the pearls,' said Janet. 'My friend loved them, said they are worth fifty thousand. It's all in there.'

'Fifty? Thousand?' Amanda frowned. 'I don't understand. Didn't they need to go to auction or something?'

Janet paused and Carole came to her side.

'She said that she already had a buyer who would pay above asking price, because they wanted them so badly. It's a win-win.'

Amanda looked at the cash. 'It's a huge win but…' She looked up at them both. 'The last time I won something it wasn't really a win, so excuse me if I'm being a little suspicious.'

'Absolutely. You can call my friend if you like. She's more

than happy to speak to you. Or you can return the money and go to auction, but that won't be until after Diana comes back to Moongate.'

Amanda paused, looking at the cash and then looking at Janet.

'I can't argue with this amount of money and I trust you. We can go today and then we can engage a contractor to do the bathroom first.'

Janet jumped up, relieved. 'Excellent idea, now let's go to Shelley's and then make our way to Moongate.'

Carole clapped her hands. 'You might want to pop that in the bank, dear. Not safe wandering about with that amount of cash.'

'Good idea,' said Amanda. 'Let me go and hide this and I will take it to the bank in Newcastle when I visit Diana later.'

Amanda disappeared and Janet turned to Carole.

'You weren't worried about me carrying that amount of money back from the hotel. I could have been robbed.'

Carole snorted. 'You are a self-proclaimed angry dyke with pink hair and badges and Doc Martens. You're intimidating. No one will rob you.'

'You think I'm intimidating?' Janet asked. 'I like that.'

'No, I don't think you're intimidating because I love you and I know you talk to the tomato vines when they're fruiting, but some might find you a little unnerving.'

Janet nodded. 'That's good enough for me.'

'Okay, we ready?' asked Amanda, who was wearing a bright blue Hawaiian shirt over her T-shirt.

'Aloha and yes,' said Janet. 'Let's go and visit Moongate.'

40

Amanda

With a coffee in one hand and a warm cinnamon bun in the other, Amanda braced herself to see Moongate Manor again.

'I'm nervous,' she admitted to Janet as they drove down towards the sea.

'That's natural,' said Janet as they rounded the corner. 'A lot happened there that last day.'

Amanda tried not to think about that awful morning; there was so much still unfinished. She hadn't told Diana she knew, Simon had gone, and her plans for her future at Moongate seemed impossible now.

The car rounded the bend and Amanda steeled herself to see the mess of the garden.

'I can't look,' she said, covering her eyes. 'It's going to be horrific and I'll cry.'

The car stopped and Amanda opened her eyes and gasped.

'What in hell?' she said, and she opened the car door.

Janet had parked on the side of the road, opposite the house, and Amanda came around and stood at the front of the car.

'It's done,' she said aloud.

The house sat proudly amongst the most beautiful garden Amanda had ever seen.

The wisteria had been tamed into order, the vines enveloping the wall, while the pink roses climbed over the moon gate, framing the view to the house and beyond to the sea.

The lawns were as green as a billiard table and new plants sat amongst old plants in the beds, planted out as they were in the maps that Diana had drawn so long ago.

'Who did this?' Amanda turned to Janet but Janet was back in the car.

'Go and see,' she called from the car window and then drove away, leaving Amanda on the side of the road.

As though in a trance, Amanda crossed the road and opened the moon gate, and then entered another world.

She swore she could hear the bees announcing her return as she walked up the gravelled paths and touched the different plants as she passed them.

The vegetable garden was planted up with new seedlings, with the runner beans that Simon had planted weeks before now climbing up wicker tepees. There were nasturtiums falling from the beds onto the paths and Amanda smiled as she passed them, remembering her mom's favourite flower.

Amanda looked around but couldn't see anyone and so she walked towards the pond in the shade of the side of the house.

'Hello,' she heard as her eyes adjusted to the dark.

She jumped and then she saw him.

'Simon?' she cried, and she fell into his arms. 'You came back.'

'I told you I would finish the garden by the end of summer and I have.'

She kissed him over and over and then held his face in her hands.

'Don't you ever do that to me again. I've been a mess.'

'I know. It was poorly done. I'm not good at endings but then… I didn't think we were ending, I just wanted to face Charlie and Anika. And then I had to get this all arranged.' He gestured to the garden.

'But how? How did you afford it?' she asked.

Simon sighed. 'Let's just say Charlie came to realise the error of his ways and my suggestion that I make a call to Revenue and Customs to get them to audit his personal accounts wasn't well received. He suddenly remembered he owed me a lot of money.'

'And Anika?' she asked.

'Anika? Oh I didn't see her. I called her and told her that she did me a huge favour and I thanked her.'

'A favour? I don't understand.'

'Well if she hadn't run off with Charlie, and if Charlie hadn't ripped me off, I wouldn't have come here and I wouldn't have met the woman who I want to spend every day with for the rest of our lives, in the most beautiful house and garden in the world.'

Amanda cried in his arms and he held her tightly.

'I'm so sorry about Diana,' he said. 'I should have been there.'

'How did you know?' Amanda pulled away from kissing his neck.

'Janet and Carole told me.'

'Oh my God, those sneaky witches,' she cried. 'So they have known about all of this?'

He shrugged. 'I needed accomplices.'

'So who did all the work?' she asked and she looked at his hands. 'These hands are soft again – city hands – so it wasn't you.'

'Rude,' he said. 'But you're right, I did nothing. Your friend and boss David did it all. His team were amazing and he was thrilled with the commission.'

'What are you like?' She laughed.

'Something good I hope.'

'Better than good. You're so good, I'm going to let you wear my top hat,' she said.

'Oh wow, what an honour.'

They kissed again and Amanda took him by the hand and started to walk.

'Where are you taking me?' he asked as they walked by cosmos daisies that Amanda could have sworn giggled as they passed.

'To bed,' she said. 'We have a lot of time to make up making out.'

'Can I wear the top hat?' he asked.

'Let's see how good you are first.'

Simon laughed and they ran into the house.

41

Amanda

Amanda woke early and saw a large flat velvet box on the pillow next to her while Simon slept.

She picked it up and felt its weight and poked him in the shoulder. 'Hey, is this from you?'

Simon woke and feigned shock. 'No? Who has been in here? Was it the tooth fairy? Did you lose a tooth?'

Amanda made a face at him. 'No really, what is this?'

'Why don't you open it and find out?' he said, leaning on his elbow to watch her.

Amanda ran her hand over the blue velvet, feeling the fabric, and then she lifted the lid slowly.

'The pearls!' She gasped and turned to him. 'You bought the pearls? From Janet?'

'Maybe,' he said.

'Why?'

'Because I didn't know if you would want to be with me after I'd left and I also wanted to help you help Diana. And because I could. I was always planning on returning them to you, whether you wanted me or not.'

Amanda touched the pearls. 'You didn't need to do all

this. The garden, the pearls, the money…' Her voice trailed off.

Simon lay on his back. 'I know, but I have it and I can, and it feels good to be able to do something with the money.' He turned back to her. 'I had money, I lost it and during that time, I saw what mattered. The friendship and kindness I have seen here outweighs anything I had in London.'

Amanda closed the lid to the box and put it on the bedside table. 'Would you have come back if you didn't get the money back from Charlie?'

Simon laughed. 'Of course, but I wouldn't be in bed with you now, I'd be googling how to make a shower in a pantry and doing it myself for you and Diana.'

Amanda laughed. 'I love you,' she said.

Simon pulled her to him. 'I love you more.'

The bathroom was renovated with the knowledge and advice from the occupational therapist at the rehabilitation centre so Diana could move freely and safely and today was the day they brought all of Diana's things to the manor.

Simon had hired some removalists to clear the living room and to bring the heavy items from the gatehouse.

'I had new curtains installed,' said Amanda to Janet who was helping her for the day. 'You press the button and they open or close.'

'Diana is going to hate it but then she will use it and start telling everyone that she has these cool new curtains and they should get them,' Janet said.

Amanda laughed because Janet was right.

The old silk wallpaper had been stripped as it was

sun-faded and pulling away in the corners, and the room had been painted a pale cream that looked beautiful with Diana's furniture. Blue and white Chinese lamps on either side of the bed with new pretty Liberty bedding created a lovely ambiance in the room, and some Chinese screens sectioned off the living area where Janet and Amanda had arranged her sofa and chairs, the television, and books and small sentimental items.

The vase that Diana had had the dahlias in now sat on the mantelpiece with the last of the summer roses, their scent filling the room, while Amanda took out an old photo album from a box of books and opened it.

'God, look at Diana as a baby,' she said to Janet who came to her side. 'My great-grandfather looked stern,' she said, touching the photo of him and his wife standing together with Diana sitting on a small pony. 'Diana, aged six,' Amanda read the caption below the photo.

All of the photos were cold, posed, devoid of personality, and Amanda thought about the warmth in her own childhood photos that she had shown Diana.

'Jeesh, it really doesn't look like it was a fun place to grow up,' Amanda said.

Janet turned the page. 'Different times,' she said as they flicked through. 'Diana was from a well-to-do family. There were expectations from the moment she was born.'

As Amanda closed the book and picked it up, a photo fell from the pages. It was small, flimsy and worn, as though it had been looked at many times.

'That's my mom,' she said, picking it up from the floor. 'And her adoptive parents.'

'Speaking of cold,' said Janet with a raised eyebrow.

'Yes, they were pretty strict, Mom said, super religious and unforgiving.'

'That's sad,' said Janet, as she arranged the needlepoint cushions on Diana's sofa. 'You would hope that whoever took on the responsibility of your baby would give extra love.'

'Perhaps they thought it was love,' said Amanda, 'if they were ruled by the church in their personal lives.'

'Good point,' said Janet.

Amanda left the room and came back with a framed picture and leaned it against the mantel. 'I need to hang this,' she said.

Janet looked at the artwork. 'Is that one of yours?' she asked.

Amanda smiled, 'Yes, it's a goldfinch. Diana reminds me of one, very hard to pin down but still beautiful.'

'You know, they say when you see a goldfinch, it means someone is coming back from the dead to visit you.'

'I haven't ever seen one in the wild,' Amanda said, 'but I know them from the Carel Fabritius painting. You know it?'

Janet nodded. 'I do. But you should join the Foxfield ornithology club. We go birdwatching when we can and also log the sightings on our website.'

'You're in a birdwatching club too?' Amanda asked. 'Wow. Who else is in the club?'

'The gardening and historical club members.'

Amanda burst out laughing. 'You all just start clubs for the hell of it, I swear.'

Janet giggled. 'It's just an excuse to get together, really.'

Janet looked around the room and adjusted the reading lamp next to Diana's chair.

'I think we're done,' she said.

'I think we are, except for hanging this. Then it will be ready for Diana to come home.'

Amanda looked at the work they had done and knew it was beautiful and homey but would Diana like it? What if she didn't want to come back to the house? What if she felt she was being treated like a child? The fears and worries had plagued Amanda for the last week but it was too late now. It was done. She would just have to see what Diana thought when she arrived.

42

Diana

Diana was waiting in her room at the rehabilitation ward, her bags packed by the staff and her walking stick by her side. She had made a deal with the physiotherapist that she could return to her walking stick if her gait improved and she did extra leg exercises and hydrotherapy twice a week.

Diana hadn't wanted to admit to anyone that her walking was better than before the stroke. She had built up some muscle and strength, and despite her protestations, she had eaten more regularly than she did at the gatehouse.

But today, despite her new-found strength and apparent recovery, she was nervous about returning to the gatehouse. Amanda had been a source of joy through the last weeks but she would be at the manor and Diana alone at the gatehouse. It was depressing to think about but she would do her best, as she always did.

'Hello.' Amanda knocked at the open door as she came inside. 'I have a surprise for you,' she said.

'Oh? I don't ordinarily like surprises,' Diana stated, but looked around to see what Amanda was referring to.

'I found something in the garden,' she said.

'Go on,' said Diana, her interest piqued at mention of the garden.

'This funny gnome fellow, he was down by the pond,' Amanda said, and Simon stepped around the doorframe.

Diana gasped. 'Well, well, well, look who has come back to finish the job he promised to do. Kind of you to return,' she said, but she couldn't help but smile at him.

Simon came and crouched at her feet. 'I'm sorry, Diana, I had some things I had to sort out. But I'm back now – for Amanda, for you and for Moongate.'

Diana gave a small nod and leaned and whispered into his ear: 'I hope you will stay now, not for the garden but for Amanda. She loves you.'

Simon looked up at Diana. 'I'm staying, for her and for me. I've never been as happy as I am at Moongate.'

Diana patted his shoulder. 'Good boy. Now let's go. I'm tired of being here.'

Simon picked up her bags and Amanda stood by to assist, but Diana was confident on her feet.

'Apparently my core is that of a much younger woman,' she said to Amanda as they walked down the hallway and said goodbye to all the staff. 'They will be sad I'm gone. I've been a delight to care for.'

'I'm sure,' said Amanda with a broad smile.

They walked outside and found Simon waiting at the front in his car.

'An Audi?' Diana noted. 'I assume you remedied your business issues with your ex-partner?'

'Yes, I did,' said Simon, as he helped Diana into the front passenger seat and Amanda slipped into the back seat.

'Time for home,' Simon said, and Diana felt the nerves rise again.

It felt good to be outside though, Diana thought. 'I can't wait to see Trotsky. Has he missed me?' she asked.

'Dreadfully,' Amanda said. 'He can't stand Janet and Carole's house.'

'That's a lie. He's a such a bossy and greedy thing, I have no doubt they would have spoiled him. He probably won't want to come back to me now,' she half joked.

'He's already at Moongate, waiting,' Amanda said, calming her fears.

The light seemed brighter to Diana as they drove out of Newcastle and towards Foxfield and the sea.

The water was calm and the breeze pleasant as they passed the beach, a few beachgoers still braving the water in the last of summer sun.

'You must be careful swimming in there.' Diana pointed to the water. 'Lots of rips. If you get caught in one you just have to float until it brings you back. It's when you fight where it's trying to take you that you get in trouble.'

'Good to know,' said Amanda from the back seat and Diana saw her share a glance with Simon in the rear-view mirror.

They came around the bend in the road and there was Moongate in its glory and then Diana saw the garden.

'What's happened? Who did this?' she asked as Simon turned onto the driveway and drove up to the house.

'Simon did,' Amanda said.

'No, I paid someone to do it since I promised I would have it finished by the end of summer,' he corrected.

He jumped from the car and came around and opened the door for Diana, helping her out.

The front door of the house opened and Janet waved. Trotsky came bounding up to Diana.

'Darling boy, did you miss me?'

Trotsky wiggled and danced around Diana excitedly.

'Calm down or you'll send me over and I'll do in a hip. Sit,' Diana said firmly and Trotsky sat down.

'I must look at this garden,' she said.

'We don't have to do it all at once,' Amanda said. 'Why don't we go inside and have tea and then we can see everything.'

Diana looked around. The gatehouse seemed very far away from Amanda now and she felt anxious at the distance for the first time.

'What's wrong?' asked Amanda.

Diana thought about brushing it aside but she also needed reassurance. 'I'm worried about being so far away. You will come and visit, won't you?'

Amanda smiled. 'You're not that far now. Come inside, I have another surprise, and yes, I know you aren't a huge fan of them.'

'Not all surprises are good,' said Diana as they walked inside the house. 'I can smell paint,' she said, looking around.

Amanda opened the door to the living room. 'Your new suite is ready,' she said, walking back to Diana's side. 'I think it best you live here now, with me and Simon. That way we can always be there for each other.'

Diana walked through the door and looked around. It was an elegant, updated room with her things perfectly arranged and a beautiful painting of a goldfinch over the mantel.

The sofa and chairs were by the French doors, which she could easily open to let the air in, and her books were on the shelves. Everything she liked from the gatehouse was up here in this huge, airy room.

Amanda opened the door to the butler's pantry.

'And you have your own bathroom,' she said.

Diana walked over and looked inside.

'You're joking – you did all of this for me?' she asked.

Simon and Janet were in the doorway, watching, Janet wiping a little tear away.

'You don't have to look after me,' said Diana. She suddenly felt ashamed of becoming old, being a burden to others.

'I'm not looking after you – we're looking after each other,' Amanda stated. She paused briefly before adding: 'That's what families do.'

Diana looked at Amanda, blinking a few times as though trying to make out the words she had heard. 'I might need to sit,' she said.

'A cup of tea is coming,' said Janet. 'And then Simon and I will leave you be.'

Amanda and Diana moved to the sitting area and Diana sat in her special and much loved armchair.

'So you know,' she said.

Amanda nodded.

'I imagined you would work it out eventually.' Diana sighed.

'I don't understand why you went to such lengths to keep it from me,' Amanda said.

Diana leaned back in her chair and clasped her hands. 'Let me tell you about when I met your mother.'

1990s

New York was too loud for Diana. She had arrived the night before and had arranged to meet the private detective in the lobby of the hotel she was staying in. It was small but comfortable place, not the Waldorf Astoria like her mother or father would have expected, but they were dead and Diana no longer had the money for extravagant hotels. She had just had the gutters done at Moongate and the gatehouse was about to be reroofed.

The private detective she had hired was not at all like the she had expected. His name was Joe but he was Hawaiian and an ex-policeman. When she had expressed that she thought he would be like the moustached men she saw on the American television shows, Joe had laughed and said he expected her to look like the Queen, so they were even. Diana liked him immediately.

They sat in the lobby of the hotel and Joe handed over the file.

'Her name is Wendy Cox. She lives in Astoria and has a three-year-old called Amanda.'

'No husband? Where is the father?'

'He comes and goes but I don't think he does much,' Joe said.

'Is she stable? Emotionally? Financially?'

Joe nodded. 'Seems like a great mom. Amanda is in day care and Wendy has just finished doing a stenographer course. She went to an interview at the civil court last week, so she will probably work there. They are usually desperate for people.'

'Is that the person who takes the notes on those funny machines in the court cases?'

'Yup. It's a good job, pays well.'

Diana smiled. 'So you gave her my letter and she read it?'

Joe frowned. 'I did, but she wasn't happy about the contact.'

Diana pursed her lips. 'And you asked her to meet me today like I requested? At the park? And bring Amanda?'

'I did, and she said she'd think about it.'

Diana checked her watch. 'It's all I can do, I suppose,' she said. She handed Joe an envelope with two thousand dollars in cash inside. 'Thank you for your help, I wouldn't have found her otherwise.'

Joe took the cash and pocketed it in his leather blazer.

'You know, I do a lot of these cases, the reunification of adopted children and bio families.'

Diana looked up at him. 'Is it rewarding?' She smiled.

Joe shook his head. 'Not often. People come with their minds made up and they usually have their hopes smashed. Nature, nurture, I don't know, but be open to her not wanting this. She seemed angry.'

'Thank you, that's good advice,' Diana said, and Joe left her in the lobby.

The meeting was to take place at the Heckscher Playground at midday and Diana decided to walk there to calm her nerves. She had a photograph of Wendy and

Amanda that Joe had given her from an event at the day care centre where Amanda went.

Diana didn't ask how he came to have the photo but it was her most treasured possession now.

It was autumn in New York and the song played in Diana's head as she made her way to the park, noticing the leaves turning yellow and red and the cool air, making it almost cold when she was in the shade.

The sound of children playing took over the sound of the traffic as Diana entered the garden from 7th Avenue and she looked around for a red-headed woman and child but couldn't see anyone that matched the description.

Finding a seat in the sunshine, Diana sat, watching the children climb the play equipment and fly down the slides. There was a very elaborate game of hopscotch being played with some girls wielding sticks of chalk like swords and some boys playing basketball at the far end of the playground near the hoops.

It's little empire, she thought as she watched all the energy and imagination play out in front of her.

'Diana?' She turned to see a woman had come up to her.

She held her hand up to block out the sun so she could see the woman.

'Wendy?'

'Yes, I understand you are looking for me.'

Diana gestured to the seat next to her. 'Yes, I've been looking for you since you were born.' She smiled and tried to push down the tears that were threatening to fall.

Wendy leaned over so Diana could see into her blue eyes. *Douglas's eyes*, she thought.

'I don't know why you gave me up, or why you want to

see me now, but know this: the people you gave me to were horrendous. There was a reason they couldn't have children, as though biology, or God, or something had stepped in and said no to them having their own. And they were denied by multiple adoption agencies. You gave me away privately to people who should never have been around children.'

Diana tried to speak but Wendy put up her hand. 'Hearing from you, and your shady private detective has been traumatic for me and I never want to hear from you again. You will not meet my daughter, and you won't be a part of our lives. The mere fact you were so irresponsible in the first place, and then gave me away to strangers to save your reputation, tells me everything I need to know about you.'

Diana was silent.

'I will tell my daughter what a horrible woman you are, what a selfish nasty woman who gave a baby to people she never met so she could wear pretty dresses again and marry a rich man.'

Diana looked at Wendy, so full of pain and anger, and rightly so. She knew those very feelings.

'I could tell you I didn't know you were being taken away. I could tell you my father signed the adoption certificate without my knowledge. I could tell you I planned to bring you home and love you, that I already loved you before you were born, and I could tell you that I never recovered. I never married, and I never wore pretty dresses again, but I don't think it would change anything for you.' Diana heard her voice crack and she cleared her throat.

'I have a house, in England, it's the family home. I want to leave it to you.'

Wendy gave a half-laugh but it was bitter. 'I don't want your house. I don't want anything from you other than for you to leave me alone. My daughter and I have a lovely life here, better than anything I could have had in Britain. She's American and she won't want anything you have to offer.'

They stared at each other for a moment.

'Please, I ask only one thing of you,' Diana said. 'Whatever you think of me is one thing, but please don't poison Amanda towards me. She doesn't need to grow up carrying her mother's pain. It's not fair to her.'

'Now you're telling me how to parent?' Wendy crossed her arms.

'No, I'm telling you to let your daughter find out for herself one day, if she chooses to. God knows I didn't have any choice when I was a child. Please don't repeat the legacy.'

Wendy was silent and then she nodded. 'Fine. But I will never tell her I met you. I won't mention you at all.'

'Thank you,' Diana said.

'Okay, goodbye,' Wendy said, turning and walking in the direction from which she had come.

Diana collapsed onto the bench and looked ahead, not hearing the traffic or the children anymore, just the vitriolic words of her daughter as they repeated in her ears.

She looked up at the clouds and wondered if there was an afterlife and if her father was laughing at today's outcome.

'Goodbye, Wendy,' she said to the sky, and she walked back to her hotel knowing in her heart that she would never hear from her daughter again. Some pain was just too hard to cure.

43

Amanda

Amanda sat in silence for a few minutes after Diana had finished her story.

'What an idiot. God she could be annoying sometimes,' she said, and Diana laughed.

'You can't say that. She was hurt. You didn't know what she went through as a child – it sounded like it was more than them being strict.'

Amanda shrugged. 'I know but seriously, we could have known you all along. We could have hung out and I could have stayed for holidays.'

'She did what she thought was right for her and we must respect that.'

'You're' right,' Amanda said. 'But I will give her one thing.'

'Oh?'

'She never bad-mouthed you. She never mentioned you, so she didn't say anything awful.'

Diana smiled. 'That's a win, I suppose.'

'I'm sorry it went so badly,' Amanda said.

'I was so worried you had been turned against me. That's why I went to these elaborate lengths to get you here; I was so scared to be rejected again.'

Amanda nodded. 'I get it.' She gestured to the room. 'But you're here now and we can live very happily together and do things in the garden. Also, I'm having my exhibition at the garden centre, so you can help with that. We're going to have such a good time.'

Diana blinked a few times and then Amanda saw tears welling in the old woman's eyes.

'I never thought I would have this,' she said. 'I have never felt loved until now. You've done so much for me. I was lied to by Wendy's father who said he would come back – Douglas was his name – and controlled by my parents, shunned by my daughter, so I let go of everyone else because I was afraid of being rejected again.'

Amanda shook her head. 'You weren't lied to by Douglas,' Amanda said in a gentle voice.

Diana frowned. 'What do you mean?'

Amanda sighed. 'I went and met Helen,' she said, causing Diana's eyebrows to rise.

'She was so lovely and loyal to you and she told me about Douglas. She was surprised he never came back.'

Diana said nothing so Amanda went on. 'Simon and I looked into it, and I'm sorry to tell you, Diana...' She paused. 'He died on the trip he took.'

Diana took in a sharp breath.

'But he was on his way back to you. He was coming back,' Amanda said.

'How do you know that?' Diana's lip trembled.

'He was found with a gold ring in his pocket, and on the inside was inscribed, *For Diana*.'

A sob escaped Diana's mouth and Amanda was instantly by her side, sitting on the arm of her chair and hugging her.

'I'm so sorry,' she said. 'You were cheated out of so much.'

She rubbed her back and kissed the top of her head and slowly Diana stopped crying.

'I haven't cried in years,' she said. 'It feels good, actually.'

Amanda nodded. 'Nothing like a good cry.'

Diana touched her granddaughter's face.

'You're kinder and more beautiful than I ever could have imagined.'

'You, also,' Amanda said. 'And we're lucky to have each other.'

'We are,' said Diana. 'Now, where is the cup of tea that Janet promised? And then I want to see the garden that Simon bought us.'

Amanda burst out laughing. 'That's mean.'

'Not mean. It's true but if you can do it then why not? You might as well share it with those you love.'

Amanda laughed again. 'So true. I'll go and chase that cup of tea.' She stood up and looked around. 'Are you okay with being back in this house?' she asked Diana.

Diana looked around. 'It doesn't feel like it used to anymore. You have changed everything, Amanda. You have changed my path and this house's path and history. I didn't think my life was worth anything anymore but here I am, with you, mattering. I have friends, I have purpose, and I have a second chance with my health and with you, and for that, I am more grateful than you could imagine.'

'Hallelujah,' said Amanda as she opened the door and Trotsky came wandering in and sat in his bed by the mantelpiece.

'And Trotsky thanks you also, from the bottom of his Marxist little paws.'

Epilogue

'Hold her for a minute?' Amanda asked Shelley, who gladly took the baby, who then tried to eat Shelley's crescent moon earring in return.

'Celene, no,' Amanda said. 'Not for eating.'

'I don't mind. She's hungry. Would she like some watermelon?' asked Shelley.

'Probably. She has her father's appetite – never-ending.' Amanda laughed.

The garden at Moongate was filled with visitors who had all paid for their ticket to the Moongate Festival.

There was music playing and food stalls and jugglers and magicians wandering about. Simon and Frank had strung lanterns throughout the garden, which were just starting to twinkle in the dusk.

'I just need to check the chairs are ready,' Amanda called to Shelley who was already walking to sit with Diana and Maggie under the wisteria arbour.

Amanda took a moment to watch them all fuss over Celene, who had taken the red hair gene and added Simon's curls to the mix. Shelley handed Celene some watermelon and after staring at it for a short moment, the baby gummed it happily while Helen and Diana fussed around her.

Reuniting Helen and Diana had been a joyous moment for Amanda and they had seen each other weekly ever since. Diana had joined the gardening club, the historical society and the birdwatching club, and though meetings for the latter were done in the garden at Moongate, Amanda had finally seen a goldfinch in the wild, when Diana had been watching keenly with the little binoculars that Simon had gifted her for Christmas.

'All okay?' she asked Simon who was putting out the last of the chairs.

'Perfect,' he said, and gave her a kiss.

'Amanda?' She turned to see Simon's mum, Elfreda, waving at her from the other side of the garden near the gatehouse.

Amanda walked over to Elfreda. 'I've finished at the dig and am showered, so what can I do?' Elfreda asked.

Amanda looked around. 'Perhaps Diana and Helen might like a gin and tonic? Or you could take Celene for me. I've lumped her on Shelley.'

'Noted. I can and will do both of those tasks,' she said.

Elfreda had come up to Moongate for a break and then learned there was a dig by the University of Edinburgh taking place not too far away. Some Viking brooches and bullion were found in a field and so she took a sabbatical.

Then Amanda learned she was pregnant, and Elfreda moved into the gatehouse, helping out at Moongate and visiting the dig when she could.

Amanda was thrilled. She loved Elfreda and her ebullience and intelligence. She had so many stories; Amanda could have listened to her all day. Simon wasn't so thrilled initially, but then he saw how much Elfreda loved Celene and Amanda.

Simon smiled at Amanda as she came back from talking to his mother. 'Is Mother assisting or advising?'

'A bit of both, but I have her on G and T duty and Celene supervising.'

'I don't think Celene is old enough to have gin and tonics yet,' Simon said, and Amanda rolled her eyes.

'What time is sunset?' she asked for the fortieth time that day.

'In fifteen minutes,' he said. 'Maybe we should get people seated?'

Amanda nodded. 'Okay, can do.'

She walked around the garden, encouraging people to find a seat, and spotted David from the garden centre and his wife. David had understood when she told him she couldn't continue working at the centre, and his support of her art had been instrumental in getting her to where she was now.

'Hello, how are you?' She kissed their cheeks.

'This looks amazing,' said Tilly, David's wife, her toddler hanging off her skirt. 'I've brought the kids so they can see it. They're excited for sunset, mostly because it's when they should be in bed.'

Amanda laughed and smiled at the toddler.

'We sold the frog today,' David said.

'Oh the frog on the gondola? That's great,' said Amanda. 'Thank you.'

'No, thank you – the exhibition has been wonderful, brought so many new customers to the centre, and when they each saw what we did here, well, I'm booked out for next year,' he said. 'You bring luck with you – didn't I just say that, Tils?'

Tilly nodded but Amanda shook her head. 'They are just finally seeing the magic that you can do in the garden, that's all.'

'Are you planning another exhibition?' David asked, his voice hopeful.

Amanda shook her head. 'No, I'm actually illustrating a children's book. My mom wrote it. I sent it to a publisher and they loved it. It will be out next year, hopefully.'

'Gosh, that's amazing,' said Tilly.

'It really is,' said Amanda before saying goodbye and going to check on Celene and Diana.

It wasn't until Amanda pulled out the old manuscript her mother had written that she had realised the meaning. As a child Amanda had just thought it was a fairy tale but now she realised how much more it was.

The daughter of the moon was the story of a child who travelled the world searching for her mother and who found her once but didn't believe her story, and scorned her. It was only later that she realised she had made a mistake but when she went to find her mother, she learned that her mother had sacrificed herself to become the moon, so she could always light the darkness for her daughter and always be looking over her.

Amanda knew it was an apology for her mother as she had dedicated it to Diana, the Goddess of the Moon.

Diana had cried when she read it and Amanda could see it had helped her to heal, and when Amanda named her daughter Celene, daughter of the moon, Diana could not have been more delighted.

The sun was setting and Amanda saw a taxi pull up.

There were no more tickets left, so she sighed and headed down the driveway to tell the late arrival that bad news.

'Mands!' she heard, and she strained her eyes in the darkness until she could see the speaker.

'Lainie!' she cried, and ran to her friend. 'You're here! I didn't think you were coming.'

'Are you kidding? My flight was delayed and then overbooked and then rerouted but I'm here, and I can't wait. It's not every day your best friend builds a staircase to the moon and then gets married the next day.'

Amanda hugged her friend and then pulled away.

'Come and meet everyone,' she said, dragging Lainie by the hand, who was pulling her suitcase with the other.

'I will, I will, let me just take a moment to soak it all in.'

They stopped and looked out over the garden and down to the sea. It was dark and the moon was rising in the distance.

There was chatter and music and the scent of night-blooming jasmine, and it was as perfect as any night could be.

Lainie looked at Amanda, her eyes filled with tears. 'It's like you were meant to be here all along.'

Amanda nodded and squeezed her friend's hand. 'I'm finally home.'

About the Author

KATE FORSTER is the best-selling author of *Starting Over at Acorn Cottage*, *The Perfect Retreat*, *Finding Love at Mermaid Terrace* and many more books that she would want to read herself, so she wrote them. When not writing, Kate loves hanging out with family, friends, and her dogs. A dedicated houseplant lover, Kate also enjoys outdoor gardening and is the founder and moderator of one of largest online women's writing support groups on Facebook.

Acknowledgements

Thank you to Martina for your support and cheerleading.

Thank you to David for the wrangling life while I write and edit.

Thank you as ever to Tara and her endlessly good advice and wisdom.